Five Days, Five Dead

Five Days, Five Dead

THE CHINA BOHANNON SERIES

FIVE DAYS, FIVE DEAD

CAROL WRIGHT CRIGGER

FIVE STAR
A part of Gale, a Cengage Company

GALE
A Cengage Company

Farmington Hills, Mich • San Francisco • New York • Waterville, Maine
Meriden, Conn • Mason, Ohio • Chicago

LIBRARY OF CONGRESS CATALOGING-IN-PUBLICATION DATA

Names: Wright Crigger, Carol, author.
Title: Five days, five dead / Carol Wright Crigger.
Description: Waterville, Maine : Five Star, a part of Gale, Cengage Learning, [2018] |
   Series: China Bohannon series
Identifiers: LCCN 2018014455 (print) | LCCN 2018015497 (ebook) | ISBN
   9781432847319 (ebook) | ISBN 9781432847302 (ebook) | ISBN 9781432847296
   (hardcover)
Subjects: LCSH: Women private investigators—Fiction. | Women detectives—Fiction.
   | GSAFD: Mystery fiction. g
Classification: LCC PS3623.R595 (ebook) | LCC PS3623.R595 F59 2018 (print) | DDC
   813/.6—dc23
LC record available at https://lccn.loc.gov/2018014455

First Edition. First Printing: December 2018
Find us on Facebook—https://www.facebook.com/FiveStarCengage
Visit our website—http://www.gale.cengage.com/fivestar/
Contact Five Star Publishing at FiveStar@cengage.com

Printed in Mexico
1 2 3 4 5 6 7 22 21 20 19 18

I'm dedicating this novel to the City of Spokane, Washington. The town's rich and varied history provides me with a never-ending supply of story ideas. The "client" in *Five Days, Five Dead* is very loosely based on a real Spokane character. I'm sure some readers may recognize a tiny bit of Dutch Jake Goetz in my fictional Sepp Amsel. The rich and flamboyant part, anyway. Even the weather plays into the plot. In late November, 1896, record cold temperatures were set. Records for the date hold until this day, with several nights reaching between five and thirteen degrees below zero. Spokane, I thank you.

PROLOGUE

Low-lying clouds spat snow and promised more. A lot more, if the slender young man hunkered in the shadow of a small cedar tree was any judge. Across from him, two men of the big, burly sort also sought shelter from a brisk wind that had arrived during the night to drive the first flakes. An inch or better already covered the ground.

None of the three was happy about the weather, even though the leader acknowledged that winter was winter in Spokane, Washington, just as it was where he came from. Anyway, a good dumping of snow would surely hide any traces the group might leave behind. He didn't want Jutte to guess his identity too soon. No. He wanted to see her surprise when he revealed himself.

"Somebody's coming," one of the men whispered. "I heard the door."

The leader smiled to himself. Jutte was supremely predictable. An early riser, even here in this country, she kept to her habit of a walk before breakfast, rain or shine or snow.

"Get ready," he said. "Be careful. Do not hurt her. You hear me?"

"*Ja,*" said one man. "Yeah," echoed the other. And yet the leader distrusted their assurances because it was still too dark for him to see if they meant to obey his instructions. They'd better. They'd been paid well.

He had a moment's doubt about this plan. But when they'd

7

talked about it back in the fatherland, he'd been assured it would work. They'd have money. No one would be hurt. Not even the mark, really, who had a great deal of money.

A minute slipped past. What took the woman so long? His feet moved in an anxious sort of dance. Sweat formed under his arms and on his brow beneath his hatband.

Probably she had stopped to pet the cat. Jutte was fond of cats, and he'd noticed a calico slinking around the waste barrels at the rear of the hotel. His face puckered distastefully. It no doubt survived by foraging through the garbage. He would have to warn Jutte not to touch the dirty creature lest she catch some disease.

Voices, female, more than one—he cursed under his breath upon hearing the second—spoke quietly to one another as they walked down the path to where he waited. This did not suit him at all. Why today, of all days, after she'd told him she usually walked alone? Hadn't she always denied his company back in the fatherland when he would've been glad to walk with her?

A figure, outlined by the weak winter daylight, neared his hiding spot.

Yes, yes. It was she. Although he couldn't see her face through the gloom and now rapidly falling snow, he recognized her figure, so soft and lush. Another woman followed a few steps behind, similar to the other, although taller and a little thinner.

Closer they came. Jutte stepped past him, a dainty woman light on her feet, turning to say something to the other woman, who laughed.

He frowned. That laugh . . .

No time to think.

"Now," he cried, and the three men leapt from their hiding places. One of the big men grabbed Jutte, threw her over his shoulder and ran toward the river. All part of the plan.

The other woman, silent in the first several moments of at-

8

tack, found her voice, crying out as the second man roughly pushed her aside and she fell. An overly loud string of curses pierced the cold morning air.

He spun, barely able to see that one through the snow. "What are you doing?" he said to her. "Be quiet." And, to the other man, "We need silence. The plan will be ruined." Then, leaving this man to watch for pursuit, he turned to follow the one bearing Jutte away.

There was the sound of a slap. One sure to spell doom for someone.

Then blessed silence.

CHAPTER ONE

Nimble, the little Bedlington terrier Gratton Doyle had given me—for my protection, no less—peeked her wedge-shaped head around the corner and cast a wary glance at the two-wheeled vehicle propped against the wall.

I stifled a giggle. My dog was jealous of a bicycle.

"Come on in," I said to her. "It's not going to hurt you."

She looked at me, then, keeping a close watch on the offending object, trod a wide circle around the new safety model Waverley Belle bicycle. Gratton, through some of his contacts down at Moseley's Saloon, had gotten a deal on the bicycle for me. I'd paid for it out of my own money, though, with wages earned as bookkeeper, office manager, and general dogsbody at the Doyle & Howe Detective Agency.

And sometime detective, I added to myself. Don't forget that. I'm sure I never do.

Gratton, of course, is the Doyle half of the agency, and my uncle, Montgomery Howe, whom everyone calls Monk, the other. I live for the day my name is scribed on the plaque hanging in our window without the addendum of "office manager" tacked onto it. Doyle, Howe, & Bohannon has a much nicer ring.

That, drat it, might take a while. Business had slowed as winter drew in. At least for me. Miners and loggers, shut out of their jobs during the bad weather, kept the men hopping with several small jobs. Nothing had come to my attention since the

Interstate fair closed in late September, and here it was the end of November. Christmas would soon be upon us.

For now? Boredom had set in. The one good thing coming from the slowdown was the lesson it had already taught the men. Frugality, a careful accounting of monies due the firm, and precise billing practices during the good times kept the business afloat now, and the men with money in their pockets while at leisure.

All, if I may say so without seeming to brag, my doing. But here it was, a Monday morning, and I had nothing to do, no business to conduct, no hobby to pursue. Is there anything sadder than spending time in an office by oneself?

With the snow, I couldn't even try out my new Waverley Belle.

"Come here and lie down," I told the dog, at which she slipped past the bicycle—shying once in a dramatic fashion as though it had reached out to grab her—and came to nudge my legs aside. Spinning twice, she curled into her favorite spot in the kneehole where I'd put down a rug, hid her head beneath my skirt, and, with a sigh, went to sleep.

Seriously? I suspect she'd claimed the coziest spot in the whole building since she'd begun avoiding the area in front of the stove. Because of the bicycle, the silly creature. Goodness knows a cold draft blew in under the door when the wind came up. I'd noticed a snow drift forming on the office threshold when I unlocked this morning. Spokane was in the midst of a cold spell. A very cold spell.

I sighed, puffed hot breath on my stiff fingers to warm them, and went back to my typewriter. My self-appointed task for this lazy day? Creating copy for an advertisement to place in *The Spokane Daily Chronicle,* but now I couldn't decide if I should make it serious or humorous, straight-forward or invent a bit of catchy doggerel. Did I need a picture—a cartoon—to illustrate the text?

How about a drawing of a mouse running away with a chunk of cheese and the question, *Need someone to watch your mousehole? Contact the Doyle & Howe Detective Agency.* Or did I need something more serious, more professional: *For all your inquiry and investigative needs,* blah, blah, blah. Somewhat boring to my way of thinking.

My mind occupied with such meanderings, I almost fell out of my chair when the door crashed open wide enough the door knob banged into the wall. Wind swept in, seeming to push the blurred figure of a man ahead of it. But his entrance didn't stop there. No, indeed.

The man skidded, our polished wooden floor offering no purchase for his snow-clogged boots. He put out a hand to steady himself, but, instead of a firm, solid object, he found the freestanding coat rack. Under his weight, the rack tilted.

So did he.

Farther and farther, then too far.

He let go the rack and slammed into the wall nose first, catching himself at the last moment. The rack was not so lucky.

Down it came.

Right into my beautiful new bicycle, which promptly fell over, metal clanging. The handlebars banged on the floor. The rear wheel hummed as it spun as though pedaled by an invisible whirling dervish.

Nimble, who'd scrambled out to greet the newcomer, yipped a high-pitched scream. She banged into my knees as she reversed direction, headed back into her hidey-hole. One of my legs, struck at just the . . . right . . . point, collapsed under me. No big problem, except I didn't fall back into my chair as I'd expected. That had swiveled away out of reach.

The floor received me with a resounding thump, at which my teeth clacked together—or would have, except for my tongue, which was stuck between them.

I, I fear, also emitted a high-pitched scream.

"Chasus, Mary, and Choseph," the man shouted. His nose dripped blood as he peered down at me. I guess he'd hit the wall harder than I'd thought. I took a moment to be grateful he'd missed the stove.

"Ow," I cried, meanwhile. "Ow, ow."

He frowned and bent over to look under the desk. "You keep a sheep in your house?"

I ducked to avoid being splattered by his blood, only to find a driblet of my own oozing down the front of my shirtwaist. Hell and damnation!

"Of course not," I retorted. The words came out a little garbled due to pain and a mouth full of blood. I wanted in the worst way to spit. Alas. I was a lady, so I swallowed instead. And gagged. "This is my dog."

He shook his head, which didn't do his nose, or my formerly clean floor, any good.

Meanwhile, as the wind blew the door to and fro, snow drifted in and began dissolving into large goopy puddles. The temperature in the room, none too warm to begin with, dropped by ten degrees within seconds.

The physical temperature, that is. My inner one rose rapidly.

"Shut the damn door." Hoping my tailbone wasn't broken, I struggled to my feet, ignoring his outstretched hand.

One thing about being angry. And hurt. It lends a certain aura of command.

He backed up, shut the door, and leaned against it as he fumbled inside his coat.

Just to be on the safe side, I snatched open the top drawer of my desk where my .32-calibre Smith and Wesson pocket pistol resided.

As it happened, I didn't need it. He retrieved a handkerchief from an inner pocket and, thankfully, sopped most of the blood from his face. Figuring it behooved me to clean up my chin, I found my own hanky and did the same. Presently, with both of us looking not so much like one of Mr. Stoker's vampires and more or less human again, we eyed each other.

"We're closed," I said, then belied my words by saying, "How can I help you?" Habit, I guess.

He wasn't a handsome man, I have to say. He appeared shorter than he really was due to being broad and blocky— although a good part of that may have stemmed from the fact he wore a voluminous bearskin coat he filled out much as the original bear probably had. And, unfortunately, for a first meeting, his rather long nose was now swollen and bulbous. Not, I thought, its normal appearance. Or not entirely, anyway.

He had squinty little blue eyes and sandy hair, what I could see of it peeking from under a funny knitted cap with ear flaps. I also knew who he was, as did probably everyone else in Spokane. His name was Sepp Amsel, and he owned a string of gambling establishments that ranged in location from Walla Walla to Wallace, with several stops in between.

I say gambling establishments. Actually, they were more than that, or so I'd heard. Dance halls, bordellos, and whatever else men considered the entertainment industry.

Mr. Amsel ignored my remark about being closed.

"I wish to engage your services," he said. Then he faltered. "I think."

CHAPTER TWO

Mr. Amsel, after hesitating at the start, collected himself and acted the gentleman. He straightened my chair, picked up my bicycle—someone should really invent a self-contained stand in case there's no wall nearby to lean it against—and, once the flow from his nose receded to a slow leak, used his handkerchief to wipe most of the gore off the floor.

Or at least he thinned it by smearing it around.

I don't know what I'd expected upon meeting the man. Someone more dashing and daring in person than grainy newspaper photographs showed, for one thing. Certainly, someone more handsome. Not in Gratton Doyle's category, of course, impossible in any event. Nor even in my good friend Porter Anderson's. But I had expected more . . . well, not this plain, rather awkward man. I mean, after all, a rich theater/gambling hall/saloon owner? One who'd been in the news repeatedly of late?

Surreptitiously rubbing my aching tailbone, I seated myself and gathered Nimble onto my lap to comfort her. She still trembled from the shock of a big, bad bicycle attacking her.

"Please." I gestured toward the client chair across from me. "Be seated, Mr. Amsel, and tell me what I can do for you."

"You know who I am?" He sounded surprised.

"I do indeed. I've been reading about you in the newspapers."

Face flushing, he took the chair, settling himself with his spine pressed to its back slats. "You are Miss China Bohannon,

16

yes? I am told you are a firety little woman with a funny dog."

I patted my "funny" dog. "Firety?"

He seemed to search for words and came up with one. "Explosive."

I suspect he meant fiery. Harrumph. I had no objection to that. Just the funny dog part. Although . . . "explosive"? Really?

"Indeed, I am China Bohannnon, sir. How may I help you?"

"Well, see, if you heard of me, then probably you heard I am getting married." His face reddened even more, as though he'd imparted news of a slightly salacious kind.

"*Everybody* has heard you're getting married, sir. Quite soon, if I'm not mistaken." If there was a single person in Spokane—or from Walla Walla to Wallace—who hadn't heard, I'd be surprised. His bride's arrival from Austria had been the leading news story for the last week. Probably because everyone, and I do mean everyone, including me, was invited to the wedding reception.

"Saturday," he said with a smile that quickly faded. "But now—"

Hmmm. A mail-order bride, I'd read. Trouble in paradise already? Was she not quite what he'd been expecting?

An awkward silence fell. He wiped his nose, and I consciously tried to not rub the swollen spot on my tongue over a tooth.

Didn't work.

After waiting for a moment for the pain to go away, I said, "But now?"

He nodded, the ear pieces on his cap flopping. "Ja. See, Jutte, she is a strong girl. You know, a bicycle like this one," he pointed at my Waverley Belle Safety model, "maybe I buy for her. A gift."

Hmm, again. Or maybe not trouble in paradise. What then? "She's athletic?"

His expression showed doubt, but he nodded again. "She swim, she ride, she play games. And always, first thing in the morning does she take a walk." He leaned forward. "Yesterday morning, through the snow, she takes a walk. Her and sister Anka."

I waited for more.

"Out the back of the hotel they go, to a garden there." He paused. "Blume . . . flowers are all dead now, but still plenty of trees and bushes to see. Someone hides there. Three mens, says Jutte. 'Now,' yells one. Out they jump and boom, throw a sack over her head."

My tongue snagged on the tooth again, and I winced. Was I hearing the story correctly? "Throw . . . threw . . . a sack over her head? Your bride's head?"

"Yes, yes," he admonished me, waving his arms and making a kind of demonstration of what he meant. "No."

Nimble cocked her head and stared at him. Amsel stared back.

"The sack over Anka's head," he said.

Understanding dawned. "Oh. Sorry. Anka."

"Ja . . . yes. Then one slugs Jutte in the jaw. Out she goes, like blow out the light. Her jaw, it is almost broken, she says when she wakes. Frau Flynn, she comes early to the hotel with pastries. She finds Jutte lying unconscious in the path and calls for help." His feet shifted, causing Nimble to sit up and growl.

I tugged lightly on one of her ears, stilling her. "Have you reported the assault to the police?"

He shook his head. "I come to hotel when the manager calls for me. Jutte is battered, bruised. Confused. We send for a doctor. We are busy. Worried. This morning a messenger hands me a letter. I open it. Read. 'Where is Anka?' I say. It is Frau . . . Mrs. Flynn who tells me Jutte is alone when she is found. Anka has been disappeared."

My friend, Mrs. Flynn, who owns a small restaurant and bakery, had gotten a contract to supply morning pastries when the Majestic Hotel's resident baker got drunk once too often and had to be fired.

"Disappeared?" I said. "She was kidnapped, you mean?"

He shrugged. "Ja. Kidnapped. Held for money. It is in the letter. Two thousand dollars I must pay. Do not tell police, the letter says, or Jutte will be killed."

I blinked. "Jutte? But Jutte—"

"Ja, ja. Anka is gone, Jutte safe. Jutte asks for her sister when she wakes up. Says men, German men, not from Austria, carried Anka away. But they do not know it is Anka. Think it is Jutte." He nodded. "Better maybe for Anka if they do not find out any different."

"Oh, definitely," I said in heartfelt agreement.

His hands, curiously slender and fine-boned for such a blocky character—a gambler's hands—gripped the edge of the desk as he leaned forward. "So Frau Flynn, she tells us you are lady detective. That you will help and will not involve police. We must find Anka and rescue her. You know I will pay." His chest expanded. "I pay good."

So I'd heard, Mr. Amsel's generosity being famous hereabouts. But was I qualified to take on this job? I'd stumbled into my last couple cases and rescued people almost by dumb luck, me being the luckiest dummy anyone ever heard of, but this situation sounded fathoms over my head. What if I moved too slowly? Blundered into a situation where someone got killed because I was inept?

What if I couldn't help?

"Mr. Amsel—" I began, but he interrupted. Worse, he looked downright browbeaten and worried. And very unhappy.

"See you," he said, "I think I am being bamboozled. Got lots of money, and I like to spend it. Help peoples."

Once again common knowledge, thanks to the newspaper and word of mouth.

Then, after half a dozen heartbeats, he said, "But I don't like cheated. I run honest games, serve honest drinks in my businesses. Women—I don't have no use for peoples who pull a fast one." Another heartbeat, then, "Try to pull a fast one."

A warning there. I suspected he wasn't an easy man to fool.

I sucked in a deep breath. Well! This was turning into a most intriguing puzzle. "Who do you suspect of bamboozlement, sir? Do you have someone in mind?"

"Ja." His jaw took on a stubborn-looking set. "I ain't going to say who. You find out. Then we know for sure."

"I need a place to start. Your impressions could be important."

He opened his mouth, then closed it again.

So much for that train of thought. "Did you bring the ransom letter with you, sir?"

"Ja."

"May I see it?" If he said no, and I almost hoped he would, I'd turn down the job.

He didn't, though. Reaching into a breast pocket, he fetched out an envelope and started to remove the note. I stopped him. "Let me. I want to see it intact."

Shrugging, he handed it over, then watched curiously as, first of all, I sniffed the envelope. I wasn't trying to be funny. In September, a distinctive scent left on a similar note, in a similar situation, had formed a vital clue in finding a lost girl and a murderer.

Alas, this time I got no such help. The paper was dry smelling and maybe a little salty, although I thought I caught the odor of India ink and maybe something else. Something almost medicinal. Not enough to suggest anything crucial in any of that. And everybody used India ink.

Rats.

Amsel's name was scribed on the envelope's face in plain block letters approximately one-quarter-inch high. Larger than

20

most people write. This, I hoped, uselessly, as it turned out, might provide a clue. The writer had used a bit of pressure, enough to flatten the pen's nib, causing the ink to spread because of the cheap, rough paper. Even so, every letter was precisely formed, as though staying within invisible lines. Childish, in a way, except for the content.

Now if only I could find someone who wrote like that.

I lifted the flap, loose now, but which had been glued down only on the very tip, and took out the letter. Modern forensics had come up with a way to identify people by the whorls on their fingertips and were often able to "lift" prints off material they'd touched. I feared, even had I known how to do such a thing, we were too late with this. Who knows how many people might have handled the paper, smearing and blurring the marks beyond recognition?

You want Miss Kalb back unharmed? the note read. Put two tousand dollars in Deutsch Banke money bag. Hang on the door knob of Room 213, Finkle's Rooming House. 417 W. Border Street. 7 p.m. on the dot. Wednesday. Tell no one. Do Not talk to Police.

I squinted up at Amsel. "How many dollars for her release?"

"Two tousand, says right there."

"Um-hum. It does indeed. I wonder—" I stared at the spelling mistake in the note. Or the not spelling mistake, depending on who might have written it.

"What?" he demanded.

"Why two thousand?" I said, thinking aloud. "Why not three or five, or even ten?"

"Two tousand is a lot of money." He sounded surprised. "I will pay. Got the money in my safe. But not much more. I keep business deposits in the bank."

"Which bank?"

"Deutsch Banke in Spokane. Other banks in Walla Walla and

21

Colville and Wallace. Do business local."

I remembered reading as much in the newspaper. His habit of doing business locally made him popular in each of those cities.

Extracting a notebook from my desk drawer, the one without the .32, I started making notes to remind myself of Amsel's words.

Why would the kidnapper demand the ransom money be put in the specific bank pouch? I asked myself after copying the note, misspelling and all, into the record. What possible difference could it make? Maybe it was insignificant, but I thought it best to draw no conclusions as to what was significant right now.

Amsel fidgeted as he waited for me to jot down my notes, blotting his swollen nose occasionally, and wearing a puzzled expression.

"You will find Anka, yes?" he asked.

"Yes." I hesitated. "Or at least I'll try. On one condition."

"Condition?"

"Two conditions, actually."

His fidgeting stilled. "What?"

"First, I want to speak with Jutte."

He nodded. No trouble with that. He'd no doubt expected it.

"And second, no argument if you don't like what I find."

His frown deepened, an expression almost frightening considering the state of his nose. "What is this?"

"Call it a hunch. You may not like my results."

He stared at me, then, losing all expression, nodded.

We spoke of rates. This time, instead of pro bono or as near as made no difference, I charged the same for my labor as I would've billed for either Gratton or Uncle Monk, and he handed over a twenty-dollar retainer fee without question.

"I take you now to Jutte," he said, but I demurred.

"I have another witness to speak with first," I said.

"Another witness?"

"Yes."

"Who is witness?" he demanded, but I shook my head. Let him figure it out if he could.

"I'll be with you shortly, Mr. Amsel. Give me an hour, if you please."

"Time is wasting." He flapped the ransom note.

"I'm aware of the time constraints. Believe me, I shan't waste a moment." I dropped Nimble from my lap and stood up, holding out my hand for him to shake.

He grasped two fingers and pumped my arm.

"Call me Sepp," he said.

CHAPTER THREE

As soon as Mr. Amsel—or Sepp, as he said I should call him—left, I mopped up puddles of melted snow and inspected my Waverley Belle. She seemed all right, thank goodness, since I hadn't as yet had a chance to ride her beyond one wobbly trip down the block. There seemed to be a bit of a learning process, and winter wasn't the best season for it. I couldn't wait for the weather to clear so I could try out the path local wheelmen had gotten paved specifically for bicycling.

Nimble stood back and, dare I say so, scowled, barking at the bicycle as we passed it on our way up the stairs to the apartment where I lived in my Uncle Monk's spare bedroom. I'd moved to Spokane early in the summer after it became intolerable, and maybe even dangerous, for me at home after my father died. My stepmother could be a model for those evil characters depicted in children's fairytales. Not so much fun in real life.

I changed my bloodied shirtwaist and set it to soak in cold water. Pulling on boots and bundling up against the weather, I snapped Nimble's red-leather lead onto her collar. Within minutes we'd embarked on the first leg of our investigation.

We didn't head for the Majestic Hotel and my tenuous appointment with Jutte Kalb, but went in the opposite direction. Wondering if Mr. Amsel—Sepp—had figured out the other witness by now, Nimble and I turned off Riverside and walked south on Howard. We ducked our heads against snow blowing down our necks until we came to the aforementioned Mrs.

Flynn's café. Tucked into a space smaller than the Doyle & Howe Agency's office, the place always smelled of delicious food and, especially, of bread and other good things baking in the tiny kitchen. Today was no exception.

A section of harness bells chimed a cheerful hello as we entered, reminding me Christmas was less than a month away. On a wintery day like this, with the temperature well below zero, the café was delightfully warm inside, partially due to the oven's heat, and partially to the steam rising from a pot on the wood stove. Mrs. Flynn had a huge caldron of soup simmering, chicken from the aroma. Better yet, I felt certain chocolate was on the menu. After drying Nimble's paws with a piece of an old towel I carried with me for the purpose, I found a chair at one of the tables and sat down. Nimble lay demurely at my feet.

Known primarily as a ladies' café—men saying they preferred heartier food even as they glommed down Mrs. Flynn's doughnuts and cakes as fast as their jaws could chomp—the only occupant other than myself was an officer of the law, the shoulders of his blue uniform dark with damp. The officer was Bill Shannon. Rough and tough and rather frightening to look at, he perched on one of the delicate wire chairs and slurped soup.

Soup for breakfast? He must've been working the night shift.

But would he pay? I wondered, or would he simply put on his hat and leave? At least this one had the manners to remove his hat. Many of the Spokane bluecoats wouldn't bother. They'd simply take advantage of Mrs. Flynn and refuse the bill. No wonder she was looking for better paying outlets for her labors. I certainly hoped she'd find the Majestic Hotel's pastry contract profitable.

Speaking of Mrs. Flynn, her head peeked around the door to the kitchen. "Good morning, Miss Bohannon. I thought I heard the bell. 'Tis a day not fit for man nor beast. I'll be with you as soon as this loaf is out of the oven. You must be cold. Help yourself to coffee or tea."

"Thank you." I didn't feel like the ceremony of making tea. Instead, I poured coffee into one of the thick white pottery mugs sitting upside down on a clean cloth on the counter.

"Pour me a refill?" the policeman asked, waving his cup.

Mind you, I hesitated, not wishing to set a precedent of letting the police think they could take advantage of me or Mrs. Flynn. But perhaps it would be best to keep one bluecoat on speaking terms. My relationship with most of them had floundered of late, after I called Sergeant Lars Hansen out for covering up a major malfeasance.

I filled Shannon's mug, at which he nodded his thanks. Carrying my own cup back to the table, I warmed my hands with its radiating heat. I heard Mrs. Flynn moving about in the kitchen, and the clatter of spoon upon bowl. Stirring up yet another tasty morsel, I assumed.

"Fierce weather for so early in the season," I said, just to test Shannon's response.

"It is. Thirteen below last night, so I hear. And more of the same on the way from the looks of things." He swallowed the rest of his coffee, stood up, and dropped some money on the table. "Tasty soup," he called back to Mrs. Flynn. "Good coffee."

Her hand waved around the doorway.

Shannon lumbered over to the door, pausing to settle his tall, round hat on his head before stepping out into the weather. He glanced back at me from under fierce brows. "You take care, missy. Watch your back. You and your uncle and Doyle, all three. You've got enemies."

I gasped. "What . . ." I started, too late. He'd already gone. Well, no question. He knew my history. On the plus side, he hadn't sounded as if he condemned me out-of-hand.

And he'd paid for his meal.

Mrs. Flynn, drifting a cloud of fine, white flour as she brushed at the apron covering her severe, black dress, bustled from her kitchen. She carried with her a plate of bite-size eclairs, each with a drizzle of chocolate and a powder of fine sugar on top. She put the plate on the table between us and took one.

"Give them a try," she said. "It's a new recipe."

I wasn't about to say no.

Mrs. Flynn was a tall, attractive woman just on the shady side of thirty, though thin as a rail due, no doubt, to working harder than any lumberjack. She tasted her work with a frown that swiftly cleared. She nodded, as though telling herself they'd passed inspection.

"Delicious," I confirmed, reaching for another. "Are they for the hotel?"

She nodded. "I take it Mr. Amsel contacted you," she said when she'd swallowed.

"Yes." I took itsy bites, working around my sore tongue while savoring each delectable morsel. They were filled with some creamy concoction I couldn't begin to describe. "I believe I have you to thank for the recommendation."

She shrugged. "Tit for tat, Miss Bohannon. It's due to you my pastries are serving the Majestic Hotel's customers."

"It's due to you I was alive to suggest your bakery." We smiled at each other.

She'd saved my life a while back, or at the very least prevented a man from marking me with his knife. I may have put her name about for the hotel job, but I figured I still had the better part of the deal.

Under cover of the tablecloth, I gave Nimble a bite of eclair and wiped my fingers on a napkin. "Mr. Amsel tells me you discovered Miss Kalb unconscious yesterday morning. I'd say Mr. Amsel, when he told me about it, left out a few things. I'd like for you to give me the details. Everything you saw and everything you heard."

She smiled. "Of course. I've been expecting you, you know. Except I wasn't sure Mr. Amsel would actually contact you, or that you'd brave the storm."

Outside the café's windows, snow pelted down at a fine rate, covering the frozen ruts in the road and the boardwalks in a thick layer of clean, fluffy white. Footing would be treacherous on the way to the hotel, my next stop.

"No choice." I lifted my heavy, woolen skirt and showed her my boots. "I'm prepared."

She sighed and gazed wryly around the empty room. "Apparently you're the only one. You and Officer Shannon. I've had hardly any business to speak of today except for a few of the telephone operators coming off night duty. What do you need to know?"

"Everything. Tell me about when you first caught sight of her. Of Jutte. What time was it?"

Mrs. Flynn pondered a moment. "A few minutes before seven, I think. The hotel starts serving breakfast at seven on the dot and I always try to be prompt with my deliveries. Besides, it was snowing then, too, coming down harder by the minute, and I wanted to finish up. I have a wagon, a child's toy really, but it works well to haul several boxes of pastries at a time so I only have to make one trip. Anyway, it was still quite dark when I rattled down the path behind the Majestic. I spotted this bundle stirring along the path. It was slumped under some bushes, possibly an attempt at concealment. When I got near, I found a woman. She was quite woozy, bleeding from the mouth, and she told me she'd been knocked out."

"Shocking," I commiserated.

"Yes. I didn't know who she was, of course, but I could see she was young and well-dressed," she continued. "I rushed over

28

to her and tried to help, asking her name and was she hurt and all sorts of the stupid things one always asks in that kind of situation. After a few minutes, she sort of woke up and started talking—in German, unfortunately, so I didn't understand more than a word or two, but when I asked again for her name she said, 'Anka.'

"You should have seen her eyes, Miss Bohannon, they opened so wide. And then she said, 'Where is Anka? Where is my sister?' Oh, and 'Who are you?' "

She seemed quite unconscious of mimicking a German accent.

"I told her to lie still and stay where she was while I ran with my pastries into the hotel, where I called for help. The manager alerted Mr. Amsel before we went out to where I'd found the young woman. She was lying down again by then and seemed quite dizzy and discombobulated. When Mr. Amsel arrived, he carried her into the hotel. She passed out about halfway there. Mr. Amsel had a doctor called; then we waited for what felt like hours. Nobody asked me to stay, mind you, but I was curious."

"Of course. Who wouldn't be? How badly is she hurt?" I wanted Mrs. Flynn's perspective.

She shrugged a bit disparagingly. "I don't really know. Not much, I think. A small knot on her cheek and a swollen lip are the only injuries I could see. She didn't regain consciousness, though, for quite some time. Or at least . . . well." Mrs. Flynn stopped, lips mashed together as though to hold back what she really wanted to say.

After a moment, she continued.

"When Dr. Barrow arrived, he applied smelling salts and revived her. After some tests, he found her eyesight quite normal, as well as her reflexes. The doctor advised her only to rest. Perhaps to put some ice on her various hurts. Then this morning, when I brought 'round my deliveries, I went up to inquire about her. Mr. Amsel was there with the doctor and received a message. He read it and promptly booted the rest of us out of the room. I don't know any more."

"What about Anka?"

Mrs. Flynn stopped just short of poking a bite of eclair in her mouth. "Anka? Why, I don't know. She wasn't mentioned again."

Now that, I thought, was odd. If my sister—providing I had a sister—vanished under those kinds of circumstances, I'd kick up a fuss of the first order. Why hadn't Jutte Kalb?

CHAPTER FOUR

While I'd been talking with Mrs. Flynn, the storm had turned into a blizzard, sweeping down out of the north and obscuring the city in swirling tunnels of white. She hastened me out of her café with the advice to "scoot on home before it gets worse."

"It's too early for this kind of weather," I grumbled to Nimble, tugging on my mittens.

We bent into the wind as we trudged homeward, the dog's ears flying out behind her like wings. The scarf wound around my head did nothing to keep my face dry. Snow stuck to my eyelashes and melted on my skin in icy rivulets. Within a block, balls of snow had formed on Nimble's curly hair, clogging her chest and feet until she paddled like a goose. Whining as annoyingly as a tired child, she stopped and sat down.

"Shame on me for bringing you out in this." I was breathing hard myself with the effort of walking into a north wind. "Here, I'll carry you."

The dog took this as her due, snuggling into my arms and shivering. I could tell I'd need to make a stop before going on to the hotel and meeting with Jutte. Maybe, while I was at it, I'd put bloomers on under my skirt for extra warmth. Men didn't know how lucky they were to wear pants.

Well, maybe Scotsmen wearing kilts.

Yellow light shone through the window as I approached the office. That meant Monk, or maybe Gratton, had decided to put in some work time today even though we had no cases.

Probably a wasted effort with the storm. The sidewalks, as I could attest, were nearly deserted. Today, of all days, I'd anticipated Monk and Grat spending convivial time with their friends at Moseley's Saloon. I'd already decided not to discuss my case with them. Not yet, I mean. They still had palpitations over me being shot—not seriously, thank goodness—during my last investigation.

Monk had tried to put his foot down, saying my sole job at the Doyle & Howe Detective Agency was that of office manager. Gratton's strategy was to bribe me, hence the bicycle.

I don't take bribes, even though I'm not averse to a good deal. Which is why, although I paid for my bicycle, I allowed Grat to negotiate the deal. I suspect more went on than I was told, as I'd paid only fifty dollars, nearly my whole savings, for the Waverley Belle.

"Where have you been?" Grat demanded, looking relieved to see me as I entered the office.

Entered? Make that burst through the door—the knob blown from numb fingers—propelling me as though caught in a dynamite explosion.

Much, I admit, as Amsel had done earlier. I skidded to a stop before I hit the wall and nudged the door shut.

Gratton had been slouched in his chair, feet propped in front of him, toasting before the fire roaring in the cast-iron stove. Now he sat up straight. "This wind is enough to blow a little thing like you away. And why are you carrying the dog? Is she hurt?"

"No, just bogged down with snow." Avoiding Grat's "Where have you been" question, I set Nimble down close to the stove, although not near enough for her to scorch, and reached up to unwind my scarf. Which is when Nimble, sensing an ally in Gratton, once again spotted the bicycle lurking in the corner.

Setting up a frenzied barking, she scooted around the room,

sliding on her ice-balled feet as though wearing skates. She knocked into my legs, whereupon my feet, for the second time in one day, swooshed out from under me.

Safety lay in Gratton's arms. He caught me before I hit the floor. We fell back into his chair, me sprawled across his lap. I found it dangerously comfortable.

He held me, apparently impervious to the snow melting onto his shirt, and fixed me with a concerned—I hope it was concerned—stare.

"Your nose is red," he said. "A good sign when it's this cold out. Where were you?" He turned to Nimble, still carrying on about the bicycle. "Nimble, behave yourself. And be quiet."

She, the little traitor, obeyed.

He probably wouldn't give up until I, too, did as he demanded.

I shivered. "I went to visit Mrs. Flynn. It wasn't snowing like this an hour ago."

"You could've come home before the snow settled in." He dabbed water from my eyelashes with the back of his hand.

"Yes." I sighed. Might as well get this next part over with. "And I have to go out again as soon as I warm up. I just stopped in to drop off Nimble."

His storm-colored gray eyes narrowed in suspicion. "And what, may I ask, is so damned important you think you have to go out in this weather?"

I loosened myself, creating a little distance between us. He was making me breathless, although that may not have entirely been the fault of his grasp. "I've got a job."

"A job? What kind of job?"

I'd signed on to create advertising copy for Mrs. Flynn's café a while back—part of the reason she got the contract at the Majestic Hotel—an agreement that had worked out well for both of us. I could tell by the look on Grat's face that he hoped this was more of the same.

Unfair as it may seem, I was tempted to let him think so. In the end, I couldn't do it. I told him the truth. "A kidnapping to investigate."

"What?" The thundercloud I imagined hovering over Grat's head seemed lit by lightning. "I thought we agreed no more investigating. My God, China, you're barely over being shot. Why do you want to poke into this kind of affair, anyway? You're supposed to leave the dangerous stuff to Monk and me. You promised."

I removed myself from his lap and whipped off my coat, flapped my skirt, and stomped my boots. Hard. It didn't help much, either the clinging snow or my temper.

"I did no such thing. It was you and Uncle Monk, talking so loud and fast you must've convinced yourselves. I made no promises, I assure you."

He breathed in deeply, his nostrils pinching. "Well, you should've. What's the matter with you, anyway?" Oh, he was full of bluster, for sure. "Why do you always get bound up with kidnap victims? Some kind of fairy dust? What is this, the third or the fourth?"

Goodness gracious. He was right. The manner of my cases was becoming habitual.

"I haven't been keeping track." I managed to sound pleased. "I'm thinking of hanging out my shingle. I shall specialize in kidnap victims."

He jumped to his feet and stood there as though thinking of barring the door. "Over my dead body."

I hadn't been serious. I don't think so, anyway. But Grat is easy to provoke, and sometimes I get carried away. For instance, when he thinks he can lay down the law to me.

"Don't be silly." I went into the hall, found another old towel, and used it to wipe Nimble's paws, rubbing it over her wet fur

34

for good measure. She, of course, basking in the attention, wriggled happily. "Anyway, I've taken a retainer. I'm obligated. And I must say the case sounds interesting."

"What do you mean, interesting?"

"Well, two girls were out walking together, but only one was taken."

He frowned. "How old are the girls?"

"Marriageable age."

"Huh." He seemed to be thinking. "Might be difficult to snatch two women at the same time. How many kidnappers?"

"Three, according to what Mrs. Flynn said the remaining woman told her. And they apparently knew the women's schedule very well. They were well prepared."

"Yeah?"

"Yeah." I corrected myself. "Or so I'm told. I haven't actually talked with the woman they left behind as yet. I have an appointment with her as soon as I can get to the hotel."

"Hotel?"

"Yes. They're staying at the Majestic. But here's the interesting part. So far, at least."

Grat had perked up by now. "Which is?"

"The man on the receiving end of the ransom note thinks someone may be trying to bamboozle him. His words. He didn't say exactly how. That's for me to discover, along with finding the kidnapped woman and precipitating her rescue." Finished with Nimble, I warmed myself at the stove.

Grat turned his chair to the desk, pulled a blank piece of paper toward him, and picked up a pencil. "You're just full of suppressed excitement, China. What is it? The case or the people? Who's the man?"

I grinned at him. "Oh, nobody much. Only Sepp Amsel."

"*Sepp?*" He jumped to his feet. "Holy . . . cow. You mean his bride has been kidnapped? Or is it her sister?"

"Indeed, I do mean that. The victim, perhaps by accident, is the sister, not that it seemed to make any difference to Mr. Amsel. For which I commend him."

Grat bustled into the hall, rummaging through the closet for more outdoor gear. "C'mon," he said, his impatience clear. "What are we waiting for? Get your coat."

Grat, not exactly one of the teetotaler contingent, had been known to voice his admiration of Amsel's business acumen. He, like most men who enjoyed a game of chance and unwatered drinks, appreciated Amsel's reputation for running an honest joint. Even so, he spent more of his evenings at Moseley's. Small and friendly, he said, where they knew him well. I think he enjoyed the Irishmen who gathered there, as opposed to the more numerous German faction at Amsel's.

Still, if I, as a representative of the Doyle & Howe Detective Agency, managed to solve Mr. Amsel's problem quickly and safely—not to mention discreetly—our reputation was bound to be enhanced. Business would flow our way.

I didn't know what to think about Gratton horning in on my investigation. After all, Mr. Amsel . . . Sepp . . . had hired me. And yet I couldn't help thinking Grat, provided he didn't try to take over, might prove a valuable ally. He had entry into places I could not go.

"Amsel's bride has only been in this country a couple weeks. First thing is to find out who she's been in contact with." His eyebrow arched as he wrapped a muffler over the top of his hat. "Or the sister. A case of jealousy, maybe?"

Calling to Nimble, I took her upstairs to settle onto my bedside rug, well out of range of that nasty old bicycle. True to plan, I donned bloomers, changed my wet stockings, and found a dry coat—my best and most fashionable, as it happened—a warmer scarf, and thicker mittens. I can't say I relished the idea of going back out into the storm, no matter how loudly duty called.

Grat locked the office, and we trundled off to the hotel for my meeting with Jutte. He, bless him, used his body to buffer me from the wind. It helped immensely as we broke through drifts growing steadily deeper. So did his arm, to which I clung. Sometimes it felt as though he were dragging me. Even so, the six blocks felt more like six miles.

Once there, Grat argued against my demand to enter through the back entrance, but I insisted. I wanted to see if any small thing jumped out at me.

Nothing did. If there'd ever been anything to see, snow had covered it by now.

Several large shrubs behind which the kidnappers had probably hid. Check.

The bush where Jutte, according to Mrs. Flynn, said she'd been shoved. Check.

Other than that, the area was quiet and serene. I figured the kidnappers were fortunate the only other building overlooking the walking garden was the hotel's maintenance shop and storage shed. The area had been built for privacy.

Convenient.

We entered the Majestic through the kitchen, pausing to first stamp our snowy boots while still under the roof overhang. Although we heard the clatter of pans and people talking in the scullery, we found the cooking area unoccupied at this particular moment. The enticing aroma of roasting beef and baking hams issued from the huge ovens. An empty box that had once contained Mrs. Flynn's pastries sat open on a counter.

The ease with which we passed unnoticed through the kitchen was another convenience for would-be kidnappers or thieves. I made a mental note to speak with the hotel's owner. Perhaps Doyle & Howe could subcontract a security force. My uncle and Gratton knew several men looking for jobs.

In the hotel's main dining room, waiters—in no particular hurry, I daresay—were setting up for their daily high tea, so very British. Crisp white cloths cloaked pedestal tables, fancifully folded napkins at each place. Silverware glittered against the pristine linen. Voices murmured from the lobby, while servers and bellboys wandered around, apparently without much to do.

Business was slow, due, no doubt, to the storm.

Grat and I mounted the grand staircase, keeping to the middle where a garnet colored Persian runner rug prevented slipping on the polished oak steps. We stopped on the second floor.

People were quarreling inside room two-ten, their angry sounding voices rising, falling, then rising again. A man and a woman; both spoke accented English. I caught a word here and there.

"Fault . . . pay . . . ransom . . . who . . . life . . . care?" I recognized the voice. It belonged to Sepp Amsel.

I looked at Gratton; he looked at me.

I shrugged and rapped on the door.

The voices stopped mid-word.

CHAPTER FIVE

We stood outside the Kalb sisters' hotel room through several seconds of silence. Presently, I knocked again. Footsteps, a heavy tread, sounded from within.

Grat glanced down at me and whispered, "I'm thinking we've arrived at an inopportune time."

"Or else the perfect time," I replied. I smiled as Mr. Amsel—Sepp, I mean—opened the door a crack.

"Hallo." Seeing me, he flung the door wide and said, "We been waiting for you. But who is this?" He eyed Gratton up and down.

"My partner, Mr. Gratton Doyle." Beside me, Grat gave a start. Partner? I could almost hear him thinking the word, complete with question mark. "He agreed to provide an escort for me today. The storm is quite severe."

Sepp and Grat shook hands, certainly with more force than necessary.

"Ja. The storm. Come in here. Meet my fiancée. Meet Fräulein Jutte Kalb."

He said the last part as though with pride, beaming at the woman, who appeared less than happy to see us. And looking at Miss . . . Fräulein . . . Kalb, I could see why. Although Sepp was not old by any means—being in his mid-thirties, a fact known to most from those oh, so informative newspaper articles—his fiancée was much younger. Probably closer to my own age of twenty-one.

In height and build she was quite tall and full-figured. Her hair was pale blonde, of a shade called flaxen, as sleek and shiny as a seal's, and done up in a high, stylish pompadour. Her eyes were blue, the vivid light blue of a summer sky. Her complexion was clear and pale with a flush of brighter pink over the cheekbones.

She was very handsome, and she knew it, but at this moment, Fräulein Kalb struck me as being uncomfortable in her own skin. I don't know why I thought this, for sure. Maybe the way her shoulders twitched in a kind of figure-eight pattern, as if she were trying to shake her dress into a better-fitting configuration. Or maybe she just didn't like my looks.

But I thought perhaps she liked Gratton Doyle's well enough. She stared at him, big blue eyes wide and somehow childlike.

Harrumph.

The newspapers declared Jutte a beauty. Frankly, I didn't see it.

I don't suppose what I thought mattered a whit.

"How do you do, Fräulein Kalb." I stepped forward to greet her. "It's so nice to meet you. I'm sorry to hear of your troubles. As Mr. Amsel has no doubt told you, I'm here to help."

Her eyes narrowed. "What can you do? A . . . Anka is gone. Herr Amsel must pay or she will die."

She spoke excellent English.

"We don't mean to let anything happen to her." I meant to sound reassuring, even as my mind raced. What had the ransom note said? I didn't remember it mentioning actual killing. Perhaps I was not thinking along harsh enough lines, but it seemed to me Jutte thought enough for us both.

"You think you find her, yes?" Her stare flicked over me. Disparaging. She obviously didn't think me capable.

Her slow glance at Gratton showed more approval, more interest.

"That is my intention." I spoke loudly enough to regain her notice. "With your help."

"What can *I* do?" Posture drooping, she went over to a slipper chair cushioned in garnet silk and sank onto it, wilting-lily style. "Is sad. Poor, poor Anka."

Yes, poor Anka, to be missing from these sumptuous rooms. Sepp had rented a suite for his bride and her sister, and it was as luxurious as you'd find in any private South Hill mansion. Perhaps more so.

Through an open door, I spied an apple-green satin comforter stretched across a bed large enough for a small family. What I could see of it, anyway. The whole bottom half of the bed was covered by a sprawl of colorful gowns, the white froth of unmentionables, and a half dozen (I counted them) hat boxes from Mamzelle's Parisian Boutique. A couple empty boxes had held beaded purses from Colored Crystal, a specialty boutique inside Mamzelle's store, for which I'd recently seen an advertisement in the newspaper. An ornate chandelier over the bed highlighted the shimmering silks and satins.

The outer room, where Sepp and Jutte—Jutte a bit unwillingly, I thought—received us, seemed smaller because of an overburdening of furniture. Tables for every purpose, a secretary, its niches filled with stationery and envelopes, all bearing the Majestic's letterhead, a couch, two easy chairs, two slipper chairs. Plants and flowers, appropriately innocuous paintings, knickknacks in abundance. Too bad much of the ambiance was spoiled by trays of half-eaten food, paper wrappers, and the smell of wet wool.

Without waiting for an invitation, I followed Jutte and sat across from her. Although pretty, I found the seat uncomfortable. What a good thing a lady of quality never actually rested her back against the chair. I sat bolt upright. She did not.

Behind me, the men spoke quietly as Sepp filled Gratton in

on the circumstances. He interrupted himself to say, "You must be cold. Jutte, vill you order coffee?"

She glanced over at him, wrinkled her nose, and shuddered delicately. "I have tea, thank you."

He opened his mouth, closed it again, reached over, and gave a tasseled pull a yank, summoning an attendant.

I forced a smile at Jutte. "Now, if you please, tell me everything you remember about the attack yesterday morning."

"Everything? I do not remember everything." She pulled a dainty handkerchief out of a handbag flung down on the table and dabbed at her eyes. The handbag was unique, beaded and embroidered with a pattern of white lilies. From Colored Crystal, I supposed, accounting for one of the boxes. "I was scared. The men were big. One hit me. Knocked me out, like a prize fighter."

"How awful for you. And what else?"

"What else? Nothing. That is all I know."

I brought out my notebook and a freshly sharpened pencil. One slow day in the office I'd prepared a short list of standard questions suitable for most occasions. All I had to do was fill in her answers.

"You may remember more than you think, Miss Kalb. Just relax, please, and take me through the incident. Start from the moment you and your sister left your room. Did you see anyone? Anyone at all?"

Her bisque-doll eyes blinked at me. She shrugged and shook her head.

I sighed. "Not one guest? Not even a maid, or perhaps the boy who cleans the shoes? Anyone you wouldn't ordinarily pay much attention to. I understand it was early." Sometimes, if an investigator can give a witness a little poke, they'll proceed on their own without urging.

Jutte, I soon found, proved a more difficult case.

She shook her head. "Nobody," she said. "Shoes all done. Mine and Anka's, set outside the door."

"I see. And as you came down the stairs?"

"Nobody," she insisted. "Too early for Americans. All still in bed, except the kidnappers."

Admiration for her new country seemed lacking. I opened my mouth to contest her statement but changed my mind, instead asking, "What time was this?"

She shrugged again, a trait beginning to annoy me.

"Six and half." She pointed at an ormolu clock sitting in pride of place atop the fireplace mantel. "So says that clock. American made. May not keep time like a good German timepiece."

I gritted my teeth and let her observation slide. "Close enough, I expect. Tell me, Miss Kalb, from which door did you and your sister exit the hotel?"

She frowned, realized what she was doing, and put a forefinger on the vertical lines to smooth them. "Kitchen door. Shorter than to front door. No reason to walk around the building. Also, the alley is dirty." She coughed, the scent of horehound mint lozenges blasting in my face. Unconcerned, she poured a fragrant tea from a pot into a matching cup and sipped from it, steam rising before her face. Any offer to share was not forthcoming, even though I still shivered from our walk through the storm.

Eyeing us from across the room, Mr. Amsel knit his brow above his swollen nose. A knock on the door revealed a young man who quietly took an order for coffee.

"Did anyone see you leave?" I asked Jutte. "Open the door for you, perhaps? Or seem to be watching you?"

Her annoying shrug came again. If she wasn't careful, she'd put her shoulder out of joint. "Everybody here watches me. I will be rich soon."

Merciful heavens! A little shocked, I concentrated on my writing as I noted down her exact words.

So, this was no love match between Jutte and Sepp. Not on her part, anyway. On his? I couldn't make up my mind.

A quick glance at Sepp showed he and Gratton standing by the window, where Sepp pointed at something on the ground. The shrubbery where Mrs. Flynn found Jutte, I imagine. From a certain stiffness in his carriage, I also suspected Sepp had overheard Jutte's comment.

I knew for certain Gratton had. Our eyes met, and he shook his head the least little bit.

One last question occurred. "Did your sister say anything before the kidnappers made off with her? Did she walk on her own or did someone carry her? Anything to suggest she may have known who they were?"

Jutte's blue eyes swiveled toward me. "How could she know?"

"That's what I'm asking you." My pencil poised over the paper, but she gave me nothing to write down. Another of those shrugs was all the answer I got. Which, when you come down to it, is neither a yes nor a no.

My patience stretched thinner and thinner as we progressed. "Had you seen any of these men before, Miss Kalb? Perhaps in the dining room?"

Her baby blue eyes widened. "I do not look at other men. I am to be married."

Funny, she'd certainly looked at Gratton.

Extracting information from Jutte was like pulverizing a stone into sand. One had to grind determinedly for so much as a dribble. But then, when I'd almost given up, she gave me something to go on.

"They speak in German," she said. "And Yiddish." She glanced at Sepp. "I do not know Yiddish. Only hear it." She said this with a pride I didn't understand.

"Nothing wrong with Jews," he said calmly, as though answering a hidden meaning.

What a relief when our coffee came. I directed my questions to Sepp as I drank the hot brew, warming me from the inside out.

Except Sepp wasn't much more informative than Jutte, able to report only on the note and on what Jutte had told him immediately following the kidnapping.

"Let me know right away if you hear anything more from the kidnappers," I said, receiving another of his funny two-fingered hand pumps as Gratton and I, finished with our coffee, replaced scarves and gloves. "And . . . about the ransom. Are you going to follow the instructions in the note?"

His expression grew quite wooden. Or . . . I take that back. It grew stony, the muscles in his jaw like snow covered rock. A light had gone out in his eyes, a change dramatic enough to make me ask if he wanted my investigation to continue.

"Ja," he said. "Is for Anka."

I glanced at Grat.

"I should deliver the ransom," he said, as though reading my mind. "Maybe we can find a way to follow whoever picks up the money. Be best to discover the woman's whereabouts sooner if we can and avoid that part. I'm afraid—"

Sepp nodded. "Afraid they kill her after. I know." He looked over at where Jutte was perusing an advertisement in the newspaper. As far as I could see, it was announcing a shoe sale at the Palace department store.

"Miss Kalb didn't give me much of a place to start an investigation, I'm afraid," I said. "She was remarkably unobservant."

Jutte ignored my remark, although Grat gave me a warning look. "No reason she should've been looking for trouble."

"Scared now," Sepp said. "She don't know what she says."

"I'm sure you're right." I thought she knew very well.

"Some ladies scare easier than you do, China," Gratton said as the door closed behind us. "Could be you oughta take a cue from them."

Or a cue from him advising me not to worry the clientele.

I waved a hand. "Pooh. Nothing would get done or figured out if we all let our fear take control."

We caught up with the room attendant in the hall as he backed out of another room carrying a tray with the remains of someone's breakfast.

"Oh, hello." I snagged his sleeve, stopping him before he could escape. "You're just the person I wanted to see."

"Me?"

"Yes." I didn't care for his expression. He looked entirely too anxious to escape for my taste, which made me all the more determined to detain him. I tried a smile. "I just wanted to ask if you were working early yesterday morning."

"Yeah," he said. "I work six days a week, sometimes more if they're short-handed."

"I see. Could you tell me, please, the time you came on duty yesterday morning?"

"Six." He shifted the tray, rattling the crockery. "Always at six. I set up the trays for room service orders, early, so they all get delivered at the proper time."

"How do you enter the hotel? Through the front door?"

"Oh, no." He shook his head. "That wouldn't do. I'm just the hired help. I come in the back, through the garden."

I noticed Grat's interest in the conversation pick up.

"Did you see anyone loitering about?"

The lad's brown eyes opened wide. "No, ma'am. Why? Is something wrong? Has there been a complaint? Was somebody robbed?" Coffee dregs spilled from an overturned cup onto a crumpled linen napkin. "Her?" His chin pointed toward Jutte

Kalb's door. If so, he didn't sound particularly sorry.

"Are you speaking of one of the young women residing there?"

"Yeah, I mean, yes, ma'am. Lucky Sepp Amsel's fee-an-cee. She's the lucky one," he added under his breath, so low I barely heard him.

I studied him until he fidgeted. "You don't like her?"

He flushed. "Ain't my place to say whether I like her or not. But the sister is nicer. She says please and thank you. I don't mind so much not getting a tip from her."

"Hmm," I said. I thought of the clothes I'd seen, the lavishly appointed room. No tip for the service attendant? That seemed strange.

"Why?" he said pugnaciously. "Is she accusing me of something? She better not be. I could tell you things—"

"What things?" Grat asked, which only served to put a damper on the attendant's loquacity.

The boy rattled his tray. "Aw, never mind. I don't know nothin' about those women. This tray is heavy. I got to get back to work."

"She's not accusing you of anything," I assured him. In fact, she hadn't seemed to see him at all, but I didn't think I'd tell him so. "Just one more thing. Have you noticed any strangers inside the hotel? Anyone who seemed out of place?"

He stared at me like he thought I belonged in the insane asylum out at Medical Lake. "Ma'am, practically everybody here is a stranger. And they all seem like regular folks to me."

Beside me, Grat snorted. I suppose the question had been rather poorly phrased.

"Sorry. I'm not being clear. I meant anyone hanging about without any apparent purpose," I amended. "Or maybe watching the Kalb women."

"No, ma'am," he said, almost too fast.

I didn't quite believe him, but thought I'd get nothing more at present.

Still . . . "What's your name?" I asked.

He frowned. "Eddie. Eddie Barstow."

"Well, Eddie, here's a little something for your trouble." My smile at him, I hoped, looked friendly. Using Gratton's own method of tipping the "little" people who are in a position to see things, I gave him twenty-five cents and told him my name and address. There was still a chance he'd overhear something important and report back. Perhaps he'd even make a concentrated effort to do so.

So. Nobody knew anything about anything. How on earth was I to find Anka Kalb when I had nothing to go on?

What's more, and so I told Grat as we walked home, this time with the wind at our backs propelling us along a great deal faster than when we'd arrived, I'd seen no sign Jutte Kalb feared for her sister's life. Disgust, impatience, ruthlessness. All those and more, but not much that stemmed from the milk of human kindness.

"Ah, sweetheart, you didn't like her. I can see why. She's a man's woman, for a fact."

I cast a peek at him out of narrowed eyes. He was holding his hat on his head with one gloved hand, guiding me along with the other. "A man's woman? What do you mean?"

"You should know. You've met women like her before. Women comfortable alongside men and who take on a man's role. Mrs. Green, for instance. Remember her running a crew of timber thieves? And Leila Drake, hijacking ore out of the Flag of America mine and setting the owner's wife up for murder?"

As if I'd ever forget his last example, since I'd been the one thrown off a steamboat into Coeur d'Alene Lake in the wife's place.

"Not that Jutte Kalb is like them. We don't know if she is or not, although, I'll admit she comes across as a cold-blooded gold-digger. But even the mother of your new young friend, Neva O'Dell, was an opportunist." He went on thoughtfully. "And a pickpocket who came within an ace of getting away with it. This kind of woman is not like most. And they've got a certain aura that's hard for men to resist."

I must have made a sound because he shot me a wary look. "Some men, I mean. Hard for some men. I'm not taken in."

Harrumph. Wasn't he?

He had forgotten one thing, though—the main thing, actually—in his reminder about those men's women.

I'd been the one to come out on top and bring them all to justice.

So what kind of woman did that make me?

CHAPTER SIX

Gratton stopped me as we passed in front of a post-1889 brick building with two glass doors in a recessed entry. "German Club" was written in gold leaf on one door in an elegant Olde Worlde script, with the translation, Deutsche Club, below. The club was locked on this Monday afternoon. The second of the doors opened into Mannheim's Haberdashery. Apparently, it too was closed.

"The German club might be a good place to ask about the Kalb sisters," he said. "Amsel told me he brought the sisters around to meet the society secretary a couple days ago. We can ask if anyone else has met them yet. Most immigrants check in at the various organizations that represent their home country. Ask our neighbor, Cosimo Pinelli, about the Italians, sometime. He credits them with helping him learn English and set up his business. Someone from there pointed out the other side of Monk's building was for rent."

I, I'm ashamed to say, hadn't known this.

Through the haberdashery's opaque glass door, we could see no lights illuminated the showroom part of the business. The shop was empty, unless one counted a mannequin without a head. I rubbed snow off the glass. I thought I saw a faint gleam at the back of the haberdashery, so I knocked.

To no avail. No one stirred.

"We'll talk to them," Grat said, "when the storm dies down."

No sign of it abating appeared as yet. The snow blew sideways out of a low, dark sky. "Will it? The storm die down, I mean."

His teeth flashed briefly as he grinned. "They always do."

No further progress on the case seemed likely at the moment, so we made our way back to the office, stepping at last into blessed warmth. Uncle Monk had returned from wherever he'd been and stoked the stove while we were gone. Nimble was with him, lying on her rug with her eyes closed as the heat washed over her.

Monk looked up from some scattered paperwork, actually letters I'd typed ready for his signature. "I wondered where you two disappeared to. I was beginning to think I ought to send out a search party. When I got here, there was water all over the floor, stuff scattered around, and the dog howling fit to wake the dead. I thought maybe we'd been robbed."

He didn't sound as concerned as he might have. However, my bicycle was nowhere to be seen, and I had a moment's trepidation.

"Where . . ."

Monk guessed what I'd been about to say. "I put your two-wheeler in the closet. Back there." He gestured toward the hall, where a storage closet held all sorts of odds and ends, from old coats to shovels to Monk's stock saddle and, now, my bicycle. "The dog doesn't like your new toy, China."

The dog lifted her head and looked at me. Really! Did I see signs of resentment on her fuzzy little face?

I touched my tongue, still sore though on the mend. "Yes. I noticed. Thank you for putting it out of her sight."

A huge sigh from Nimble repeated the thanks.

My uncle divided his attention between Gratton and me. "You plan on telling me what took the pair of you out on a day like this? You must've been the only ones . . . brave . . . enough to risk the weather."

Brave? Or did he mean stupid?

"Just about." Grat grinned at my uncle, taking off his hat and slamming it against his leg, scattering chunks of snow around the room. A few landed on the stove, sizzling as they evaporated. His coat was next. He hung it on a peg to drip. "But we— China—had some people to meet at the Majestic Hotel. I figured I'd better escort her."

"People to meet? A new client?" Hope lit in Monk's eyes. He hates having nothing to do almost as badly as Gratton does.

"Well . . ." Grat drew the word out. "China's client, if you want to be precise. I thought I might give her a hand." He bowed affectedly toward me. "With her permission."

My uncle frowned. "China's client?" His head cocked questioningly. "Not another little girl in trouble, I hope."

Should one classify Anka Kalb as a little girl? Not if she was anything like her sister. "Certainly not," I said and proceeded to tell him about this morning's events.

"Ain't that somethin'," Monk said when I'd finished. "Sepp Amsel. That's fine."

He caught my look and flapped his hand. "I don't mean fine about his bride's sister being kidnapped. I mean it's good he heard about us."

Harrumph. Technically, Sepp had heard about me. But if I was ever going to be accepted as one of the detectives, I must include the whole agency as well. Grat and Uncle Monk, in other words.

"If we can get Miss Kalb back and Sepp can avoid paying the ransom," I said.

"Alive." Grat warmed his hands over the stove. "Get her back alive."

I'm afraid Gratton's remark was more to the point than either Monk's or mine.

"Of course. That's what I meant." I drew my chair over to huddle next to the stove. "But right at this moment I don't know how we're going to do it."

Wind gusted down the stovepipe with a howl, making me shiver even though I knew the room was warm. Comparatively, at any rate. The idea of a woman held captive and at the mercy of some unscrupulous man—or men—did more to cause the shivers than the outside temperature.

"We didn't accomplish much in the way of clever sleuthing today," I confessed to Monk. "I'm afraid our star witness lacks something when it comes to simple observation. She says she doesn't remember anything."

"No, and it struck me and China she wasn't trying real hard, either." Grat turned away from the stove and took a chair at his desk, positioned so his back was to the wall. Monk usually just pulled a chair up to either Grat's desk or mine. Mine, at the front of the room, provided either a greeting station or a barricade to whoever entered the office. Depended on if the visitor was a friend or an enemy. The enemy part was why I kept a .32 Smith & Wesson DA revolver in the top drawer. It had come in handy more than once.

My uncle pointed his feet toward the fire, his brow puckered in a pensive frown. "And you say Amsel thinks somebody is trying to pull a fast one on him, eh? I don't suppose he hinted at who this somebody might be."

I nodded. "I think he went out of his way to avoid doing just that."

"Yeah, lambie, but you're quick. Who were you talking about just before he said it?"

I tried to think. "I don't remember. I don't think any names were mentioned. We'd discussed him paying Anka's ransom, then he said Mrs. Flynn had recommended me. I—" I spoke more firmly, "nothing we said indicated why he thought somebody was bamboozling him, or who is involved. Or even the nature of the swindle, if swindle it is."

Grat cleared his throat. "You want to start with the shakedown or the kidnapping, Monk? Or split the difference?"

My uncle used his forefinger to smooth his mustache, although to my eyes it looked perfectly groomed already. "The clock is ticking. Saving the woman comes first. And the best rescue comes from finding who took her before payment becomes due."

"No question." Grat got up and went over to look out the window. He had to clear a peep hole first, scratching away frost with his fingernail. He grunted. "I'll go poke around at Amsel's saloon. One of his bartenders is fresh off the boat, and another runs a mean game of faro." He glanced at me and winked. "Or so I've been told. One of them might've heard something."

Monk's knees creaked at he rose from his chair and scooted it over in front of my desk. "And I'll go talk to the fellers who tend the outside portion of the hotel. See if they've noticed anything. They'll probably be holed up in the shop around the stove when they aren't shoveling the boardwalk out front of the hotel."

Grat wrapped a gray wool muffler around his neck and over his nose, then struggled into his still damp coat. The muffler, I noticed, was a match for his eyes, but not one for the brown coat. Which, I daresay, didn't appear to warm him much.

"What do you want me to do?" I asked. "Where do you think I should start?"

Grat cocked a dark brow. "Stay here and keep the stove going, China. It's too cold for you out there."

My uncle agreed. "This wind is like to blow you right off your feet, lambie, a little thing like you."

As if to punctuate his advice, another down-blast of wind rattled in the chimney pipe. Nimble raised her head and emitted a mournful *whuff*.

I bit my lip. Oh, how I hated to give in to the vagaries of the weather—and the patronizing tone the men took with me. Just because I am a woman. Still . . . "I shall make up a list of people to talk to and questions to ask while you're gone. We can divide it up later."

Monk nodded. "Good idea. You do that."

A sop. He didn't mean it.

Which was all right. I didn't mean it, either. Or not entirely. I had plans and the fortitude to carry them through on my own.

Which meant that, as soon as they were gone, I donned my outdoor clothing for another trip into the storm, this time leaving Nimble to toast before the fire.

A perilous trip of slipping, sliding, and pushing my way through two-foot snowdrifts brought me to the door to the Cozy Corner Café. It, like every other business on the street, was locked up tight. The sidewalk in front had not been swept in a while. Still, after the struggle of getting there, I wasn't about to leave without asking Mrs. Flynn one more question. To tell the truth, I was a bit worried over whether I could even get back home without a warm-up.

She, thank goodness, lived in an ell behind her business, much as Monk and I lived above the agency.

I banged on the glass in her door until I feared it would break. At last, a light came on, and I saw a tall female shape hurrying toward me. Mrs. Flynn's face peered out, saw who it was, and yanked me inside.

"Miss Bohannon! Whatever are you doing here again? Are you out of your mind? You must be frozen."

"Y-yessss," I agreed, answering her last statement, not the questions.

She made a production of taking the hammer of her derringer off cock. "Come in. I'll make coffee and warm you up."

I could only nod, my whole face so cold my lips barely moved.

"Are you still pursuing your inquiries about the Kalb

woman?" Mrs. Flynn answered herself. "Well, of course you are, or you wouldn't be here. I can't imagine anything less than an emergency taking you away from your own fireside." In an absolute first, she invited me into her spotless kitchen, which smelled of cinnamon and was neat as a picture in a magazine, with every pot, pan, and bowl in place, where she helped me shed my coat. Shifting a pretty black-and-white cat out of the way, she sat me down in an old rocking chair. "Don't tell anyone you saw a cat in here," she warned me. "There are some who wouldn't like it."

I nodded. "C-c-cozy," I managed to say.

She smiled as the cat climbed into my lap. "His name is Jerry. He'll keep you warm until the coffee is hot."

"J-j-Jerry."

It always surprises me how much heat a cat can generate, and my legs, smothered by purring cat, were grateful. Quite soon, as the rest of me warmed, my lips thawed enough to talk.

"I'm so sorry to bother you." I accepted a big white mug of steaming coffee. She'd stirred in cream and sugar, which I don't usually take, and added a little something extra—whiskey, I think, and cinnamon. It was delicious. A glow lit in my innards.

"No bother. I need this myself." She settled herself on one of the wire-frame chairs from her dining room and sipped her own coffee. Or maybe I should call it a beverage since it was like no coffee I'd ever tasted. "I take it you've met Fräulein Kalb."

"Yes." I breathed in alcoholic steam. Delicious, indeed.

Mrs. Flynn smiled. "What did you think?"

"About her?"

She nodded.

"I think Sepp . . . Mr. Amsel, should find himself a different wife." I had no time for niceties.

Mrs. Flynn nodded. "Looking at the situation from a bystander's point of view, it's not hard to think the kidnappers got hold of the wrong woman."

I couldn't help myself. I giggled as Mrs. Flynn smiled a little grimly. "Yes," I agreed. "Abducting Jutte would serve them right." I sobered. "I just hope the sister is more cooperative or she might not live long enough for us to rescue her. Mrs. Flynn—"

"Call me Rose," she interrupted. "I believe we know each other well enough for first names by now."

"Yes. And I am China."

Rose settled more firmly on her chair. "And so, China, what is of such great importance it brings you here twice in one day?"

I leaned forward, carefully, to avoid disturbing Jerry. "Something Miss Kalb said. And something she didn't say."

"Well, now," Rose said, "you've got my attention. What is it?"

CHAPTER SEVEN

Monk arrived home from his scouting expedition first, just at dark and as the wind faded to a fitful breeze. Actually, I wondered if Gratton would be back tonight at all since his self-imposed duty consisted of visiting a gambling house/drinking establishment.

And then I thought it might be better if he didn't make the attempt. As Monk said when he came in stomping his feet, his nose red with cold and his mustache and eyebrows frosted with snow, "A man could freeze to death out there without half trying. They've got a thermometer at the hotel mechanical shop. One of the men told me it read minus five at three o'clock this afternoon."

I can't say as I was surprised. It had been no warmer for my own dash through the storm.

"Did you learn anything from the Majestic's crew to further our investigation?" I asked.

My uncle, coughing a little, shook his head. "Nothing worth mentioning."

His expression was not encouraging. To the contrary, in fact. I'd call it downright glum.

"Yet," he added, as if trying to reassure me, "one young feller gave a twitch when I asked if he'd noticed any funny business in the hotel garden yesterday morning. Could be he knows more than he's saying. It might take a pay-off to get at the truth. I'm just not ready to go that far yet."

"Do we have time to wait?" My nerves had been jumping with tension all afternoon. "This is an awful time for a person to be kidnapped. Not that there's ever any good time, of course. But what if they're keeping her tied up in a drafty barn or a dark, dank basement? She might freeze. Don't forget I've had personal experience with both those kinds of places in conditions less dire than this, and I was always cold. Fear makes one cold."

I'd never admitted as much before.

My uncle sent me a sharp-eyed look. "It does?"

"It does."

My uncle's face puckered like it sometimes does when he's thinking. "Too damn bad we can't make 'em have her telephone before the ransom drop. Prove she's alive."

"If only we could!" I filled the teakettle and set it on the stove. I thought my uncle could use a warming drink.

After my visit with Mrs. Flynn, I'd kept warm—and gotten my exercise—by running up and down the stairs, killing time as I waited for the men to return. In between stoking the fires in the parlor, the Monarch kitchen range, and the office stove in an almost futile attempt to keep the place above freezing, I'd made up a batch of split pea soup with ham hocks, an internal warmer on its own. Comforting food at the end of something other than an ordinary day.

At nine o'clock, and I daresay it felt more like the middle of the night than the middle of the evening, my uncle and I gave up on expecting Gratton and went to bed. Thank goodness for Nimble, burrowed against my side helping to keep me warm. Or maybe the other way around and I was helping her.

Not that I slept any to speak of. My thoughts rolled and tumbled together like salt grains thrown into a pot of boiling water. Eventually, each melted into nothing, just like every piece of information that had come my way. My uncle's inquiries had fared no better.

We had until Wednesday to discover Anka's whereabouts, with one day already gone. What had we accomplished?

Nothing, as far as I could see.

Unless, given the amount of time he was taking, Gratton had already cleared the case.

As it happened, he hadn't.

He had, however, cleared the boardwalk outside the office of drifts by early the next morning, throwing snow into the street to be trampled into ice by horses' hooves and wagon wheels. The exercise did nothing to improve his temper.

Nothing to improve mine, either, since he woke me up to the racket of his shovel scraping against the sidewalk beneath my window. Oh, yes. And he was cursing.

Even before I'd swung my legs over the side of the bed, the chill in my room warned me to pull on slippers before my feet touched the floor. Nimble jumped down, too, stretching her hind legs first, then her front. Voilá. She was ready for her day. Me? Not so much.

The sunshine outside my window seemed an insult.

Time was wasting, moving inexorably toward the hour when, unless we could free her, Anka Kalb's ransom must be paid. Or else . . .

I hastened to pull clothing over my goosebumps, run a brush through my hair, and wash my face, the water cold enough to feel like frostbite. Nimble skipped ahead of me downstairs, she to dash outside, me to poke only my head around the door, shiver, and call to Gratton that I'd start breakfast.

He grunted without pausing his shovel work, his breath clouding the air.

Judging by his response, I assumed his investigations last night had been more assiduous than one might suppose, involving, no doubt, a quantity of demon rum—or, more likely, Irish whiskey—and gambling on cards. Gratton, I regret to say, becomes quite surly when he loses at poker, his game of preference.

Hearing Uncle Monk stirring about in his room, I hollered "good morning," outside his door, poked more wood into the Monarch's fire box, and set about breakfast. The coffee came to a boil about the same time the men and Nimble showed up in the kitchen.

Grat's nose twitched. "Who made the coffee?"

"I did," I said.

He scowled. "I don't know which is worse, Monk's witches' brew or your dainty tea party stuff." He grabbed a pottery mug from the shelf above the stove and filled it to the brim.

My uncle huffed out something that sounded like a laugh.

"I suppose the bacon won't be cooked to your liking either," I said, pushing Grat out of the way. "Perhaps you should try one of the restaurants. I'm sure they'll appreciate your business. Just don't forget to tell them what a fine cook they have."

Silenced, he pulled out a chair opposite Monk and sat.

Monk winked at me.

"Any success at Amsel's place last night?" he asked Grat, who dipped into the jam pot and piled strawberry preserves onto a piece of toast.

"Dunno for sure. Maybe. Maybe not." He picked up a slice of crisp bacon and stared at it a second before sticking it in his mouth.

I scooped a scrambled egg into Nimble's dish and set it on the floor for her to wolf down before I settled on my chair. "What do you mean?"

He held up his hand in a "stop and wait" motion. "I'm still thinking about it."

Funny. I would've said he was too busy eating.

In his own good time, he began his narrative.

"First of all, you'd have thought you were in Berlin or wherever Amsel hails from, guzzling big steins of beer and singing drinking songs," he said. "Seemed everybody in the place was a Dutchman but me. Made conversation a little difficult."

Monk and I nodded our understanding.

"Seeing as the kidnapping is on the quiet, I couldn't just start asking every disreputable looking character in there if he'd heard anything about a woman being snatched, so I joined a game and kept my ears open."

Did, or did this not sound encouraging? "And?" I passed Nimble a snippet of bacon.

"Nobody said a word about anything but the game. And the weather. And the quality of the beer, about everyone's tipple of choice. Those Dutchmen wouldn't know a good bourbon from panther . . ."

At Monk's glare, his mouth snapped shut. Panther what? I wondered. Something rude, I'd be bound.

Disappointment made me lose my appetite, although a handful of Mrs.—Rose's chocolate drizzled eclairs wouldn't have gone amiss. "Rats! A dead end then," I said. "It's hard to know where to go from here."

"Too bad Miss Kalb—the remaining Miss Kalb—turned out to be such a bad witness." Monk wiped his mustache and got up to pour another round of coffee. He, like Grat, may have complained of my coffee being weak, but he always managed to drink his share.

"Yes," I agreed, warming my hands around the cup. "Which I don't mind saying I find a little strange."

Gratton tossed Nimble a toast crust—which she snapped up in an instant—and leaned back. "I said nobody was talking about a kidnapping. That's not to say something fishy isn't going on. Could've been an advantage for me *not* to understand

62

half of what they were saying out loud. Sharpened me up some, having to read physical signs."

Monk sat straighter. "Such as?"

"What do you mean?" I leaned forward. Grat looked too smug, by far. His comment about reading physical signs had to signify something. Hopefully, something that carried our search for Anka Kalb forward.

He grinned. "While I was watching them, I noticed a particular contingent of fellers watching me." He shifted in his chair. "I have a certain reputation around town, you know, and Amsel's place isn't my usual watering hole. Some men there paid me no mind, but I made a few others nervous. Those are the ones who caught my attention."

"Who are they?" Monk asked.

"Here's the funny part. Nobody seemed to know. Evidently they're new in town."

My heart took a little jump, but then the wheels in my mind revolved, bringing the brief moment of euphoria to a halt. "Isn't that odd, then?" I asked slowly. "You making them nervous, I mean? Do you think . . ."

We paused, me to ponder a bit on the scene Gratton described; the men to look at me as if wondering why I wasn't filled with delight.

"Think what?" Grat's fingertips drummed on the table, a sure sign of aggravation.

"Is there any reason you should've been making anyone nervous? In the normal course of things, I mean, them being strangers and all. Were you winning large sums from them, perhaps?" I was reasonably certain, going by his demeanor this morning, he'd done no such thing. I let the little dig rest a moment before I went on. "Or was one cheating? Or is someone involved in another of your cases?"

"We don't," Uncle Monk said with grave emphasis, "have any

63

ther cases pending at the moment."

Grat nodded. "So, given the people concerned, we must be looking at the only open job on the table."

"Looks that way to me," Monk said.

I shook my head, unbound hair flying wildly about my head until I latched it behind my ears. "Do either of you see the flaw in your thinking?" Pausing for effect, I waited in vain for the penny to drop. "No? Then how about this? The ransom note Mr. Amsel received instructed him to tell no one. No police. According to what he said, I'm the only one he told, then I told you. If news of the kidnapping gets out, the woman might be killed. Am I correct?"

Two pairs of eyes stared at me. Three if you counted Nimble's. She must've sensed the tension in the room.

"Yeah," Grat said at last. "So?"

I sighed. "So, what possible reason would any of those men, strangers to you, have for being disturbed by your presence? What gave them cause—if anything did—to rouse their suspicion?"

Grat's jaw clamped shut.

A moment later, Monk nodded. "I see," he said.

The table shook as Gratton's palm slapped down on it. "You're saying either the kidnappers have learned the news is out, or I'm seeing a false clue."

"Yes."

He got up to pace the kitchen, stepping over Nimble where she lay sprawled in front of the stove. He seemed to be arguing with himself. Two circuits around the room later, he stopped in front of me.

"I know a nervous, suspicious man when I see one, China. And I know when I'm being watched. Which can only mean one thing."

"Yes," I said again.

"What—" Monk shook his head.

"Somebody has been spreading the word," Gratton said.

I added, just to clarify, "The kidnappers have learned we're on the job."

"The question is," Grat finished, "who told them?"

CHAPTER EIGHT

Our next step, or so the three of us decided after a half-hour's heated discussion, lay in following up on what we knew and going from there. Not a lot to begin with, I must admit. Three men, German speakers, had abducted a woman and sent a ransom note. They wanted their money on Wednesday. That much we knew for a fact. Everything else was guesswork.

According to a recently developed methodology, I made a list of questions in need of answers. Monk, still coughing from a recent cold, volunteered to mind the office, keep the fires burning, and make sure Nimble didn't follow me.

Gratton and I planned a visit to Mannheim's Haberdashery and the German Club, where he'd take the lead in questioning the subjects. Then he'd return to Amsel's saloon for another go at the bartender while I revisited the hotel and spoke again with the fair Jutte. This time, I vowed, I'd get her alone. I felt sure she'd speak more freely if Sepp wasn't there to overhear. And, if the bellhop was on duty, I wanted another word with him, too.

With Gratton pacing impatiently in the office below, I, hoping to stay warm, bundled up until I resembled a rag doll stuffed to overflowing. Still, I didn't get away without a severe word of warning from Monk.

"You be careful, China," my uncle said as we left. "I don't want you becoming a victim like last time. And the time before that." He thought a moment. "And before that."

I must say I had no desire to play victim again. "I'll be careful," I promised, and with a wave, Grat and I set off.

Gratton had done a fine job of shoveling the length of boardwalk in front of the Doyle & Howe offices. Many of the other business owners, except for Mr. Pinelli at the cabinet works, had ignored their drifts and blocked doorways. Evidently, they expected customers to blunder their way through. We found ourselves walking in the street more often than not.

"You think Jutte Kalb had something to do with her sister's kidnapping, don't you?" Grat lent me his arm as we slipped and slid our way along Riverside.

"I'm not sure," I said as we turned the corner onto Post Street. "She doesn't seem unduly concerned about her. And she knew I . . . the agency had been hired. What do you think?" I gripped his arm harder as my feet flailed once again. The thought occurred to me that I would've made better, and safer, progress if I'd been wearing skates.

He held me upright until I steadied myself. "I don't know what to make of her. On one hand, she acts oddly uncaring. On the other, she appears to be trusting her fiancé to manage things. Remember, the ransom note was delivered directly to Amsel."

I snorted. "Ah, yes. The demand for payment."

"Everybody knows he's got money. I'd be surprised if she has two dimes to rub together."

"Yet she appears to be spending like she has it. You may not have noticed, but her hotel bedroom is filled with expensive clothing. Hats and accessories from Mamzelle's Parisian Boutique—only one of the most expensive shops in town. Gowns from Spokane's own couture dressmaker. Not Mamzelle. I mean the one who actually studied in Europe. And I saw her looking at ads for shoes while we were there. I can guess where the bills are going, can't you?"

"Yeah, well, it doesn't seem like Amsel minds. Could be she's a more dependent type of woman than you're used to, China.

otta hunch that's why a lot of these women emigrate to the United States. They're scared and alone, got no place to turn and no prospects. They want more and better opportunities than they're used to in the old country."

Needless to say, I thought he was wrong. Oh, perhaps not about the majority of women, but wrong about Jutte Kalb. And probably her sister, too. I figured Jutte wanted not simple opportunities, but a life of ease, and the only prospect she had in mind was the one of using a man to fulfill her desires. Why else would a woman agree to become a mail-order bride?

"Is that how Jutte struck you?" I asked. "As a woman afraid she'd be abandoned with no place to turn?"

The corner of his mouth quirked. "Now that you mention it, no."

A figure appeared behind the frost covered window of the German Club's door when Gratton knocked. A man's round face, complete with a double chin, peered out at us a moment before he unlocked the door.

"Hallo, hallo." He spoke through the six-inch crack he opened up. *"Was kann ich für dich tun?"*

I understood the "hallo" part. The rest I wasn't so sure about. "How do you do. Do you speak English?"

"Ja. I speak it goot," the rotund little man said. "You are not Deutsch?"

"Sure—" Gratton's brogue grew broader, "—we're as Irish as they come. Afraid we don't speak your lingo."

I elbowed him. Without much effect, what with my arm being well-padded with layers of clothing starting with a thick knit sweater over a long-sleeved shirtwaist as well as my heaviest coat.

He winked at me.

"Are you, then, in the wrong place?" the man asked.

Grat pointed to the lettering on the door. "Nope. German

Club. This is it. Want to ask you a couple things."

The man's brow puckered low over deep-set eyes. "*Herein-kommen, bitte.* Come in, please. I am Herr Schultz. Is cold today, yes?"

"Indeed, it is," I said.

Herr Schultz stood back, beckoning for us to enter, then led the way into a mostly empty, rather cavernous room. A stove, undersized for the area, fought a losing battle against the chill. Although the door had been locked, two men wearing heavy coats hovered beside the stove. A few tables and chairs in rough condition were scattered about. A counter mounted on sawhorses supported a dishpan, and beside it, a stack of chipped plates and some mugs. Kettles were stored on rough plank shelves behind the counter, with forks and spoons standing upright in tin cans.

"How may I help you?" Schultz asked.

Grat didn't waste any time pussyfooting around. "Are you acquainted with Jutte and Anka Kalb, two women recently arrived from Germany?"

One of the men at the stove, the one clad in a navy-blue pea jacket like sailors wear, cleared his throat, sounding as though he had a chunk of phlegm lodged there. I glanced at him. He had a large, red, printed handkerchief over his face, obscuring his features. Hopefully it would keep his cold from spreading. I certainly didn't want to re-infect Monk.

"Jutte and Anka Kalb." Our host's gaze traveled the room as he thought about whether he was or whether he wasn't acquainted, then nodded. "Ja. A little." He held up a space between his thumb and forefinger. "A little. Only they are not from Germany. They are from Austria. They do not like it here, at our German Club. Too many of our people are poor immigrants looking for help. They are hungry. The Kalb women, they are embarrassed around the poor. One of the ladies says she does not need our help to learn the new language, that we should help others. Already, she says, does she speak the best English."

"And does she?"

"Oh, yes. Very good," he said grudgingly, but brightened to say, "Better than the sister. But Herr Amsel, he is a generous man. Money he gives to us every month. With it we feed the poor. Then, when the men find work, they help the newcomers."

Somehow, I wasn't surprised.

"When did you last see the Kalb women?" I asked.

The little man paused for thought, his eyes rolling up as though to see the inner workings within his own forehead. "Three days, maybe, or four," he said at last. "No. Five. On Thursday. They came with Herr Amsel when he brought a donation. Meat. We do not have much meat. Men need it for strength to work, ja?"

Yes, and so do women and children. I stopped the words before they escaped.

"Was anyone else here at the time?" Grat glanced around the room, settling on the two men who stared back at him and then at me.

Herr Schultz fidgeted as he pondered the question. "Ja. Herr Amsel brought the beef. At same time, he brought man who is hiring for mines in Idaho. *Sieben . . . acht* men came here to put in app . . . appla . . ."

Gratton helped him out. "Applications?"

"Ja." He twinkled and put his numbers into English. "Hired four. One with family, six *kinder*. A happy day."

"I can imagine." I smiled, too.

"Did the Kalb sisters talk with any of the men that day?" Gratton took it upon himself to snag a chunk of wood from a small stack on the floor behind the stove and stuff it into the firebox.

There wasn't, I noticed, a great deal of wood on hand. Perhaps I, though not on the same plane as Sepp, could do something to alleviate the shortage. Mr. Biddlestrom, whose family the agency had saved from a major scandal earlier in the year, had mentioned a couple dead firs leaning over the roof of his mansion. I'd bet he'd be happy to contribute the wood to the German Club, and maybe even pay the men for taking the trees down.

Meanwhile, as though uncomfortable with the direction our questions were going, Herr Schultz refrained from immediately answering Grat's question. He looked toward the men again, one whose mouth tightened as he shook his head a fraction of an inch.

In connection to what we were saying? Or a reply to something the other man murmured to him?

"A little talking, maybe," Schultz said, adding, "but is not wrong to speak with men. To take their thank-you."

"No, no. Of course not." My elbow went into Grat's ribs again. This time he flinched. "We were just wondering if the ladies may have known some of the men. Acquaintances, you know, perhaps from the boat coming over."

The man shook his head but soon stopped. "Maybe," he said. "I forget which sister, but she did speak with two or three of the men. One, at least, I remember, who was hired by mining company."

A frill of excitement stirred in my stomach. At last. Something that looked like a promising lead.

"Who were the men?" Grat asked.

"Who?" He smiled a nervous little smile and spread his arms in wonder. "I do not know their names. All but one were strangers to me. I will ask that man when next he comes to club."

"And when would that be?"

"Next week maybe. When he comes to visit wife."

Grat's eyes narrowed. "Not soon enough. Does Amsel know the men?"

The man shrugged. "Ask him."

"Just one sister spoke with the men?" Evidently there'd been something in the club host's voice to intrigue Gratton. Or perhaps he'd noticed the way the other two men in the room listened.

"Ja. The other sister—I forget which is Herr Amsel's bride—" Schultz stopped, a wary expression dropping over his fleshy face. His gaze flicked toward the men, then the door—or no— toward the business on the other side of their shared wall and as quickly away. What did that fast-moving expression mean? Something to do with Mannheim's Haberdashery?

"I did not notice," he said, his cheeks growing pink above a neat, blond beard.

The interview ended on this note. He'd seen nothing, heard nothing, and for sure was saying nothing. Nothing further, anyway. Even though Gratton and I both prodded at him a few minutes longer, the only thing of possible use was the name of the man, a certain Herr Berger, who'd been hired by the mining magnate. It seemed Berger frequented the club. The problem being he was out of town for now. Even so, I thought we'd done well, and now I was eager to get Grat outside.

Speaking our thanks to Herr Schultz, we left, me sort of urging Gratton along.

"What's the matter with you?" he complained. "That feller knows more than he's saying. I'm sure of it. And I think maybe those other two, as well." He pulled away from me. "I should go back in there and hammer it out of him. Them."

"Wait! He may know more, but I think he's done talking. For now, at any rate. We should leave him be and let him stew for a bit." Perhaps that load of firewood would loosen his tongue.

"Yeah? Well, he did leave the barn door open more than a crack, didn't he? By accident?" He looked thoughtful. "Might've been intentional." Grat's breath steamed out in great puffs of vapor. Mercy, but it was cold, and with the sun out, blindingly bright under a blue, blue sky.

I nodded toward the haberdashery's door, which lay directly opposite the German Club's. Its frosted window bore a small Open sign in the corner, placed there since we'd entered Herr Schultz's domain. "I think we should pay Mr. Mannheim a visit, don't you?"

The tension went out of him, and he grinned. "Sweetheart, I wouldn't miss it for the world."

I love it when he calls me sweetheart. Except when he's being sarcastic. This time, he wasn't. Butterflies fluttered in my stomach—or thereabouts.

Mannheim's Gentleman's Haberdashery sported a considerably more efficient stove than the German Club. The large, well-lighted room was warm enough I felt safe removing a mitten to feel the quality of one of the shirts on display. I'd been wondering what to give my uncle and Gratton for Christmas. Now I knew, even as I winced at the cost.

A man barely escaped from his teens was folding handkerchiefs, three to a box, in such a precise manner I would've sworn a specialized machine had done it. He ceased his labors and smiled at us, his narrow face genial.

"*Guten tag,*" he said. "Good morning. *Was kann ich für sie?*" The same phrase Herr Schultz had used. I doubted I needed a translation now.

"Good morning." I strode forward. "These shirts are very nice. Are they made on site?"

Gratton looked at me as if I'd suddenly become unhinged.

The young fellow grinned cheerily. "Oh, yes. My uncle, he is the tailor. A very good tailor, famous in the old country. Suits, trousers, jackets, vests—and shirts. Anything a gentleman needs. Except hats. Hats we import from England." His grin expanded. "But nothing for ladies. Sorry."

We heard the burr of a machine and a rhythmic clack as the treadle worked the needle up and down. His uncle, no doubt, in the back room busily sewing.

"But the gentleman," the clerk said, indicating Gratton hovering behind me, "for him, a medium size, with the shoulders a little more broad. I could interest him in a jacket, yes? The one he wears—" He hesitated. "Something a little warmer, perhaps?"

Oh, such tact. Such finesse. And, dare I say it? Grat actually seemed to agree. As far back as September, after a man with a knife slashed his old jacket almost to shreds and inspired a giant mending job, he'd mentioned the purchase of a new one. I guess it took a cold snap to make up his mind.

Somehow, the young clerk maneuvered Grat over to a rack where several jackets hung. He picked out one in a muted charcoal plaid.

The clerk slipped it off a wooden hanger and held it out. "A good color for you, yes? To match your eyes." He glanced over at me. "Your lady will swoon."

Grat blushed. Truly. I grinned and wandered over to the doorway leading to the work area. Brushing aside the curtain separating the two rooms, I peered inside. My first impression was that they could've used more light. An older man hunched nearsightedly over a Singer sewing machine. A skull cap clung to the back of his head. Jewish, then. His foot on the treadle pumped so fast it was a blur.

I cleared my throat. "Ahem. Excuse me. Are you Mr. Mannheim?"

"Talk to August," he said, not bothering to look up. Probably a good thing at the speed the needle was going. "He will help you. Out front."

The machine slowed as he turned the fabric, then picked up speed again. Another of those wonderful shirts spilled over the side of his table as he attached a sleeve. More bolts of fabric were stuffed into individual cubes on wide shelves. Huge wooden spools of thread hung from spikes pounded into the wall.

I squinted. My breath caught. Something other than thread dangled from one low spike.

"I'm sorry, I really need to speak with you." I suspected the answers I wanted more likely lay with this man instead of the young clerk—presumably the aforementioned August.

Or perhaps with him. I'd spotted a slim, younger man of medium height bent over a broad table at the side of the room. I hadn't even seen him until he moved and his pale hair caught the light. He held a pair of scissors in his hand. Still and silent from the moment I darkened the doorway, I'd evidently interrupted his labors as he snipped around a paper pattern set out on a thick, brown fabric.

"What do you want?" this man said. He didn't sound friendly. He sounded . . . um . . . worried, I believe is the applicable term. Worried people arouse my curiosity and make me wonder at the cause.

"I want to talk about a young woman with whom someone here may be acquainted."

He looked down at his scissors, reflexively opening and closing them a couple times. When he met my gaze, I saw his eyes were as light as his hair was blond. Also, he was very handsome in an insipid sort of way. And not, of course, as handsome as Gratton Doyle.

"What woman?" He took a page from August's book. "We have nothing for women here."

His English was self-consciously precise, a monotone really, sounding as though he read from a schoolbook.

"So I've been told." I stepped forward, edging closer to the item that belied his statement and studied it closely. "And yet—" I paused dramatically and pointed. "What is that?"

CHAPTER NINE

The sewing machine's clackety-clack stopped. I heard an indrawn breath.

My accusatory finger apparently transfixed Herr Mannheim, if only for a moment. He aimed a fierce frown at the younger man and said something that sounded angry. Hard to tell since he spoke in German or Dutch or perhaps another dialect. Something other than English, at any rate.

The younger man flexed his scissors again. *"Nein,"* he said in sharp reply. I understood that well enough, but not what he said next. From the scowl he turned on me, I wished I'd thought to bring my trusty pocket pistol, a Smith & Wesson .32. I hadn't imagined I'd need its cold weight in the special pocket I'd had made in my skirt. Not when I had Gratton as an escort.

Speaking of Gratton, I let out a sigh of relief when he stepped through the doorway behind me. He carried a bulky package under his arm. It took only an instant for him to grasp the tension in the room.

"What's happening? Find something interesting?" He took his time studying the two men and, take my word for it, he has an intimidating stare when he chooses to put it in play. Mannheim, still hunched over his sewing, tapped a nervous foot on the treadle of his sewing machine—though not quite enough to start it running. The younger man appeared to take no notice of the scrutiny.

"Yes. A lady's purse." I indicated the object, which Grat eyed re he shrugged.

"Which means what, exactly?" he asked.

I turned toward him and whispered. "It means our missing woman is here—" I glanced around. There seemed no place to hide unless she'd been stuffed in one of the large packing crates supporting the table top where the cutter had his work laid out. A grisly thought I'd as soon hadn't occurred to me. "—or she has been. Recently."

"What makes you think so?"

There'd been two empty purse boxes in Jutte's room. I'd bet ten whole dollars this pocketbook had come from one of them. "Trust me. I just know."

"Another of those crazy hunches of yours, I suppose," he muttered, evidently forgetting my hunches often, no, usually proved quite accurate. Neither Grat nor my uncle cared to acknowledge them.

"No hunch this time," I assured him. "A fact."

Facing the Mannheim contingent again, I said, "That's a pretty purse. I would like an identical one. If you didn't make it, where did it come from?"

The younger man shifted from one foot to the other and spoke up. "I do not know. I found the purse in the hall a few days ago and set it aside to keep safe for her in case she came back."

"For whom?" I shot the question at him. "What day?"

His gaze flicked to the older man, who looked down at his work. "I think perhaps a woman who came from the German Club, one day last week. Two women came with the saloon man, Amsel, when he met some men who look for job."

Mannheim growled something that ended with, ". . . Dieter?"

Dieter being the man's name, or so I assumed. What had the rest of the sentence been about?

German people are, for the most part, polite and quite

formal—or so I've found. Why did this man not address Sepp as Herr Amsel, or perhaps, since his English was very good, Mister Amsel? Sepp showed a certain amount of sartorial panache. Did he shop at Mannheim's? Or did he not, which provided a reason for the disrespect, or maybe just dislike, I sensed.

Meanwhile, I pondered Dieter's answer.

"Has a certain ring to it, China," Grat said, which I took to mean he thought the excuse plausible.

And it was, except for one minor thing. A thing that required further inquiry before I leveled any accusations. I decided not to speak to Gratton about it just yet, either. If I'm proved wrong about something, I don't like to point it out beforehand.

The older man spoke to the younger, who bowed. "I must work. Herr Mannheim says we will find lady and say to her to come get the purse."

And why, I wondered, hadn't they done it before now?

Herr Mannheim barked something else, which Dieter translated. "No time, no more interruption."

We were dismissed.

The streets were much emptier than on a usual Tuesday morning as we made our way back to the office. The cold was enough to stop most sensible people from stirring from their firesides. But sense notwithstanding, Gratton and I had a job to do.

Grat hustled me along, the freezing air sticking my nostrils together with every breath I took. After a few moments made difficult by the icy roadway underfoot, Grat's long strides became too much for me to keep up with. I came to a dead stop.

"Why are we running, for goodness sake? I can hardly catch my breath."

He'd gone a full three strides beyond me. "I need to hop the noon train to Kellogg, that's why. And I want to talk this over with Monk before I go."

Just like that, he abandoned his plans to talk again with the bartender.

"Kellogg? Why are you going to Kellogg?" Galvanized into motion again, I caught up with him. "Why do you need to talk with Monk?"

"Didn't you hear Schultz? I need to talk to those men hired on at the mine."

"Really?" I puzzled the logic for a moment. "Maybe. I don't suppose it would hurt, but the purse, Grat. That's the best lead to Anka's whereabouts. Those people at Mannheim's know something, especially Dieter."

"What makes you think so? Which one is Dieter, anyway? And how did you get on a first name basis with him?"

I confess to feeling a little smug about this, but a bit impatient, too. Opening one's ears is not complicated sleuthing, as Grat himself had been known to tell me. "He's the one with the scissors. I heard Mr. Mannheim call him Dieter."

"Oh." Grat waved this aside. "Why are you so concerned about the pocketbook, China? Wouldn't surprise me if every other woman in Spokane has an identical one."

"I beg to differ. It would surprise me right out of my stockings."

"That I'd like to see."

And just maybe I'd like for him to.

Heat rose in my face. Quashing the vision, I grabbed his arm and let him tow me along as I returned to the subject at hand. "Those purses are new stock, fresh in this week. I saw them advertised in Saturday's *Spokesman-Review*. Only a person with plenty of money can ever afford a purse from Mamzelle's Parisian Boutique, and these happen to be very expensive. I can't believe any woman who lost such a bag wouldn't miss it immediately." My voice sounded a little choked. "Jutte Kalb had a similar one on her tea table. Perhaps Anka had . . . has one, too."

His face twisted. "Something else Amsel paid for, I expect." He helped me off the walk, lifting me over a shin-high drift as we crossed the street. "He can afford it."

"Yes, but—"

"I'm more interested in those men who hired on at the mine, China, and I'll tell you why. They had the opportunity to snatch the woman and make the last train out yesterday evening, probably taking her with them. Or, if it wasn't them, maybe they can name the men who didn't get hired. Those are the ones, broke and down on their luck, most likely to take a desperate action like kidnapping a woman for ransom."

I have to say his hypothesis made sense. "Yes, but—"

"Don't forget, Schultz said he's acquainted with only one of them. As far as he's concerned, the others are strangers who happened to show up at the hiring."

Had those two in the German Club showed up for the hiring? I wondered.

"And," Grat went on, "he mentioned Amsel most probably didn't know them, either. Amsel just brought in the mine owner. You've got to admit it was a golden opportunity to hatch a plan and set it in motion."

"Yes, but listen—"

"Those men at Mannheim's . . . well, they don't seem like the kind of people who'd abduct a woman. A man who sews? One who cuts up fabric? Or the salesclerk kid?" Shaking his head, he enumerated the three jobs with a certain attitude. They were not the kind of men he was comfortable around.

I smiled and didn't try to argue further, or even get in a word of my own. He'd take his own course in the investigation. So would I.

★ ★ ★ ★ ★

Uncle Monk, needless to say, agreed with Gratton, although he did concede that asking Jutte about the purse was also a good idea.

"Cover all our bases," he said. "I expect the woman would've gone back for it if she hadn't been kidnapped."

"Assuming the purse actually belongs to Miss Kalb," Grat put in. "We don't know if it does or not."

"This supposedly happened before she was kidnapped," I reminded him. "She would've had plenty of time to retrieve her purse."

"Yeah, well, maybe she didn't attach as much importance to getting it back as you would, lambie."

Harrumph. He had no idea of the connection between a woman and her purse.

"And," he added, "could be you're mistaken about who the purse belongs to."

My eyebrows drew together in a pained frown, something I'd been doing a lot lately.

Gratton grinned as he cut the string binding the package containing his new coat. "Don't think she's mistaken this time, Monk," he said, surprising me as he came to my defense. "I think we pretty well established the purse belongs to the missing woman."

"Exactly." Even though he still didn't agree it was a vital clue.

Moving the coat rack closer to the stove, I hung my outdoor things on it as I peeled them off, layer by layer. "I'll follow up on the purse with Jutte while you're gone."

"You do that," Grat said. He shook out his new coat, which, when he shrugged into it, looked even more resplendent on him than it had in the store. Off the rack, but looked as though made just for him. And yes, the clerk had been right. The color did go well with his gray eyes.

"Where'd you get the coat?" My uncle sounded interested, reaching over to pinch the fabric between thumb and forefinger. "Looks good on you. Good quality, too. They got any more like it?"

Heavenly days! Since when did my menfolk think past comfort and utility to how they looked.

"Guess I might buy one like it for myself," Monk said, rather to my astonishment, as he so rarely buys himself anything. "Mavis has been nagging me to dress warmer when I go out."

Mavis Atwood, if I haven't said so before, is not only my uncle's housekeeper, but his lady friend of long standing. And she was right. Given my uncle's cough, he did need to dress more warmly.

"Mannheim's Haberdashery." Grat preened the least little bit. "Warm as a buffalo hide at half the weight. They've got a whole rack of them ready-made."

Monk yawned and stretched. "I'll pay the outfit a visit when we get back."

"You're coming with me?" Grat asked, appearing a bit surprised.

"You don't know who you'll be up against," Monk said. "Never hurts to have somebody along to watch your back." With the prospect of action, he appeared perkier than he had for days. I guess there's nothing like a real objective to get a man's blood running. Or a woman's.

Before they left, saying they'd catch the late train back to town, Grat warned me to always carry my .32. And to ask Mr. Pinelli for help should any word, any action, any anything strike me as wrong. I also got a surreptitious kiss that went on for several delightful and breathless moments while Uncle Monk was upstairs searching out a muffler to tie over his ears. I almost forgot the danger part.

But who, I wondered, as they left for the train station without packing more than extra ammunition for their pistols and a few dollars out of our petty cash drawer, did they leave to back me up?

Easy answer. Nimble, of course.

CHAPTER TEN

Getting Nimble ready for the next task on my list, another trip to the Majestic Hotel, turned into a bit of a tussle. With business slow over the past few weeks, I'd knitted the dog a sweater, a pretty little cable-stitch affair in red yarn to match her leash and collar. I'd amended the sweater from a child's pattern, and it had turned out well.

The thing is, she fought like a tiger when I pulled the neck cuff over her head. Or tried. I'd worked up quite a sweat by the time I succeeded. I had no fear my outdoor things, also nicely warmed after their sojourn near the stove, would fail to keep me snug. I turned the Open sign in the window to Closed and, with my pistol a reassuring weight in my pocket, locked the door behind us.

Outside, the sun shone on snow glittering as though crusted with gemstones. Here and there, thoughtful retail proprietors had cleared drifts and sprinkled the sidewalk outside their stores with sawdust, providing traction underfoot. I made a note to do the same when I returned home. And to clean Nimble's paws before she tracked it all over.

More people were stirring about than had this morning. I found the hotel humming with activity. Ladies emerged from their rooms to take tea in the spacious lobby, where huge fires blazed in the massive fireplaces. Waiters with white cloths over their arms toted trays heavy with fine silver, steaming jugs, and plates of delicate sandwiches and pastries. I supposed the credit for the treats was due to Mrs. Flynn . . . Rose, I mean.

Nimble drew a few looks as we passed through the lobby to the stairs. She always did, of course, but this time I heard a comment or two regarding her red sweater. She flapped her ears to show she heard them as well. I was pleased even if she was not.

The hall outside Jutte's room had breakfast trays still sitting outside doors. Remnants of bacon and sausage proved too much for Nimble. She snatched a bite or two as we went along, no matter that I reprimanded her severely.

"Inattentive bellhops," I muttered as I raised my fist to rap on room number two-ten. If the same sullen young man we'd seen yesterday worked this floor today, he was remiss in his duties. What did he say his name was?

Oh, yes. Eddie. The very person I intended to speak with when I finished with Miss Kalb.

Jutte took her time answering the door. "What is it?" The knob held in her hand, she stared down at me from her superior height. "Oh, you, Miss Bohannon. Have you found my sister?"

"Not yet, I'm afraid." I hauled Nimble away from a nasty looking egg just before she bit into it and snubbed her against my skirt. "Have you heard anything new from the kidnappers?"

I hardly thought Sepp would've omitted sending word if he had, but one never knew. And if they'd contacted Jutte, I figured hell would freeze over before she'd let me know. The puzzle remained as to why.

She stood in the doorway looking beyond me. "Where is the detective? Where is Gratton Doyle?"

"He's out of town following a lead." I smiled at her. "We have made some progress towards finding your sister, I assure you."

An odd look crossed her face. "What progress?"

"May I come in? I have a couple things to ask you."

"Me?"

"Yes. About Anka."

With obvious reluctance, she moved out of the way and opened the door far enough for me, holding Nimble close, to slip into the room.

"What need you to ask? I told you all yesterday."

I tried the smile again. The result, a sober stare, was the same. "As I said, there have been a couple developments."

"What developments?" She spoke precisely, showing off her English. Leading the way, she went over to sit in the same slipper chair she'd taken yesterday and waved me into the one opposite. I sat, Nimble beside me. Jutte didn't so much as spare the dog a glance.

Just as well perhaps, as Nimble's black nose was busy sniffing at the tea table. She seemed almost offended by a dish of horehound lozenges residing there. Not that I blamed her. I dislike the smell of horehound myself. Even so, I ignored the scent, being much more taken by the lovely beaded and embroidered purse lying casually amongst the clutter.

"Down, Nimble." For a change, she obeyed, almost instantly.

My mind raced. My heartbeat quickened. Yes. I'd seen a purse on the table yesterday. Yes, I'd seen a purse at Mannheim's Haberdashery this very morning. The thing is, the purse on the table now was a duplicate of the one at Mannheim's, but different from the one here yesterday.

Was I certain?

Yes.

Interesting that the purse had been returned so promptly after Grat's and my visit to the haberdashery earlier. Especially since the man, Dieter, had feigned ignorance as to whom it belonged.

I decided to give Jutte a little test. "What a beautiful purse. May I ask where you bought it?"

She lifted a shoulder in her trademark shrug. "Some shop. Is a gift from Herr Amsel. One for me, he buys. One for Anka. Very expensive."

An implication I couldn't afford one? I rather thought so. She didn't give me an answer, either, not that I needed one. Where else but Mamzelle's Parisian Boutique?

"I see," I said. "How dreadful if you should lose it, and brand new, too."

Jutte blinked and, snatching the purse off the table, put it in her lap and closed her hands over it, hiding the design from my view. She hesitated, then said, "Yes. Dreadful, but not for me. Anka, she loses hers. This one is found and now returned for reward."

"How fortunate for the kindness of strangers," I murmured. "It will be waiting for her when she returns to the bosom of her family."

Her face flushed pink at my words. Her shoulders twitched.

Hadn't whoever returned the purse mentioned the visit Gratton and I paid to Mannheim's? Or told her I'd specifically noticed the purse?

He must have, but she wasn't letting on.

How very odd.

Maybe I was reading too much into this whole thing. A purse had been dropped, picked up, and returned to its owner. Perhaps Jutte felt guilty because Sepp's gift had been treated so carelessly, the reason she reacted in such a peculiar manner. But I still couldn't see why she bothered to prevaricate about something so easily verified.

Even if she didn't know that was the very thing I planned to do next.

Jutte breathed in and, looking at me directly, which she didn't often do, asked again, "What developments?"

I smiled again and allowed her to change the subject. "Even

as we speak, Mr. Doyle is preparing to check with some men we think may have seen your sister. The thing is—"

Her blue eyes widened. "Seen her? Seen Anka?"

Have I mentioned I've been known to tell a fib or two in the course of my investigations?

I lifted a cautionary hand. "Perhaps. There's a chance. In order to be certain, I'm hoping you might have a recent photograph of your sister. One Mr. Doyle could have to show around."

She twitched. "Kidnapping is a secret. If told, Anka may die."

"I promise you, we are not telling anyone she is being held for ransom. We have an excuse in place if anyone should be curious enough to ask."

"What excuse?"

I blinked. "We plan to say news has come about one of her relatives dying, and we're looking for her to pass on the word. We aren't even saying her name. Nothing, you see, to put her in further danger. And, more importantly, nothing to connect the detective agency to her abduction."

What can I say? Yes, an implausible story with a great many weak points, but all my brain managed to come up with on the spur of the moment.

Anyway, it served to back her into a corner. Reluctance to comply showing in every move she made, Jutte went over to the large breakfront along one wall and poked around amidst what appeared to be a deal of clutter in the top drawer. Presently, she drew forth a brown cardboard photograph folder and brought it over.

"See," she said and waved a graceful hand, "this is Anka. And me."

The folder held two photographs, although I don't believe Jutte was aware of it. Somehow, one had gotten stuck behind the other, and, as she handed the folder to me, the stuck one slipped, its edge peeping out below the other.

Just then, Nimble, as though she'd been reading my mind, provided a most fortuitous diversion. Crusts of toast having provided a temptation too great to ignore, the plate she was licking on the sly clattered to the floor.

Jutte spun to look. *"Schwein hund,"* she yelled, adding a few more incomprehensible words to a diatribe.

Nimble whimpered.

Jutte having even more to say, this one time I let my dog be chastised. Flipping up the top photograph, I took a careful look at the one below, memorizing what I saw.

"Control your dog," Jutte snapped at me, yanking Nimble's leash and dragging her over to me as I smoothed the photographs.

"I'm so sorry," I lied, which seemed to mollify the woman as she directed her attention to the photograph again. I think she just wanted to get me out of there.

I patted Nimble, soothing her hurt feelings. Such a good dog.

The two women Jutte pointed to were similar in coloring—or seemed so in the sepia-toned photograph. Both wore hats that placed their faces in shadow. One, whom Jutte identified as herself, was quite a bit slimmer than the other. Anka was nearly as curvaceous as a Rubens nude. Otherwise they looked very much alike.

Both photographs had been taken at a picnic or some such festivity. Outdoors, at any rate, as they showed a background of grass with trees and a lake. In the topmost, the girls were seated on a bench with steins in hand, lifted as though saluting something or someone. In the other picture, the one she didn't know I'd seen, people, mostly men, stood behind them, the focus a little blurred. But all in all, an adequate photo.

"A bon voyage party?" I asked.

"Yes."

"How sad if you never see your friends again."

"Ja," she said, doing her best to appear woebegone. "Never again."

And then, because I wanted to see what she'd do, I pretended to notice the second photograph. My word, she snatched the folder out of my hands so fast it almost burned.

Jutte ripped out the top photo and handed it to me. "Other is a copy," she said, looking me in the eye. "I will keep the copy."

Liar, I thought, standing up to take my leave. And not even a good liar. But why lie? I wished I could go back for a second look.

Nimble, who'd sat beside me watching Jutte with distrust, got up, too, and went to the door, pawing at it.

I took the hint, and we escaped the rather poisonous atmosphere lingering in Jutte's room.

Breakfast trays still littered the hallway. I knew for a fact, as Jutte's much disparaged American-made clock had told me so, that the noon hour had passed. Time for lunch trays to be delivered. I'd think hotel policy demanded the bellhop's morning duties be complete beforehand. A puzzlement, for certain.

More aggravating to me was the thwarting of my desire to speak with Eddie again. I felt sure he had more information about Anka's recent activities than he'd let on. One of my friends from the mansions on the hill south of downtown had told me their servants heard and saw everything that went on in their house. They knew their employer's friends—and lovers. They knew where said employer went, what he or she ate, who she hated, and how much he bet on horse races. I'd wager all of Sepp's retainer fee that the hotel maids and bellboys were no different.

Spying another boy who wandered within hailing distance, I cornered him and asked about Eddie. He'd seen neither hide nor hair of his friend since they arrived together this morning, he said. When they'd donned their uniforms in the employees' basement changing room getting ready for work. I could tell the fact he hadn't worried him.

It worried me, too, with a nagging, unsettled feeling.

In the end, though, it was Nimble who found Eddie.

The other bellboy and I, our conversation finished, separated, he to take the back way down to the kitchen while I started for the main staircase. Then, taking me by surprise, Nimble yanked the lead from my hand and dashed past me. Past the boy, too, until she stopped right in front of him and scratched frantically at a half door set in the wall. A laundry chute, I thought, or perhaps a dumbwaiter.

The boy looked back at me. "What's the matter with your dog? Better catch her. She's going to disturb the guests."

"Sorry."

He spoke truly. She was barking now, along with jumping up and digging at the door.

I froze where I stood. This couldn't be good. Nimble had a mind of her own, but she didn't usually act like this.

The boy set down his tray. "For pity sakes, dog, you're gonna get us all in trouble."

Indeed, a door further down the corridor opened, and a woman's tousled head poked out. "Shh," she whispered.

Nimble, of course, ignored her.

"Miss?" The boy looked at me.

I blew out a breath and grabbed Nimble's lead. That close to the floor, it was easier to see the stain dampening the carpet. A red stain. I didn't think it was wine.

"Hell and damnation," I breathed, evidently loud enough to earn the boy's sharp look.

"What—" he said, but I was already lifting the half door.

It opened onto a dumbwaiter. The cavity didn't contain dishes, though. It contained Eddie's crumpled body. Needless to say, he was dead.

The scream that echoed down the corridor came from the bellboy. Not from me. I swear.

Although I'd vowed during last fall's race meet to never again speak to Sgt. Lars Hansen of the Spokane Police Department—an officer who took bribes and brutalized women, including me when he got the chance. Need I say more?—I had no choice. I suppose it figured he'd be the first to answer the hotel manager's frantic summons.

"You," he said without any discernible pleasure. "I might've known."

We'd flirted and teased each other once upon a time. He'd even helped save my life once, but that was before I discovered his true colors.

"Indeed." I infused the word with ice. "My bad luck."

"Or that damn dog up to her tricks," he returned.

Nimble showed him her teeth.

At least Hansen wasn't alone. A couple of beat policeman accompanied him, one, happily enough, being Officer Shannon.

Shannon shook his head at me. A warning. *Keep your mouth shut,* it seemed to say.

Good advice.

Hansen gestured the policemen forward, one to stand guard over Eddie's body. I'd forcefully had to prevent the crowd of people, including the manager, from disturbing the evidence. The manager had hoped to save the boy, but anyone could see the back of his skull was crushed and oozing out all the matter that fills one's head.

Nauseated, I swallowed and looked away.

Officer Shannon, without being told, produced a small tablet and a pencil stub and stood ready to take down my words.

"Who found him?" Hansen loomed over me as if he'd like to

accuse me of murder. "You?"

I puffed out a sigh. "Nimble. At least, I imagine she smelled the blood and other—" I didn't want to think about the "other" part.

"Nimble's the dog," Hansen informed Shannon, who dutifully wrote this down.

"We were in the corridor, where I'd been talking with him," I nodded toward the live bellboy, "when the dog started acting up. I opened the dumbwaiter door, and we found the body together."

The bellboy who, upon Shannon's soft-voiced question, gave his name as Squirt Williams, nodded agreement.

"What were you doing here in the first place?" Hansen asked me. "What were you talking to the kid about?"

Prevaricating crossed my mind, but with Squirt right there to dispute my words, I didn't dare. Keep this simple, I told myself.

"I asked if Squirt here had seen Eddie." I'm practically positive my innocence showed through. "Eddie did me a little service the other day, and I wanted to tip him."

I might've know it wouldn't work.

"What service?" Hansen demanded. "Are you mixing in other people's business again?"

A number of answers came to mind, none of them wise to repeat. I settled on something fairly innocuous. "Well, I am a detective, Sergeant Hansen. But this was personal. Nothing that has to do with his murder."

Except, of course, with Eddie dead, I was certain it did.

Hansen, as I figured he would, droned on and on, questioning my activities, my motives, and, most of all, my proclivities, stopping just short of a murder accusation. In the end, having decided he couldn't dig up any probable cause to arrest me, he ordered me and my dog to leave and to let the real detectives get to work.

"Real detectives?" I feigned astonishment. "Do you mean yourself? Ooh, I wish I could stay and learn from the master."

He understood sarcasm when he heard it. His eyes flashed.

Shannon, standing behind him, understood it, too. He shook his head. "I'll see her out, sir." He stepped forward and took my arm—none too gently, I might add—propelling me toward the stairs. By this time every guest on the second floor had come from his or her room to see what all the commotion was about.

All, that is, except Jutte Kalb. Her door remained closed, almost as if nobody were there.

CHAPTER ELEVEN

After Sergeant Hansen more or less shoved us into the snow and ordered us to go away, Nimble and I headed off to visit Mamzelle's Parisian Boutique. I'd never been there before and was looking forward to it. A short tramp of only a couple blocks gave me ample time to dwell on Eddie's murder. I wanted answers to the same questions Lars Hansen asked me during his inquisition. When? How? Why? And most of all, who?

Had I read the situation wrong? Was Anka in more danger than I'd first assumed? It began to seem so. I missed Gratton and Monk. Why did they go off on a totally unnecessary wild goose chase, just when I needed them most?

At least, I supposed their excursion unnecessary. It depended on what they turned up.

"Hell and damnation," I said aloud, startling a man walking down the street.

He looked up from watching his traction. "Beg pardon?"

I smiled sheepishly and picked up my pace.

Although the square footage of Mamzelle's store just about equalled that of Monk's apartment front room, the quantity of exquisite goods arrayed there nearly struck me dumb. And, as I'd feared, temptation set in with a vengeance.

I mustered all my willpower in resisting the urge to spend. Even the small front display window, certainly set up by an inspired artist, was enough to lure in the random customer and almost a destination by itself. I wouldn't be surprised to find the clerk had to wash nose prints off the outside glass several times a day.

A tinkly brass bell attached to a petit-point streamer chimed on the note of C as we entered. Nimble pranced beside me, on her best behavior. I noticed Mamzelle, whoever she might be, certainly had her customers' welfare at heart. The room was warm as hot bread.

A young woman of about my own age glided forward with a greeting. Small and thin, her raven hair was arranged in an elaborate pouf atop her head, helping lend her height. Severely garbed in black bombazine with stylish puffed sleeves, her appearance suited the elegant shop. Even so, she appeared so happy to see me I thought she must've been bored. Something about her struck me as familiar.

"Mademoiselle," she gushed in a rather unlikely French accent, "welcome to zee Parisian Boutique." She glanced at Nimble, one fine eyebrow arching. "We have in stock, a new shipment of gloves and handbags from which to choose. Arrived from Pareez only last week."

Pareez. Her pronunciation, not mine.

I glanced around. "I've heard your shop has the most charming handbags in town for sale."

"Sure does," she said, then, *"Oui, merci."*

Her voice—"Philly?" I said, staring hard at her. Black, slightly slanted eyes. Unique. Not quite Chinese because she was only one fourth, but oh, so exotic.

My pseudo Frenchwoman stared back. "China? Is that you?"

"It is me. And it is you!"

We fell on each other's necks causing Nimble to create a bit of a fuss, unsure, I believe, whether we were hugging or fighting. For the record, we were hugging.

"Gawd," Philly—or more precisely, Phillippa Kim drawled as she knelt to make friends with my dog—an act soon accomplished. "I didn't figure I'd ever in my life see you again."

"Nor me you."

Phillippa's mother had worked for my mother when we lived in Seattle. My father, a successful businessman, in order to keep our societal standing in good order and my mother avoid the stigma of cleaning her own house, hired Mrs. Kim to do it for her. Phillippa often came to work with her mother. We had become friends.

I was thirteen when my mother died. My father moved us to Walla Walla for a fresh start and shortly thereafter married Oleatha, my evil stepmother. Phillippa was left behind in Seattle.

And now? I sensed an ally in meeting with Philly again.

A full quarter hour slipped past as we caught each other up about how we both came to live in Spokane. My route had been easy compared to hers. Her mother "married"—I seemed to hear quotes around the word—a wastrel who worked her to death. Philly, on her own at fifteen, successfully made her own way, became a Gibson Girl model for an advertising artist, and landed in Spokane a year ago when he expanded his business here. It hadn't lasted long. He'd already moved on. Philly decided to stay.

"I'm glad you did," I said.

The C note chime sounded as a customer interrupted our reunion. I recognized a matron, a casual acquaintance, who lived on the exclusive south hill area of town. We nodded cordially. When Philly went into her sales pitch, speaking with her faux French accent that almost made me laugh, I took the opportunity to look around.

A dozen or so faceless heads, not decapitated people but simple mannequins, bore hats. Some of the hats were light and frothy, some wide-brimmed and sophisticated. Two were suitable for the winter weather, both warm and beautiful at the same time.

A case of gloves sat in the middle of the room. Gloves of leather so fine it was like silk, more of silk, some of lace. Wool gloves or mittens were available at almost every mercantile. Mamzelle's stock rose miles above such plebeian offerings.

There were boas, shawls, shrugs, belts, combs and brushes and silver backed mirrors, all elegantly displayed. Philly had always been artistic, probably accounting for her becoming an artist's model. She'd already told me she was in charge of the shop and responsible for its style.

Shoes lined one whole wall. I spied a pair in blue with kitten heels that I coveted.

And in a corner with signage introducing the Colored Crystal Boutique, there were handbags. A nest of special occasion leather ones, dyed in vivid colors to match the shoes. Another grouping hung from the ceiling on velvet ribbons, the bags themselves at eye-level to a tall man. Beaded and embroidered, they were like Christmas ornaments in their beauty. These were the ones from which Sepp Amsel had selected gifts for Jutte and Anka. The ones I'd come to see.

Just as I expected, no two were alike.

Philly, having sold the matron one of the warm winter hats and a belt, rejoined me. "You like those? They're pretty, aren't they, although a bit expensive. Even so, I've already sold four, and we just got them in."

"Direct from *Pareez*?" I grinned at her.

"Oh, you." She gave me a little push. "The ladies like my accent, and their gentlemen like it even better. They can pretend they're all international beauties."

"Who? The women or the men?"

"Both."

I regretted the necessity of introducing a serious note to our meeting. It'd been nice to avoid thinking of murder even for a short while. Philly's occupation seemed much more sophisticated and fun, not to mention a deal less dangerous, than mine, but I consoled myself in the knowledge that possessions, even beautiful ones, fade with use and time. Helping keep someone alive, or striving for justice, were worth my hard work. And right now, I had to concentrate on freeing Anka Kalb from her kidnappers.

I waved my hand at the purses. "Are any of these patterns duplicated?"

"Certainly not. Each is unique. It's what makes them so costly."

"I thought so." I pondered a moment. "Do you keep a record of who buys what, Philly?"

"Sure I do." She eyed me like I'd insulted her. "How else am I to keep track of my customers' likes and dislikes?"

"Can you tell me who bought the purses?"

At this, she looked a little uneasy. "I don't know, China. Don't you think that sort of counters our customer's right to privacy? Why do you want to know?"

Speaking of privacy, I was bound by the same sort of circumstances as Philly, only more so. Keeping Anka's kidnapping secret might actually figure into saving her life.

I left her question without a direct answer. "If I tell you that I already know who bought two of them, do you think you'd trust me with the other purchaser's identities? Just so I can eliminate her—or him?"

"Oh, definitely him. Two of them." She rolled her eyes in a suggestive manner.

Evidently Philly's business clientele split between two factions. One being rich women, or those who had rich husbands, who bought whatever they liked for themselves. And two, rich men, likely some of those self-same husbands, who bought for their mistresses. Sepp Amsel, I guessed, fell somewhere in between.

She thought a moment before growing serious. "Eliminate him—them—from what?"

I'd thought of a story, one close enough to the truth to be plausible.

"One of your purses was found where it probably shouldn't have been. Its ownership is in question. But you say each purse is unique. I should be able to establish the owner from this. Depending on your answer, I might not need those other customers' names." I leaned closer to her and added, "I know Sepp Amsel bought two, one for his bride-to-be with a pattern of white lilies, and one for her sister with big, red cabbage roses. Pretty things."

She stared at me in surprise, then nodded. "You are the smart one, aren't you? And you're almost right. The exception is that the bride chose the red roses, and the sister took the lilies."

"Really? Are you sure?" My mind raced. Turning a little aside, I dug my note pad out of my mundane leather purse and read what I'd written. The photograph I'd cadged from Jutte was stuck between the pages.

"What's that?" Philly asked, peeking over my shoulder to look at the rather grainy picture.

"Recipients of the purses. They're the Kalb sisters. This was taken before they left Austria for the United States." I took a second glance. "They appear to be having a grand old time, don't they?"

"They do." She studied the photo a little longer. "Which one did you say is the bride?"

"Jutte. The slender one."

Her eyebrow arched. "Hmmm. This isn't a very clear photograph. I could swear . . ."

"Swear what?"

"Oh, nothing," she said.

I found my notes and started to read. "Yes. It says here the bride took the white lilies."

"You write everything down?"

"Mostly. I make notes of what people tell me, in case I'm called to testify in court or something."

Her slanted eyes narrowed, an expression I recognized as alarm. "Is this a case for court?"

"I'm hoping it won't become so drastic. Not about the purses, anyway. This is just to clarify things in my own mind."

"You're sure your notes don't get mixed up?"

Something in her voice compelled my attention. "What do you mean?"

"I mean the sister took the white lilies purse. I distinctly heard the other woman say her name. They seemed to be fighting over who got what, but only when Mr. Amsel had his back turned. And there's something else." She hesitated. "This photograph, do you know when it was taken?"

"A few months ago, I believe."

"Hmm. The sisters are very similar in looks, aren't they?"

"Yes." What was she getting at?

Her slim forefinger touched the photograph. "You see the plump one? Well, she's no longer this plump. Not thin, by any means, but they look even more alike now. I can't tell which is which."

It took a minute for what she meant to sink in. "What? Why that miserable . . ." I stopped short of name calling, but only by the width of a frog's hair. "She didn't tell me that. So it wouldn't do a particle of good to show this photograph around."

"Not so much." Philly smiled. "Except to me. I learned a little something from my artist . . . friend. A discerning eye, for one thing."

"Yes." My heart beat hard. It appeared possible the future Mrs. Amsel might be fooling around. "Only one more question, Philly. When were the purses bought?"

Her mouth puckered. "All of them or just the Amsel purchase?"

"Just the Amsel purchase." The others had only been a smokescreen anyway.

"Saturday morning."

My heartbeat accelerated to a full-blown gallop.

Philly eyed me with some consternation. "Are you all right? You just gasped like somebody stuck you with a pin."

"I'm fine, just mad. And a little surprised."

But was I really? I'd been certain there was some funny business going on between the Kalb sisters and the man at the haberdashery from the moment I saw the purse. I just didn't know if it concerned the bamboozlement Sepp had mentioned, or if it was connected to Anka's kidnapping. Or were those two things one and the same? I thought I had my answer now.

A sudden vision of the bellhop, Eddie, dead and stuffed in the dumbwaiter filled my head. I had no doubt his death tied in to the kidnapping, and I couldn't help wondering if he'd been waiting to speak with me.

Although she'd been sitting at my side like a properly trained dog should, Nimble whimpered suddenly as though she sensed my distress.

I shuddered. This case had turned into more than a simple ransom or a way to con money out of Sepp. Promising Philly I'd see her again soon, I told her thanks and good-bye and departed the splendor of Mamzelle's Parisian Boutique.

My childhood friend had answered everything I asked of her, only now the investigation appeared more muddled than ever. Was Anka a victim or an accomplice to her own kidnapping? Or should one even consider her disappearance a kidnapping? Was she likely to be murdered, perhaps by her own sister? Or, after Sepp paid the ransom, would she come traipsing home healthy, happy, and secretly a couple thousand dollars richer?

I wished Grat would hurry and get back from Kellogg. And Monk, too, of course. I needed to report these latest developments.

And truthfully? When I took Eddie's murder into account, I was downright frightened.

CHAPTER TWELVE

Police still swarmed the steps outside the Spokane Hotel when Nimble and I trudged past on our way to the office. The poor constables shuffled their feet and swung their arms in an attempt to stay warm, their noses red with cold. Lord only knows what they were guarding against since Eddie's murderer must be long gone.

Sepp Amsel emerged from the front entrance as I stopped to gawk and to eavesdrop on what a couple of oblivious officers were saying to one another. To be honest, it didn't amount to anything. A complaint about the weather. Anyway, Sepp called my name and strode over to meet me, his stocky physique gliding across the slick sidewalk as if he were on bare ground. Galoshes covered his shoes, the rubber an improvement over plain leather soles on the ice-covered boards.

"Mr. Amsel," I greeted him. "Just the person I wanted to see. I wasn't sure how to reach you. I can hardly stand outside your establishment and yell!"

I wasn't being entirely truthful, and it had nothing to do with yelling. Right at this moment, I'd rather have avoided him. How much dare I say about the woman he intended to marry?

He grinned as though amused by the vision of me yelling from the street, then turned serious. "You send a messenger boy. I will answer." He hesitated a moment. "The police, they say you are person who found the dead bellhop. You and some boy. And your dog." He glanced down at Nimble and bent to give her a pat.

"Yes. Nimble showed us." I shivered. The cold, I tried to tell myself, and not the horror of the boy's murder rising in my head once more. "What's happening in the hotel? Have the police made any progress towards finding Eddie's killer? An arrest, by chance?"

Sepp snorted. "What do you think? They talk to hotel staff, this one and that one. Nobody knows anything. Sergeant Hansen, he speaks to me. Says to leave hotel since I am not a guest here. I pay for room but can't stay. Can't even buy one of Mrs. Flynn's good pastries."

I eyed a bored-looking policeman. "Murder is not good for business, I'm afraid. From the look of things, I'd say the police are wasting their time as well as discommoding the hotel."

"Ja. I waste time here, too. So I go now to talk to pastor at church where wedding is held. Tell him to hire organ player for Saturday."

Somehow, he didn't seem as joyous as a bridegroom should be.

I glanced around. "Miss Kalb isn't with you?"

He frowned. "No. Is upset over sister."

"I see."

Amsel lowered his voice, a good tactic due to his tendency to speak loudly. "You and Gratton Doyle. What about you? What have you learned?"

I wasn't ready to face him with what scanty information I'd gleaned so far. Not with the bamboozlement factor looming large.

"We haven't found Anka as yet, I'm sorry to say. But even as we speak, Mr. Doyle and my uncle, Montgomery Howe, are pursuing a snippet of information that takes them to the Kellogg mining district."

Sepp, being quick on the uptake, nodded. "Them men at the

106

German Club, I bet. They was strangers to both me and Schultz. Good work."

"I've spoken with some people here in town who may have been among the last to see Miss Kalb." I faltered over my next statement. "I have an idea the murdered bellhop knew more about events than he was willing to say. I'd questioned him once and meant to speak with him again. Too late, I'm afraid. I—" I stopped. My next plan was best kept between me and myself.

Sepp swallowed. "You think the bellhop was involved?"

"I think he may have seen or heard more than he owned up to. I question whether he was one of the kidnappers."

"Ja. Jutte said kidnappers were big men. Not like young bellhop."

"He could've been their informant. But then why would they kill their own man?" I was thinking aloud.

Sepp shrugged. "One less to share in ransom, ja?"

I nodded. "Ja." Gracious. Now he had me speaking German.

"Rose . . ." He hesitated as his face turned even more ruddy, and changed it to, "Mrs. Flynn, she says she talks with you, too. She says you ask about what Jutte says when she is found. What she says about kidnappers. What to do next." He got all his *wh* sounds right. "Why do you ask these things?"

Rose, eh? Apparently he and Mrs. Flynn had become quite friendly in the last twenty-four hours. And meeting rather often.

But he still asked the hard questions.

And I gave him a hard answer. "No one is closer to the missing Miss Kalb than her sister." I met his eyes. "Some things about the kidnapping don't make sense."

"What things?" Sepp demanded.

His voice had risen. I untangled Nimble from the leash, which had somehow gotten wrapped around one of her legs and, taking Sepp's arm, urged him out of earshot of the police, hoping all the while Lars Hansen wouldn't catch sight of me talking to the notorious Herr Amsel.

"Has it occurred to you Anka may be involved in her own abduction?" Steam floated into the air in front of my words. "It doesn't really make sense that the kidnappers took *her*. Why not Jutte? Surely they would expect you to pay more ransom for your fiancée than for her sister."

His lips compressed. "They did not know which woman is Jutte."

Doubtful of this excuse, I shook my head. "A photograph of the Kalb sisters has been in the newspaper. Not a particularly good picture, I must admit, what with both ladies half-hidden in the background, but . . ." I hesitated. Wait a minute. Maybe Sepp was right. Jutte had given me a terrible photograph, but the newspaper one was even worse. Seen in person there'd still be a lot of guesswork in deciding who was who. "But," I continued, "why, when those men demanded ransom, didn't they ask for more money? Two thousand dollars? A tidy sum, but—"

He said nothing. He'd told me at our first meeting he kept around two thousand dollars in his safe. A smart man, I felt certain the ramifications of that specific amount had already occurred to him.

I pressed on. "Another puzzle is why Jutte can't give a description of the men. Not even of the one who slapped her. But she says they weren't wearing masks. I find that odd."

He stiffened and squinted into the sun. "She was frightened."

"Yes. So I'm told." I did my best to keep my tone neutral.

"And she is frightened for Anka. She thinks talking will put her sister in more danger. She just wants me to pay so Anka comes back safe."

His sigh spoke volumes. He didn't believe in this happening any more than I did. We walked a few steps farther before he said, "What you want to see me for?"

I'd almost forgotten I had one question that shouldn't make him mad. "Kidnappers tend to keep in touch with the person who's going to be paying the victim's ransom. They send further warnings to remain silent, to tell no one of the abduction on threat of death. That sort of thing. Have you gotten another note, by any chance?"

"No." He was still short with me.

"Who brought the first note to you, by the way? Was it, as I suppose, Eddie, the murdered bellhop?"

I knew what he was going to say before he said it. "Ja, was the bellhop."

"Hell and damnation," I said, and in no soft mutter under my breath either. "I should've seen it coming. Of course they had to kill him. He knew who at least one of them was. I should've gotten to him first."

Goodness, such a look he gave me. Clearly he thought me an idiot, as well as much too slow in comprehending the clues. I'll wager he wondered why he'd hired someone as inept and incompetent as I.

Even so, Sepp walked me all the way home, dropping me off before he continued on. He had a further word. "You be careful, Miss China. Crooks killed that boy. Maybe they want to kill you, too. Think maybe I should fire you, keep you safe. You're just a girl, easy to catch."

His heads-up didn't have the effect he may have intended. I took a deep breath, determined not to let him frighten me any worse than I was already. Besides, I had my gun. And a sturdy nine-inch hat pin. I'm a tough detective, a crime fighter, or so I told myself. I won't be scared off by maybes. It's bad for business.

I told Sepp the same. I don't think he believed it any more than I did.

Besides, what would Gratton think? I'd never make full partner if I gave in to my fears.

When Sepp left me outside the office, the direction he took led toward Mrs. Flynn's Cozy Corner Café. He'd mentioned lunch, and in the next breath spoken of Rose. An interesting development, unless I read the signs wrong. I hoped not. I liked Sepp (mostly), and I liked Rose. I didn't much care for Jutte. As for Anka? Who knew?

Once in the office, I locked myself in before turning the Closed sign to Open. I didn't want to be interrupted without fair warning. Sepp's cautionary words struck home in a more forceful fashion than I cared to admit.

Older editions of the *Spokane Daily Chronicle* were crammed into the closet under the stairs. We always saved the paper to help start the morning fires, and I was glad of it. Fortunately, we hadn't yet burned the editions in which a reporter's two-part article on the Kalb women's arrival in the United States had been published.

I gathered the papers, shook them out on my desk, and settled down to read. Just as I remembered, Sepp Amsel's upcoming nuptials had been front page news on November thirteenth, when his bride and her sister reached Spokane by train from New York City. Representatives of the paper—consisting of a reporter and a photographer—had accompanied Sepp when he met them at the station. The picture illustrating the article, also as I remembered, was indistinct and less than flattering.

The ocean voyage from Germany had been nerve-racking and frightful, the Chronicle quoted Jutte. There'd been storms. Her sister had suffered most dreadfully with seasickness the whole time although she, herself, hadn't been much affected. Bored by the dreary weather, she said, although Herr Amsel had provided her and her sister with a first-class stateroom.

After complimenting her on her proficiency in English and

asking where she learned it, the reporter inquired about her background.

"My sister and I come from Bregenz, in Austria," she'd informed him. "Not from Germany like American peoples think. Our parents are dead. Nothing in the old country was left for us."

Asked how she liked America, she burst forth in complaint. A story of lost or perhaps stolen luggage on the train west. Her trousseau gone. She and her sister had only what they stood up in.

A sad tale of woe, to be sure, although from what I'd seen, Sepp had made it up to her and to Anka—many times over. Even so, I understood now why she'd seemed rather disgruntled with everything American.

If true, a sour little voice whispered in my inner ear. Perhaps the reporter thought so, too, for, when I turned to the next page, where he asked how Jutte and Sepp became acquainted, he poked a little "fun" at her. For the rest of the article Jutte's replies were verbatim in English a great deal more broken than I'd heard her speak.

"We write to each other," she said. "Chust fall in love from letters."

Actually, she added, they corresponded for more than a year before any mention of marriage. And then events moved fast. Herr Amsel booked passage for her, and here she was.

Omitted from this particular newspaper article, although accounted the most trustworthy version of events by in-the-know gossipers, Sepp had signed up with an agency that helped procure wives from the old country. According to the gossip mongers, he selected her letter from among several others as someone whose further acquaintance he wanted to pursue. Liking the fact she could speak English, he agreed to pay her way to the United States. She bargained for her sister's passage as well, and Sepp agreed.

I daresay what she told the reporter sounded more romantic, although her answer to him on where she learned English was terse in the extreme. "School," she said.

The second part of the article, relegated to the next day, detailed plans for the wedding on this coming Saturday. Sepp took over the interview, announcing the date, time, and place, and the city-wide invitation.

"All come," he'd said with a broad smile—according to the reporter. "Vill be humdinger party."

Would it?

I suspect that depended on if I could return Anka to the bosom of her family in the next couple days.

Chapter Thirteen

Blinking, I looked up from the newspaper and stared into space. I may've been looking at Anka's kidnapping all wrong. Oh, maybe not all wrong, but I'd been focusing more on discovering the wrong-doers than on rescuing the victim. I needed to find her. The where, at this moment, mattered more than the who.

Except Eddie Barstow's murder meant we had more than a kidnapping on our hands. Events had suddenly become infinitely more dangerous. Gratton and Monk, in gallivanting off to Kellogg, had no inkling of the latest goings-on. After September's murder case, in which I'd been slightly shot, they'd have a conniption over me investigating another killing on my own.

The police, unless someone—Sepp or Jutte for instance—had decided to tell them, still didn't know about the kidnapping. I doubted it would bode well for Anka if they discovered Eddie's murder was tied to an abduction. Go in with guns drawn and Anka's life would be over—perhaps—if she was even still alive. Those last few words were never far out of my mind.

As an exercise in deduction, I needed to start thinking like a kidnapper and try planning a kidnapping based on the few facts in my possession. See where it led me. Hopefully, straight to Anka Kalb.

So that's what I did. Tried to do, at any rate. I threw a hefty chunk of wood on the fire, brewed up a pot of strong coffee in hopes of stimulating my brain, and settled down behind my desk.

If I intended to snatch someone off the street—or from a garden path—where would I confine her while I waited for the ransom to be paid? I should be able to figure it out. All I had to do was put myself in his/her/their place.

I did, after all, have some personal experience. Oh, not of being held for ransom, but certainly of being held against my will. A list seemed in order. Out came my trusty notebook, which I opened to a blank page.

One: I wrote, then stopped and chewed the end of my pencil.

"Hell and damnation," I muttered.

Nimble, who'd settled for a snooze in the kneehole under my desk, poked her head out and stared at me with intelligent dark eyes. I had nothing to lose by asking her opinion. "If you were a kidnapper, what is the first thing you'd do?"

Her ears twitched.

"Got it, thank you. Select the best place for the abduction, of course, with the least risk to oneself." Using my best penmanship, I wrote that down and finished with a remark about location. "It would help if one knew where she'd be," I said to Nimble, "which seems to say she's either been under close observation so people know her personal habits, or someone tipped the kidnappers off. Someone in a position to know. I think I need a separate list of possible suspects, don't you? I'll work on that in a minute."

Nimble scratched her ear with dedicated enthusiasm.

"Knowledge of opportunity," I so noted and left room for more information.

"Then you'd hire your crew, right? And we know there were three of them. Or so Jutte says. Find one and we can track them all." I mulled that over. "Maybe. Grat might have to persuade that one into talking." I nodded to Nimble. "Gratton is a very good persuader, you know."

Two: *Crew,* I printed. *Who is the leader? What connection?* Information I'd likely not know until the end.

On to number three.

I thought a moment. "I know. Act fast. We have to keep her quiet and get her out of sight before we're seen. So, we need to think of likely escape routes."

Made sense. I felt certain Nimble's lifted ears meant agreement, so I wrote it down to think more about later.

Four: "Next? Hmm. Where is the first place I'd take my victim? Rats. I'd better turn three and four around."

Nimble sighed, turned around twice, and, putting her head on my feet, went to sleep. Apparently, I was on my own.

So . . . I'd rush my victim off somewhere close, convenient, and totally out of sight. Oh, yes. And someplace where any screams or cries could go unheard. If there were any screams or cries, which remained to be seen.

Anyway, didn't that all depend on who took her and what they were going to do with her? Trouble is, when boiled down it all came back to where I started. I needed to find who took her before I'd know where. Or reverse it. Find out where, and then I'd know who.

The purse must be a clue to the where.

Mannheim's Haberdashery was only a couple blocks from the hotel; easy and quick to slip down an alley and there you'd be. There'd been a faint light in the shop's back room yesterday even though they'd been closed when Grat and I first went there. Who kept a light burning when the place was unoccupied? Not a frugal German Jew, I'd be bound.

So, Mannheim was probably not personally involved. I'd heard him complain of losing a work day to the storm. But Dieter? Or August, the young clerk who'd fixed Gratton up with a new coat?

I tapped the pencil on my teeth.

Probably not August, either, I decided. He appeared too young to be mixed up with the Kalb sisters. But Dieter, a handsome man who'd struck me as sinister as he clicked the scissor blades together? Dieter, who'd made an excuse regarding the purse?

Anka hadn't been concealed in the haberdashery today. Unless, and here I returned to an earlier fear, her body had been stuffed in one of those crates, and, frankly, I doubted it. Not with three people working in the shop, and customers passing back and forth all day. Still . . .

I made a note next to the four on my paper. *Look into Mannheim's.*

Literally look into the shop, I meant. I needed to physically enter the building and see what I could see. And I had to do it after they were gone for the day.

I checked the time on the watch pinned to the front of my shirtwaist. The shop wouldn't close until six. I had some time in which to set myself up for a bit of undercover, and highly illegal, work. To scare myself. To talk myself out of it. The latter no doubt being the wisest course.

But not what detectives were paid to do.

Striving for calm, an item number five raised its hand, demanding attention.

Five: *Ransom site,* I noted. Paging through the notebook to Sepp's and my first meeting, I found the address where the ransom was to be delivered. There. Finkle's Rooming House. Not, according to the street number, in the best part of town.

But also, I assured myself firmly, not in the worst. And not the one where I'd once found a man dead, with his throat cut.

I swallowed coffee, cold now, wishing I hadn't revisited a memory that lived in my brain as though it happened only yesterday. Because I rather thought it my duty to familiarize myself with the drop site before tomorrow night and the appointed hour.

This was not going to be the most enjoyable excursion of my life.

Leaving my lists incomplete, I turned the agency's Open sign to Closed and went upstairs to prepare. Nimble, as though sensing she'd once again be left behind, snuffled at my heels.

In some cities, a woman can be arrested for dressing as a man. I didn't know if Spokane had such a silly law, but, if they did, I intended on breaking it. Fingers crossed no one would ever learn of my lawbreaking, of course. Lars Hansen would be tickled to catch me out. He'd make my life miserable and be happy to do it.

Over these last few weeks—dull weeks, hence Monk's and Grat's ennui and my knitting of Nimble's red sweater—in anticipation of a clandestine operation of some sort, I'd cut down a pair of Uncle Monk's old britches to fit me. Wearing those and an oversized barn coat with a plain knitted cap covering my hair, I figured it would be well nigh impossible to tell my sex when hidden by the gloom of night.

Darkness fell at an earlier hour than usual on this snowy late November afternoon. I peered out the window to discover the sky clouded over again, as if another storm were brewing. The temperature didn't seem quite as cold. Or maybe that was only because I was in a dither over a little breaking and entering.

I exited via our building's rear door, hearing Nimble pawing the woodwork at being left behind. I slogged through snow drifts in our backyard to the alley, my breath billowing out in front of me, until I came out on the street in the middle of the block. The sidewalks were nearly empty at this time of day. Not quite quitting time, but past the hour when housewives ran their errands. I trusted it to be the perfect time to pay a call at

Finkle's Rooming House, when most cooks would be in their kitchens preparing supper for their boarders. I preferred, you see, to be unobserved.

Mind you, my trusty .32 was in my pocket—I patted it to make double, or perhaps triple sure—and even though this part of the investigation might be better left to Grat or Monk, I felt safe enough. No one could recognize me, after all, in my boy's disguise, and I didn't plan on putting myself in danger. All I meant to do was spy out the lay of the land. What could it possibly hurt?

I always expect these things to run smoothly, even though they never have before. This time just followed the pattern.

In the first place, the lady of the house was not in her kitchen fixing supper as I'd anticipated. I found her outside a rather ramshackle two-story house in the near dark, almost as though lying in wait for my arrival.

A heavyset woman, she wore only a sweater over a woolen dress. She didn't seem to feel the cold at all as she swept her steps free of fluffy, dry snow with great swoops of a wheat-straw broom. A medium-sized dog of indeterminate breed sat well out of the broom's reach, watching her work.

The house needed paint, I noticed. A shutter at one of the windows had come loose and hung by a single nail. Piles of snow at the side of the stoop showed a dusting of black. A soot trail, I guessed, from carrying in coal for the furnace. The dusting was scant, which probably meant the rooms were as cold as ice boxes, pity the poor boarders.

A small sign on the side of the house read, "Finkle's Rooming House, Rooms To Let," so I knew I'd come to the right place. Now I had to talk my way past the woman and her broom. I approached her with a certain amount of trepidation.

"Howdy," she said as I trod the short path between the road and her stoop. "You here about the room?"

118

Well, that made things easier. I made sure to drag my feet as though tired out from a day at work and kept my head bowed, hiding my face from her scrutiny. "Yeah. How much you say you want for it again?"

"Three-fifty a week, room and found. I'm the landlady, Mrs. Finkle."

"How'd ja do." I coughed and deepened my voice to make it sound raspy. "I dunno. Three-fifty. That's purty dear."

She banged her broom on the side of the steps, throwing up a shower of the black-dusted snow. "Take it or leave it. It's a clean room. Got a good bed." She eyed my shabby form, squinting as though nearsighted. A malady helpful to my cause, I assumed. "Growing boy like you needs a good bed. And I'm a good cook. You can tell by looking at me."

Her chuckle didn't seem particularly amused.

"Yes'm," I said meekly. "I dunno." Now what? I needed to get inside and see the layout. Finally, inspiration struck. "Can I see the room?"

"See it? You want to see the room?"

"Yes'm." She didn't expect me to hand over money sight unseen, did she?

"What for? It's a regular room. Bed, chair, a table, and a washstand. Ain't fancy, but it'll do for a working man."

Quick, think of an excuse, China. Nothing came to mind. "Rats," is what slipped out of my mouth. As though I'd said the magic word, the dog pricked its ears and came over to smell my boots.

Mrs. Finkle reacted to the word, too. Her eyes narrowed to slits. "Rats?"

"Yes'm. Last place had rats. I durn near stepped on a big'un this mornin'. I ain't stayin' there no more."

She slapped her broom on the stoop hard enough to bend the straws. The dog jumped.

Me, too.

"There are no rats in my house, young man," she said.

"I wanta see for myself."

Her glare turned steely. "You think you're funny? Who told you I got a rat problem?"

Oh, my. My stomach turned over. Did that mean she did have a rat problem? "Nobody told me nothin'," I said. "I just—"

She spun around. Slamming the door open hard enough to shake the glass in the window frames, she motioned me into the house with a jerk of her thumb. At a hand signal from her, the dog rushed inside ahead of us and ran up the stairs to the second floor, barking fit to warn off scary monsters—or rats.

"Well, come on in and look at the room if you think you gotta. It's up this stairs. Parlor, kitchen, and eating and my quarters are on the ground floor. All off limits to the boarders except at meal time. Understand?"

"Yes'm." Hesitantly, I entered, ducking my head as I followed her.

"I'll show you rats," she muttered under her breath. That much I heard clearly, but she also said something about somebody telling the world, and she'd have his guts for breakfast when she found out who. All interspersed with fervent mumbles that sounded a lot like curses.

I sneaked a touch on my pistol, just in case she turned dangerous when I refused the room. Or on the off chance the dog scared any rats my way and I had to shoot them.

The stairs, as is often the case in a house like this, were dark and close. Even I, with no carpentry experience, could see the house had been built on the cheap. The steps creaked as though they were about to fall through. Quite creepy, all in all. I half expected a ghost to appear.

Once past the upper landing, five closed doors about ten feet apart lined a narrow hall lit by a small gas lamp at the top of the stairs. Three doors were on one side of the hall, two on the other. Number 213—and heaven only knows why the two-one part of the numeral was attached. Why not a simple three?—was in the middle towards the front.

The dog, quiet now though obviously on guard, stood at attention at the very end of the hall, near the brick chimney stack.

I shuddered. Rats for sure. I was quite certain I smelled them.

Mrs. Finkle led me right to 213—evidently the room for rent—and flung open the door. A shiver ran up my spine as something with sharp-sounding toenails skittered in a dark corner as the door caught on a high place in the floor. Sure enough, as advertised, the room contained the aforementioned bed, nightstand, chair, and small table. As for clean? Well, perhaps she went by a different standard than some.

"Suit ya?" she demanded as I examined the interior. Frankly, it stunk.

"Well—" I started, as a man spoke from the doorway of a room across the hall. He appeared big and hulking to me, like the proverbial ogre, and had a German accent. To tell the truth, it was becoming so familiar I had nearly acquired one for myself.

"This room is not for rent. Frau Finkle, you are saving the room for my friend, yes?" he said. "You agreed to hold it until Thursday morning. My friend, he paid you two dollars in advance."

Aha. And the ransom was to be delivered here on Wednesday night.

"First come, first served," Mrs. Finkle declared, sounding a little unsure.

"Not so. You, boy," the man said, "you go. There is no vacant room here."

If I'd been Mrs. Finkle, I do believe I would've been kowtowing to the man. He sounded cold and angry, a threat implicit. Determined, as well. She was a brave soul to stand before him.

Or maybe a stupid one. Who knows? But I, for one, didn't like his tone.

I peered more closely at him. Tried, anyway. Backlit by the lamp burning on a table, he became a mere silhouette, his features obscured by the darkness of the hall. Even so, I thought I'd know his voice if ever I heard it again.

"See here, Mr. Klein . . ." Mrs. Finkle started. Over by the chimney, the dog growled.

Mr. Klein cut her off. "Our agreement says you are to hold the room until Thursday," he repeated. "Now you must hope the house does not catch fire before then."

The landlady heard the threat as clearly as I. Beaten, she yelled at the dog to hush before she spoke to me. "Guess this room is taken after all. You better scat."

"Yes'm." Backing away, I turned tail and fled for the stair.

One thing for certain. I had no desire to go into the boarding house business. Or to stay five minutes longer in one, either. Especially this one.

There is, after all, more than one kind of rat.

CHAPTER FOURTEEN

Shaken by the encounter, I retreated as fast as my legs would carry me. Even so, the landlady's dog passed me on the way down. Mrs. Finkle's heavy footsteps weren't far behind.

"I'll put you out if'n you don't mind your manners," she shouted over her shoulder at the man. I admired her bravado, if not her good sense.

At least I had a general picture of the ransom hand-off site. Getting inside the house, and maybe the room, to observe the ransom pickup would take some finesse. Apparently, Mr. Klein stood as lookout for the kidnappers, and getting past him might be a trick even for someone as wily as Gratton Doyle or my uncle Monk. Thank goodness, I could depend on one of them to handle this part of the operation. As long as they were back from Kellogg. If not, I didn't know what I'd do.

I was pretty certain of one thing, however. With Mrs. Finkle on the watch, I doubted Anka Kalb was being held in this rooming house. But where on earth could she be?

My only other clue led to Mannheim's Haberdashery. It wouldn't hurt to look around there, to see if anyone was keeping an eye on the place.

Perhaps I could peer in a window. Check to see if any lights showed. Put my ear against the door. Or what if someone had forgotten to lock it? People did forget sometimes.

But first, I went home and wrote up notes regarding my visit to the rooming house, including my impression of Mr. Klein.

Who was he? Was Klein his real name? What part in the kidnapping did he play? All questions that went unanswered, for now.

Two hours later, I set out again. Snow spat icy pellets against my face as I traced a route through the dark to the haberdashery. Low clouds floated at rooftop level. Sound was muffled. Another storm stirred itself as the wind picked up. Once again, the streets were deserted, and I felt lonely and exposed without Nimble at my side. I found myself darting from doorway to darkened doorway, furtive as a thief.

Not for the first time, worry struck me that Monk and Grat might not make it home on the late train. The mountains leading into Kellogg were notorious for snowfalls deep enough to block the tracks. Sometimes it took days to dig out. And then what?

I guess I knew what. I was on the job. Saving Anka would be up to me.

Buoying myself with brave words, I cut around to the back upon reaching the German Club/haberdashery building. The only shoveling done here was a path barely long and wide enough to reach a depleted woodpile and a small privy. On the whole, it hardly counted. The previous storm's snow had been trampled into ice. Even an experienced tracker like Uncle Monk would've been hard-pressed to trace anyone from here.

No lights had shone out front, but a lamp flickered through the German Club's rear window. Not a welcome surprise. I heard voices, too. One, I was certain, raised in anger.

Or glee. I suppose it could've been glee.

The lamp went dark.

I barely had time to fling myself onto my stomach behind the woodpile when the door opened and Herr Schultz and two other men stepped outside.

Their previous conversation hadn't, I soon surmised, been gleeful.

"Gott dammit, man," Schultz grumbled. "Why you do that? What you going to do now?" He sounded quite horrified about something. "I don't want mixed up in—"

"Shut up," the bigger man said. "He had it coming."

I knew the voice, having heard it only a couple hours before. Herr Klein sounded just as menacing now as he had then.

"Ja," Schultz said, "but—"

The other man took Schultz's elbow, silencing him. "Leave it," he said. "You don't know anything. I don't know anything. If anybody asks, we have seen nothing. Understand?"

Schultz stuttered, "J . . . Ja. We have seen nothing."

"These police, they don't ask questions," the other man went on smoothly. "Money has changed hands to make sure. Polacks, they call us, no matter where we're from. They don't care what we do to each other. Just more ignorant immigrants, they say, who have nothing better to do than kill each other."

Kill each other? Now who was dead? My heart beat like a drum roll.

Peeking around the edge of a largish block of wood awaiting the axe, I spied one man, Schultz, I think, reaching up into the eaves overhanging the door. A single door that served both the haberdashery and the club.

"Not right," he kept insisting. "Not right to leave the body there."

"Won't be for long." Klein shrugged, the movement of his heavy shoulders clearly outlined against the snow. His features, worse luck, were hidden not only by the dark, but by a turned-up coat collar and a pulled-down cap. "They will find it in the morning."

"Ja, but—"

"I can do something with it, boss," Klein offered, his voice rough and growly as he looked to the man still holding Schultz's arm. "Drop him off behind Amsel's saloon. Be funny."

This man chuckled. "I like the way you think. But best not. He will serve as a deterrent to the others, in case they wish to speak."

Schultz, for one, wanted to speak. His repeated protests went unheeded as they walked past me. And really, I couldn't help noticing he didn't insist. Klein, a dyed in the wool thug if I've ever seen one, seemed very persuasive. He had the deterrent part pegged.

"Come." The second fellow slapped Schultz on the shoulder in a friendly sort of way. "Leave it. Go home now. Forget this."

Schultz gave in. "Ja. I will forget." But something in the way he sounded made me think it would take a while.

Wavelike tremors shook me for a full minute after the men were out of sight. When I thought it safe, I rose from my snowy concealment. Cold, yes, but terrified, too.

Whose body? Whose?

I didn't want to know.

I had to know.

Dragging up the wood chunk I'd been hiding behind to stand on, I fumbled in the area I'd seen Schultz conceal something. Sure enough, a door key dropped onto the stoop.

Should I or shouldn't I?

I stepped down and unlocked the door, leaving the wood chunk where it was so I could return the key when I finished my search.

The door opened with a squeak. Quickly, I slipped inside and closed it.

Once there, I had the choice of either the haberdashery or the German club. I was in a short hall, which held a coat rack and a lamp sitting on a tiny table. Much to my regret, I deemed it too dangerous to light the lamp. Believe me, there's nothing worse than blundering around a strange place in the dark, but that's what I did. More or less.

I couldn't get into the German Club. The outer door key didn't work, and I didn't want to force the lock. No such problem deterred my entry to the haberdashery. To my surprise, I simply turned the knob and went in.

The room seemed hot after my sojourn outside. Silence hung in a layer. More than an hour after the shop's closing, a Franklin stove still churned out heat. Chilled from lying on my stomach in the snow, I was thankful for that but sorry, too, as the warmth accentuated the odors of blood and excrement.

"Oh no," I breathed, my mouth turning dry. Had I said it aloud? I hoped not.

One would think me prepared after the conversation I'd overheard. And I was, sort of. But two corpses in one day? It was too much.

There'd been sulphur matches on the hall table. While I dared not light the lamp, I did gather up a handful of the matches and strike one. A curtain covered the open arch into the showroom. I closed the hall door behind me and looked around. The workroom seemed much as I'd seen it before. A little untidy with bolts and stacks of cloth. The pegboard with its row of scissors and large wooden spools of thread.

The match soon burned down to my fingers. I shook it out and struck another. This one flared brightly, and I went a few steps farther. Most of the room was in view. It was just behind the fabric cutter's table that I couldn't see. Even though I moved quickly, I had to strike yet another match. I guess I wasn't going as fast as it felt.

I found the body there, on the floor behind the table.

Not Anka. Thank God!

It was Dieter. Eyes open, mouth twisted, then frozen in either pain or fear—or both—he lay on his back in a huge pool of blood, still wet and vivid red, but slowly thickening in the warm room. The blades of a large pair of scissors were stuck in his

127

body. Only the handles protruded. He'd been stabbed low in the belly, more than once, I think, ripped open and left to bleed out. Hence the horrific smells.

I gaped at the awful scene, unable to look away or even to close my eyes.

This man had returned Anka's purse to Jutte today. And now he was dead.

Eddie the bellhop. He'd delivered the ransom note to Sepp. He was dead, too.

A sudden pop in the stove made me jump. A good thing, really, as the match was scorching my glove. I blew it out, grateful for the darkness, which is when I heard a knock at the front door.

"Mr. Mannheim, you in there?" a man's voice called.

I almost wet my drawers.

After a short pause where I stood locked in place, unable to move, the knock came again, harder this time.

"This is Officer Jim Blake. Mr. Mannheim? Anybody there?"

Dear Lord . . . What if he came around back to investigate?

Turning tail, I fled, kicking the block of wood aside on my way out. I dashed madly across the alley, holding my breath for fear the officer might hear me panting.

Nobody chased me, or not as far as I could tell, even though I felt as though a pack of silent hounds ran at my heels. Nobody called out to stop me. I ran past the next street until I reached Riverside. From there, taking in great gulps of freezing cold air, I jogged along the sidewalk to the Doyle & Howe door. The lamp I'd left burning upstairs in my room sent a soft yellow glow onto the street below. Snowflakes shimmered in the light.

I fumbled for the key, only to discover I couldn't slide it into the lock no matter how hard I pushed. That's when I discovered I still gripped the one to the haberdashery. God knows I didn't want anything in my possession to either remind me of or connect me to the body in Mannheim's store. My fingers felt frozen around the key, and I sobbed softly as I pushed it deep into a coat pocket and found the right one. What a horrible, horrible night.

Hands shaking, I managed at last to fit my own key into the lock and turned it.

"Where da hell you been?"

The irritated question came from my right and caused me to nearly leap out of my boots. Reaching for my .32 pocket revolver, I pushed hard against the door, only to have it stick at the bottom.

Frozen shut. Hell and damnation.

"Who is that?" I made my voice raspy, not too difficult what with my vocal cords tied in a terrified knot.

"Sepp Amsel." The reply was sharp. My client's bulky form emerged from the doorway of Pinelli's cabinet shop next door. "What you doin' out here, Miss China Bohannon, all dressed up in boy clothes?"

"I . . . I . . . How'd you know it was me?"

He snorted. "What? You think I can't tell a woman when I see one, even if she's wearin' men's britches?"

It must've been rhetorical since the answer appeared obvious.

Relieved I wouldn't need to defend myself, I let go my pistol and pushed open the door with a final angry shove. Nimble, who'd been standing directly in front of it, yelped and went flying.

"Come in," I told Sepp over the dog's chatter. "It's cold out there. We can talk inside."

But before I snapped on the electric overhead light, I went around the office making certain the blinds were closed down tight. Sepp nodded his approval, but there was a question behind it, too.

I collapsed into the chair behind my desk, leaving it to Sepp to toss another chunk of wood on the embers in the stove. Nimble, whining softly, sniffed at my boots before crawling up on my lap. I felt better with her in my arms.

"Have you been waiting long?" I asked Sepp. My voice still quivered, I noticed.

"Long enough to frostbite ears. Figured I'd better wait, though. I got one, you see. Just like you said."

"Got one?" I gaped at him.

"Note from kidnappers."

I sat up straight. "Did you bring it with you? What does it say?"

Sepp, taking the chair across from me, loosened the top three buttons of his coat and fished in an inner pocket. "You read." He withdrew a rather grubby envelope and passed it to me. "Then you tell me what you been up to."

I'd have to think before I did that.

My fingers shook, making it difficult to manage the envelope flap without tearing.

No police, the note said. *No private detective. Fire the woman before she must die. Before the Kalb woman must die. Do it now. Ransom has gone up. Pay five thousand dollars. Deliver tomorrow at Finkle's Rooming House. 11 pm. Will release prisoner at midnight.*

I gawked at Sepp. "Huh! They changed the time, raised the ransom, and want it tomorrow?"

"Ja. Is no matter. I got the money."

"They also know I'm on the job. Who do you suppose told them?"

He shrugged. "Don't know, but they make threats to you."

"I noticed." Oh, yes, indeed, I noticed.

"Best to pay ransom. Get Anka back. You safe. So maybe they bamboozle me. Don't matter. Forget it."

I opened my mouth. Five thousand dollars might not mean

as much to Sepp Amsel as it did to most people, but it was an amount that would keep several families in some style for an entire year. A substantial sum.

The thing is, there were considerations beyond whether Sepp was duped or simply allowed himself to be robbed. Considerations beyond either my safety or Anka's return, as well, although we had no way of knowing if she was still alive. Two men had been murdered. I couldn't walk away from their deaths as if they didn't matter. I had a responsibility to them.

"The thing is—" I said, starting to tell him all this, then stopped and tried to think how to go on.

"Thing is what?"

"I don't think all our problems will be over if you pay the ransom. Maybe they'll let Anka go. Maybe they won't. You see . . ."

"Why not?" Anger flared in Sepp's voice.

I sighed so deeply Nimble turned her head and licked my chin. "A matter of murder."

"Coppers are looking at boy's murder. Don't know of connection to kidnapping."

"Yet, perhaps. Doesn't mean they never will."

He shook his head. "Who knows? You, me, Jutte. Gratton Doyle. And Rose . . . Mrs. Flynn, I mean. Will any of us speak of kidnapping to police? No. Not until Anka is safe."

"Are you forgetting the kidnappers themselves?" I asked with a twitch of my lips. Not amusement. Sardonic pessimism.

He stared at me. "You think they would speak?"

My teeth ground together like a squirrel cracking nuts. "You asked where I'd been when you jumped out at me earlier." I paused. "As a matter of fact, you asked where the hell I'd been. Well, I think I've been in a little bit of hell."

"What you talking about?" He sounded impatient.

"Murder," and, over his shaking head, "a second murder, I mean."

CHAPTER FIFTEEN

Sepp froze at my announcement. Presently, his muscles flexed as he gathered himself. His face had gone from ruddy to white in the space of ten seconds. "Is it Anka?"

"No."

"Then who?" He appeared only marginally relieved.

"A man."

"What man? Where?"

"I only know the victim's first name, Dieter. He works . . . worked at Mannheim's Haberdashery. He . . . his body is there, in the shop. Killed within the last hour, I should think."

The mere thought made my stomach churn, bile rising in my throat. Thank goodness, I'd had no supper. In fact, I might never be able to eat again.

"Mannheim's?" Sepp echoed. "What you doing there?" He thought a moment. "You think Anka is there? What for?" Then, after a moment, "Was she?"

The look I gave him probably showed puzzlement. And sympathy, or maybe pity. Whichever, he seemed to take offense, because his face folded into a fierce scowl.

"Well?"

"Do you and your fiancée ever communicate?" I had an overwhelming urge to inquire if the only words spoken between them involved her demand for money and him asking how much.

"Communicate?"

"Talk to each other."

"With Jutte? Of course."

Harrumph. If you ask me, that sounded like a lot of bluster.

"Have you spoken with her today?" I pressed on, not because I wanted to be unkind, but because his reply might be important. Turned out, it was.

"Ja," he said, confirming one of my gathering fears. "Later, after I saw you at hotel, when police left we talked then, Jutte and I."

"What about?"

A flush rose in his cheeks, as if the memory of that conversation made him angry or embarrassed. Of the two, I'd say embarrassed.

"The wedding, a little. Maybe . . ." His face stiff, Sepp stopped and shrugged.

Maybe? Maybe what? Sounded to me like trouble might be brewing in lovebird land.

I arched an eyebrow. "Did you speak about the kidnapping? Or the ransom?"

"All of it. Anka is Jutte's sister. Jutte deserves to know what happens." His lips twisted. "She don't like you, Miss China. She say you ask silly question about a purse, and I tell her what you and me say. What for?"

"Silly question? Hmm, did she now?" I thought a moment. "Did she say why she thought my question silly?"

He shook his head. "She say you are jealous."

"Jealous? What about?"

He shook his head in a "bewildered man" sort of way. "We talk about price of ransom, too. About why Wednesday deadline. About who would do such a ting. I tell her be on lookout for another letter."

"Ah." I had to grit my teeth to keep from speaking out. I settled for, "How long afterward was it before you received the new ransom demand?"

"Hour. Hour and half." He breathed in through his nose, causing a peculiar whistle that made Nimble jump from my lap and go to his. Wise creature, she must've sensed his need of comfort was greater than mine. Absently, he stroked her soft fur. "You think Jutte sends note, ja?"

I breathed a sigh of relief. Thank goodness. He wasn't as blind as I'd feared.

"I think you must be prepared for the possibility that the sisters are colluding in the abduction." It seemed foolish to say things certain to alienate the most influential client I'd ever had. And yet, it wasn't fair to withhold my suspicions. If wrong, I'd be happy to apologize.

To him, not to her.

He spread his arms in a helpless gesture, barely swooping them closed in time to catch Nimble before she tumbled from his lap. "But why? I buy for her, and for Anka, too, everything they want."

"I'm sorry. I can't begin to answer that."

"I am old fool," he said, so shamefaced my heart broke for him. Yes, even though I couldn't deny it. "I thought a young woman from my own country would be honest. Soft and gentle. Not like women I meet here. Hurdy gurdy girls, bottom feeders, women who . . . who work in my business. I will not marry such a woman."

"I understand. But, Sepp, there are good women here, too. Look at Mrs. Flynn."

His nose did that pinched thing again, and his face turned the color of a ripe strawberry.

"Ja," he said. "Too bad—"

Or did he mean too late?

I got up, slipping in a puddle—the result of snow melted from my boots. A similar lake surrounded Sepp's feet. Going into the hall, I found a mop. Armed with it, I came back into the office to find Sepp staring down at the floor where I'd been sitting.

In a moment, I saw why.

"Uh," I grunted.

"Is blood from your boots," Sepp said matter-of-factly.

There went my stomach again, turning flip-flops. "I must've . . . I didn't realize . . . Oh, Lord. I stepped in Dieter's blood without knowing." Willy nilly, I applied the mop to the floor, swabbing away with all my might. Hard to do when one is shaking like laundry on a line, blowing in the wind.

Sepp rose to his feet, carefully setting Nimble onto the floor. "Did you call for police?"

"No."

"Good. Will be footprints. Must hope snow covers trail to this place. Not good if you say you find another body. That policeman, I hear him say things. He is angry with you. Why?"

"Long story. He's not an honest man, I can tell you that much, and he doesn't like me knowing him for what he is. He hit me once, a few months ago, when I accused him of graft, and he'll make trouble for me if he can." I didn't like thinking about it. "Here's another long story, one that concerns us— concerns you—right now."

With short breaks to rinse my mop and wring it out in fresh water, I told Sepp most of what I'd learned, and some I only suspected. So far.

"Do you think Jutte stabbed this man? This Dieter?" Sepp got up and put more wood on the fire, allowing me to mop where his shoes had dripped.

"I'm certain she did not." It was best, I'd decided, not to tell Sepp about Klein and the other man. Not yet.

"Sepp, I'm not even positive she is one of the kidnappers. She—"

"Bamboozlers," he broke in. "Bamboozlers, kidnappers, murderers. All are together. I think so." He sighed like a beaten man. "Next will ask for more money. I—"

"What?"

"Maybe I do a test. See what happens." His jaw set.

"She may be perfectly innocent. American justice says one is innocent until proven guilty. Or something like that." Sepp and I seemed to be losing sight of the precept.

He didn't argue but only shook his head sadly. Or maybe in disgust.

Sepp left then, although I felt guilty sending him out into the cold looking so woebegone. I went upstairs to stir the fire and change my clothes. It really wouldn't do for anyone to see me in man's garb. Not that I was expecting anyone else to come around at this time of night.

I found cold meat and vegetables for Nimble's supper and forced myself to swallow some bread and cheese. Nothing else would go down. And then it was back to the office and work.

Sepp and I had made plans and discussed what we knew and much we only suspected.

"I wish Gratton was back," I'd whined to my employer. "I'm afraid he's followed a false trail."

"Ja," Sepp surprised me by saying. "Need a tough guy. This Gratton Doyle, he is tough, ja?"

"No doubt about it," I said.

Early the next morning, after a night where visions of murdered men haunted me and kept me from sleeping, I sat down at my desk to peruse the morning paper. I was looking for reports of a man found murdered. There was nothing.

Further engaged in alternately fretting, blowing on my cold fingers, and making notes on a fresh sheet of paper, I looked up as frozen snow crunched on the walk outside the building.

Someone took no notice of the Closed sign hanging in the window. He hammered on the door as though announcing that Queen Victoria herself had arrived.

Sharp, demanding, imperious. How could a fist pounding against wood convey so much?

Alarm coursed through me. Gratton and Monk! They hadn't yet returned. Had something happened to one of them? To both of them?

Was Sergeant Hansen coming to arrest me?

Or was this a trick of some kind? A vision of Dieter's bloody corpse flashed through my mind.

The hammering repeated. On my feet without knowing how I got there, my pencil fell from nerveless fingers. Nimble, who'd been peacefully dozing with her head resting on my toes, surged from her hidey-hole and howled like an old-country banshee. I don't mind saying icy fingers ran up my spine.

Yanking open the desk drawer, I grabbed the .32 revolver and shuffled across to the door.

"Who's there?" Glory be! Did that frail quaver belong to me?

"Let me in," a man called without identifying himself. His voice was muffled. "I must speak with the woman detective."

I groaned. Hell and damnation. Here was yet another foreigner arrived to cloud the issue. *Please Lord, not German.* I suspected that particular prayer hopeless. No matter who, any new client thumping on the door so early in the morning struck me as suspicious, coming as it did at this point in an investigation where murder was involved.

Particularly in a case as tangled as this one.

I resolved to invest in a knocker or, better yet, a muted bell. No more fists on my door. Anyone entering must act civilized.

"We're closed." I stood well away from the window, out of sight. "Come back tomorrow." Slipping to the side, I tweaked the blind the least little bit and, with one eye set to the gap, peered out.

My heart sank all the way to my feet.

CHAPTER SIXTEEN

Know your enemy. Isn't that what strategists always say? A predictable enemy means a battle already halfway won.

Or something like that.

I recognized the man's face. It had been quite clear in the photograph Jutte hadn't wanted me to see. Of course, so had Dieter's. This man, however, had a thin scar tracing down his cheek from the corner of his eye, until it disappeared into his beard. Germans were said to take pride in dueling scars, weren't they? Somehow, it stuck in my mind I was seeing one now.

I cleared my throat. "What is your business with the detective?" I called, loud enough to be heard through the door.

"Let me in. I need to speak with you, not shout in the street for everyone to hear."

I wanted to know what he had to say, but I'd prefer the conversation to take place at a distance. I agreed shouting in the street was not the best approach. However, I am not without some sense. I'd heard Cosimo Pinelli, our cabinetmaker neighbor and my sometime bodyguard, only moments ago sawing away on a current project. The saw had stopped when the man outside began making so much noise, and I guessed Mr. Pinelli was on the alert.

"Wait one moment," I said. I dashed out the back and hurried next door through two inches of new snow. Another freezing day, although I hardly felt it in my apprehension.

Mr. Pinelli was waiting for me.

"I need your help, Cosimo," I said. "Have you time to come with me?"

He eyed the pistol in my hand.

"Sure. That man making the noise, he scares you, Miss China?"

"I don't trust him," I said, not admitting to fright.

He, bless him, without further question, followed me in through the back. I don't think it took us more than thirty seconds all told before we were in the agency office, ready for action.

Cosimo, a fairly recent immigrant married to a mixed-blood lady of the Nez Perce tribe, strayed from the usual preconceived Italian stereotype. A blue-eyed blond, he was large and muscular. Though sweet as could be with his friends, customers, and animals—I never hesitated to leave Nimble in his keeping—when required, he could be quite fierce. A good mix-up of fisticuffs and he figured he'd had a good time. Oh yes, and he was a new father and probably short tempered due to lack of sleep.

Just the kind of person I needed at this moment.

Cosimo stopped in the hall and leaned against the doorjamb into the office, his arms folded. Definitely formidable.

My courage restored, I tucked the pistol in my skirt pocket and unlocked the door, holding it open. The man stepped inside, preceded by the powerful scent of bay rum. Seeing Cosimo, he stopped short and fixed my friend with a cold stare. His eyes were a pale hazel, I noticed. A murky, no-color color.

"Who is this?" he demanded, upon spotting Cosimo. "Another detective?"

"Mr. Pinelli watches over me," I replied oh-so-primly and gestured for him to sit in the guest chair in front of my desk. "We at Doyle & Howe Detective Agency take security very seriously."

Behind his back, Cosimo winked.

I seated myself behind the desk, my feet coming to rest against Nimble, who cowered in the kneehole. "I am Miss Bohannon. I believe you're looking for me. What can I do for you?"

He leaned back in the chair, perfectly at ease. The neatly trimmed dark beard covering the lower half of his face made his expression hard to read.

Although leaving drips of melted snow on my floor, his shoes were polished to a high shine. He wore an elegant black bowler, which he only removed as an obvious afterthought. His overcoat was of excellent quality and fit him well. Was he, I wondered, a patron of Mannheim's Haberdashery?

A fast-moving chill shook me at the thought of that dark sewing room and how I'd seen it last. With an effort, I erased the memory.

He acted like a self-satisfied muckety-muck, or perhaps a minor lordling from the old country. Obviously an educated man of power and command, I could see it in the casual way he crossed his legs and studied me. Very superior.

His gaze, as it rested upon me, seemed cold, calculating, and cruel. Especially cruel.

For all the hurry he'd seemed to be in, he kept me waiting before speaking, and then what he said struck me as off the subject. But maybe not.

"Do you have a bodyguard with you at all times?" He flicked a wary glance at Cosimo.

An interesting start to the conversation, especially after the fuss he'd made outside.

That chill thing was making goosebumps rise again, and not because the fire had died out. It hadn't.

I looked up to see Cosimo eyeing the man with a puzzled look. He had caught on to the oddity of it all, as well.

I believe I've mentioned before that I'm not averse to a little fibbing if the situation seems warranted.

"Most of the time," I replied, as if I didn't care if the whole world knew. "Mr. Pinelli is very good, as are the others on the Doyle & Howe payroll. Only rarely does the general observer realize anyone is there unless he wants them to."

"I see. I admire your employers, Miss Bohannon, and the way they see to your well-being."

I smiled. If he only knew. "We all do our best. Now, sir, I repeat: What can I do for you?"

"I wish to hire you." Lounging in the oak straight chair, he turned far enough to extend his feet toward the stove, as though satisfied the deal was closed.

"Indeed." Not only did he frighten me, he annoyed me. And there was something, something about—"Then I believe introductions are in order. With whom do I have the pleasure of speaking?"

Another lie. No pleasure was involved.

He cast a look over his shoulder. Seeing Mr. Pinelli's impassive gaze fixed on him, he shifted his attention back to me.

"I am called Horst Werner."

I inclined my head in a ladylike nod. "What is the nature of your problem, Mr. Werner?"

"I am staying at the Portuguese Hotel. For the past two nights, I have returned from dinner in the hotel restaurant to find my room ransacked. Money was taken the first evening. Last night, a valuable gold pocket watch and chain on a diamond-studded fob went missing."

The longer he spoke, the deeper the sinking feeling in my belly. I recognized his voice now, although he'd lost the accent he'd used when I'd heard him speaking with Herr Schultz last night as they walked away from Mannheim's Haberdashery. Who was he really? And what did he want? To kill me here, in broad daylight?

But I am made of stern stuff. A sort of haze enveloped me, until I barely heard him, even though I met his eyes as he went on speaking.

"I suspect the night maid who turns down my bed," he was saying when I regained my wits. "I want you to wait in my room tonight and keep watch during the meal. Catch her in the act."

Without even thinking, I shot to my feet. "We're finished here. I must ask you to leave. Now."

His mouth dropped open. His muscles tensed, visibly flexing beneath his coat. "Here," he said as if the word meant something.

I took a breath. *Careful.* "Clearly, I must decline. You would do better to contact the police about any stolen items." My voice hardened. "Or is this a joke? It's difficult to believe any thief would be so idiotic as to rob the same man's room more than once, let alone three times. Even more ludicrous to think the man would let himself be robbed." My voice rose. "And more ludicrous still for you to think I would risk my reputation on such a claim."

He stood up, too, blinking eyes semaphoring anger. "Do you accuse me of lying?"

"Aren't you?"

"Why would I do that?"

"An excellent question, sir. Why would you?" I could think of a reason or two.

Werner gathered his coat around him, one hand burrowing its way into a pocket. "I'm not."

"Then contact the police, sir." I had a pocket, too. Reaching in, my hand closed on the butt of my revolver. "I have no wish to pursue the question any further," I said coldly.

"You may regret this."

"Is that a threat?"

I was ever so glad Cosimo stood by. The floor creaked as he stepped forward and gripped Werner's arm with a hand muscled from his work of sawing and sanding. "Miss China says go. You leave now."

Werner really had no choice considering the way Cosimo propelled him to the door.

When he was gone, I sat down, trembling. "Do you think he was going for a gun?" I asked Cosimo as he turned toward me. "Or a knife?" *Scissors?*

He shook his head. "Maybe. Don't know. That man, he lies about thief in room. But them Bolsheviks are bad people, Miss China. Dangerous. Don't ever trust them."

I thought of Jutte Kalb. "I won't." Then, a moment later, "Bolsheviks?"

I wasn't much wiser after he'd explained. "Ah," I said. "Politics."

Werner's visit having left me shaken, I had a difficult time settling after Cosimo returned to his own business. I needed counsel, and who better to confer with, I decided, than Mrs. Flynn? A stalwart friend, Rose never failed to provide me with good advice.

All right. I admit to also being curious about what appeared to be a budding . . . shall we say "friendship?" . . . between Rose and Sepp Amsel.

Although that left a surefire dilemma. What would Sepp do about his well-publicized marriage to Jutte Kalb? I sensed heartbreak ahead. Oh, not for Jutte. I figured she'd be fine as long as Sepp had plenty of money. But what about Sepp himself?

And Rose? Rose most of all.

I bundled up in my coat, a warm bonnet with a decorative hatpin stuck through the top, and thick woolen gloves. I wore an extra pair of stockings and, perforce, crammed my feet into boots. My outdoor preparations may sound like much ado, but stuffing Nimble into her sweater was an even larger endeavor. Once I'd chased her down for the second time and snapped the lead to her collar, we were ready to go. I switched the Open sign to Closed and, locking the door behind us, went out onto Riverside.

Brrr. Intermittent sunshine did nothing to warm the day, but glinting off the snow, it did do a fine job of blinding me.

I hurried south on Howard, sliding on ice buried beneath last night's snowfall. Nimble pranced, lifting her feet high, although I don't suppose it did her a particle of good. She'd soon be weighted down with snow balls clinging to her fur. Perhaps I would consult Cosimo's wife about making her a set of doggie moccasins if the snow and cold kept up. I could only anticipate dressing her in them.

Amusing myself with such scenes to take my mind off the cold, I was unaware of a person coming up behind me until Nimble shied aside, getting out of the way. Her action caused me, to avoid stepping on her, to slip.

An excellent piece of luck, as it happened.

Skidding feet saving me from more than a jolt as a man's arm swept out with what would've been a crushing blow to a spot above my ear.

I fell to the frozen ground, hurt badly enough to surprise a cry out of me. Everything went black for a moment.

Nimble's snarls did nothing to deter the man as he prepared to stomp me, an easy target now that I was down.

The man, his face covered by a brown knit muffler, panted loudly. Over his noise, I heard someone at a distance, a good Samaritan, I suppose, yelling at him to stop. Boots clumped on the sidewalk. Help was on the way.

At least it gave him pause. Long enough for me to pull the nine-inch hat pin from my bonnet and wield it like a sword.

This pin was stouter than most, with the head of a smiling cat as the decorative element. High quality hatpins, for those who aren't afraid to use them, work well as stabbers. I don't suggest trying to cut with one. My advice is good. I've attained a bit of a reputation in Spokane for my prowess in using them as a defensive weapon.

As this man discovered when, evidently figuring he had time to get away after delivering another blow, reached down to ram a fist in my mouth.

He didn't count on Nimble's sharp little teeth grabbing the meaty heel of his hand. She bit deep, too, drawing blood.

The man bellowed and shook my dog from her hold, whereupon she went tumbling out of the reach of his foot.

All this distraction gave me time to scramble up, hatpin in hand. Only instead of waiting for him to come at me again, I attacked.

The face is the best target for a hatpin.

"EEEE!" he yelled. He shook bright drops of blood from his chin onto the front of his blue pea jacket and reached for me.

He wasn't expecting me to step into him and go for a jab at his eyes. I may have even done a little damage.

Well, I know I did. But before I could get in a second jab, my pin hooked in the muffler around his neck and jerked from my hand when he batted at it.

Immediately, I dropped to the ground. Instead of rolling away, I rolled toward him. He tripped over me and went lurching straight at the man running toward us. The last I saw of him he had lumbered across the street and headed north, into the tenderloin. His hand was covering one eye.

And me? A bit worse for wear, I picked myself up, collected my dog, and, after thanking my would-be rescuer with sincere gratitude, limped on.

I tasted blood, having bitten my tongue yet again. I would

bill Sepp for the hatpin, I thought, mentally totting up expenses. It had been one of my favorites.

Why Sepp? Because I'd had a chance to think about my attacker. About his shape and the way he stood. And that I'd seen him before in Schultz's German Club.

Another of Werner's henchmen? Bound to be.

Chapter Seventeen

The group of women partaking of either a late breakfast or an elaborate mid-morning tea went silent as I stumbled into Rose's restaurant. Two tables full, which meant eight ladies with dropped forks and staring eyes. It seemed an indication my mix-up on the street had left me in a bit of a shambles.

Self-consciously, I reached up to straighten my knitted bonnet with hands clad in grubby, torn mittens. My smile wavered as I nodded to a woman whose face was familiar.

"My feet slipped out from under me," I announced, my voice pinched as though in pain. Not a complete prevarication, I daresay. "I fell."

Chatter broke out again. "Oh, you poor dear," the familiar woman said.

"Are you hurt?" asked another.

"I'm fine," I bravely assured the ladies. Yes, even though a bruise was already making itself known on my shoulder where the man had buffeted me, my hip hurt, and my tongue positively ached.

Relieved, they began chattering again, this apparently being a committee meeting to discuss "the movement," and forthwith ignored me. So much for sympathy. I only hoped it was the suffrage movement they were talking about.

Rose poked her head around the kitchen door and nodded toward the small table she reserved for herself when she had a moment to rest her feet. Still a little shaky, I sat down. Nimble cowered against my ankles and began chewing at the snow clumped in the fur on her legs.

Soon, as though my entrance had been a signal of some sort, the women adjourned their meeting, paid their bills, and departed, several of them piling into a single cab. Who says the rich don't know how to economize? Rose cleared their table and fetched her own cup of tea before she joined me.

"All right, missy. What really happened to you?" she demanded. Mouth pursed, she examined me with narrowed eyes. "You have the look of a woman on the edge."

"Edge?" I snorted. "Edge of what?"

She studied me a moment longer. "Not hysteria," she said at last, smiling a little. "More like a woman who's about to draw her six-shooter and plug somebody." One strong eyebrow arched. "Or maybe you already did."

I had to laugh. In fact, we both laughed. I felt better afterward.

"You're not far off," I admitted. "Only I used a hatpin instead of my revolver."

"Again?" Her expression anticipatory, Rose settled her elbows on the table. "Do tell."

I did. I told her everything. Not only about the attack on my way here, but also about the visitor I'd had earlier. I even told her the part about finding Dieter's body.

Blood receded from her face, leaving red spots on her cheeks.

"Wait here." Rose stood up. "I'll just get my outdoor things and be right with you."

"With me?" What did she mean? I must say this wasn't the reaction I'd expected.

"Yes. We're going shopping."

She'd said "we."

"We are?" She'd already disappeared into her rooms beyond the kitchen. "What are we shopping for?" I called.

"Use your head, China. We're going to see what the situation is at Mannheim's Haberdashery, for a start. See if we can get the police to tell us what they've found out, if anything. Officer Shannon might talk to us. Then we're going to talk to Sepp. This situation has gone far enough."

"Wait a minute. I can't let you be seen with me. It might put you in danger. Just give me your thoughts, that's all I want."

"Oh, pshaw. I'm sticking with you until that man of yours gets home. I'm going to give him a good talking to, while I'm at it. What's the matter with him—or your uncle, either one— leaving you on your own when there's a murderer on the loose. Haven't they realized by now that you're . . ."

The rest faded.

I was on the verge of agreeing until I remembered neither Monk nor Grat knew about the first murder, let alone the second. And they weren't going to be happy when they found out. Truth to tell, I wasn't any too happy myself. I'd contracted to investigate a kidnapping, not multiple murders.

Anyway, I was a little confused by her calling Gratton "that man of yours." How had she gotten that idea in her head? His occasional kisses meant nothing to him. He liked to tease me, is all. And I'd never mentioned a word about him to Rose. Nothing beyond explaining how he bedeviled me every time he got the chance, anyway. Oh, and maybe repeated a little something he'd said to me, here and there, and—

Left to ponder while Rose donned sweater, coat, overshoes, muffler, hat, gloves, and, I suspect, warm flannel drawers, I occupied myself with clearing the last of Nimble's ice balls from between her toes and piling them in the under-counter sink to melt.

I only found out considerably later about a young newspaper boy's discovery of two bodies. The first was sprawled in the alley behind a Chinese opium den down in the tenderloin.

"Frozen stiff as a poker," the newsboy said, according to the reporter sent to cover the incident. This indicated he'd been dead some hours before discovery.

Then, only a couple streets farther on, after the police allowed him to continue his route, the youngster found the other body lying alongside the road with a berm of snow kicked over him. Enough had fallen away to uncover part of a foot, a shoulder, and a nose.

"This'n was still steamin' hot and squishy," the boy said and added he was inclined to look for a different job.

The one close to the opium den had suffered an overdose. After assessing the bruises on his arms and body, the medical examiner reported the next morning that he didn't think the dead man had committed suicide but had been forcefully injected with a massive dose of heroin.

Neither Rose nor I had any thought of *more* murdered men as she locked her restaurant and we set out to traverse the seven blocks to Mannheim's Haberdashery. The sun came out even as the temperature dropped. The city streets looked like something on a picture postcard, so clean and pure. Cold enough to freeze one's nostrils shut, the air was invigorating until one's breath caught on smoke from a thousand chimneys. Both of us coughed, and even Nimble joined in.

The pristine beauty wouldn't last. All too soon horses' hooves and wagon wheels would churn the snow into mud. Ruts would freeze and streets become impassable for vehicle and human feet alike.

"Not that I don't appreciate your company," I told Rose, puffing a little to keep up with her longer strides, "but I hate for you to get mixed up in this case. I don't mind saying it's turned a bit messy."

"I should say so." Rose chuckled a little. "But are you forgetting I'm the one who got you involved? I was drawn into it from the moment I found Jutte Kalb shivering under a bush last Monday morning. And then I compounded my mistake by telling Sepp—Mr. Amsel, I mean—about you."

I glanced sideways at her. Something was in the wind between the two of them. Just the way she said his name convinced me.

"So, you think there's something suspect about Jutte, too?" I asked.

"Oh, yes. I'm afraid I do. Poor Sepp. He deserves better. I just hope you can clear this business up before the wedding on Saturday." She paused. "He asked me to bake the cake, you know. More than one, actually, if everyone invited is treated to a morsel."

Rose's tone had lost some of its briskness.

I looked over at her, but she was staring straight ahead, eyes blinking.

"He did?" I said. "Except Anka being missing is a perfect excuse to delay the wedding."

"Do you think he would do that?" I believe I heard a note of hope in her question.

"I think we'd better see he does."

"Well then." She centered her hat atop what frankly was rather tousled hair as we came even with the door to Mannheim's. "Here we go." She led the way into the shop, with Nimble and me close behind.

To tell the truth, I was surprised to find Mannheim's door not only open, but unbarred. Had the police finished their investigation and gotten out so quickly? It seemed a bit strange given their snail-like pace when attending the bellhop's murder. Perhaps the death of German immigrants, particularly if they were German Jews, didn't rate as highly as that of a born American like Eddie.

The room was chilly today, as if the fire had gone unattended, but the lights were on. Mud-clotted puddles dotted the wooden floors, making for slippery footing. As if that weren't odd enough, a stack of shirts on one of the tables was in disarray, as though someone, a careless customer, no doubt, had rooted through the pile. Probably while searching for the right size. Ordinarily, August, the attentive young clerk, would've delivered the required item into the customer's hand.

Likewise, a box of handkerchiefs had been opened and a couple of the contents fallen to the floor. August's precise, machine-like folds had gone to naught.

The room was empty of people and silent as death.

Rose and I exchanged wary glances.

"Where is everyone?" she whispered. "Where are the police?"

"I don't know," I whispered back, then, louder, "Hallooo. Is anyone here?"

Beyond the curtain separating the sewing room from the showroom, someone stirred. Feet shuffled. A man sighed and murmured. Slow footsteps headed our way.

I touched the .32 stowed close to hand in my skirt pocket, but it was only August who pushed the curtain aside and entered the showroom. His eyes, I noticed, were red, his face pale.

He forced a workaday smile when he saw us. "Guten tag. May I help you?"

Frankly, he looked like helping us was the farthest thing from his mind and he wished we'd leave. Or had never showed up in the first place. Even his accent sounded more pronounced today.

"Good day. Yes. I'm looking for some shirts." I hadn't forgotten my idea for Christmas presents. Rose, gazing about, remained silent.

"Shirts, ja," he said and gestured toward the unsteady stack on the table. "There."

"Are they marked for size?" I moved toward the display, even though most of my attention was on him.

"Size? Ja. Label is in back." August hardly seemed with us. He kept glancing toward the sewing room as if certain he was missing out on something more important than mere customers. Oddly enough, although he seemed not to see the melted snow trailing through the main room, I was certain I heard the sound of scrubbing behind the curtain. Well, I could guess what was being cleaned, couldn't I?

An all too vivid remembrance of the blood pooling around Dieter's body last night rose in my mind. Blood I'd probably left my own tracks in.

Rose, I saw, had heard the swish of rags and water, too. She edged toward the inner doorway, even as I, hoping to divert August's attention, asked, "Do you have a medium size in blue?"

August joined me in pawing through the stack, as careless as any shop-weary customer. I'd seen a shirt yesterday I thought would look nice on Grat and hoped it hadn't been sold.

The sound of scrubbing ceased. More water sloshed. There was a thud and a man cursing—it had to be cursing—in German. August drew in a shaky breath.

"You look troubled. Are you having problems? Has the cold set your plumbing amiss?" I asked August, pure innocence and sympathy in my tone. Would he tell me about Dieter?

Apparently not, although he turned a shade paler. "Nein," he said sharply. "No problems. No problems here." His head shook as though with a palsy, even more so as Mr. Mannheim started into the room. The older man stepped quickly behind the curtain again as he saw me and recognition dawned.

"August," he called, hidden once more. But not before I'd seen his shirt cuffs were stained with blood. *"Beeilen Sie sich!* Hurry."

"Ja," the clerk replied and said to me, "Have you found what you want?"

"I saw a shirt here yesterday. I hope . . . ah, here it is."

No thanks to him, I found the blue shirt lodged at the bottom of the stack. I pulled it out and quickly found another in white for Monk. Good enough. I am nothing if not decisive in my choices, particularly when I have murder, the solving of a murder, I mean, on my mind.

"These will do." I smiled at him. A smile he didn't return.

August turned away from Rose as he took the shirts and led me toward the cash register. She inched aside the edge of the curtain and peeped into the other room. Gasping, she spun and looked back at me.

Her eyes went wide as the saucer of one of her own demitasse cups. She pointed into the sewing room.

"There's a dead man in there," she announced.

CHAPTER EIGHTEEN

Unless someone else had been murdered, Dieter's body must still be very much present in the back room. Not, I thought, the best development.

It only needed for Nimble to lift her nose, scent the air, and let forth with a howl fit to rattle the mirror hanging on the wall.

I think Rose was about ready to join Nimble. I guess she—Rose, I mean—had never seen a murdered man before. To her credit, she didn't scream or vomit, even though she placed a hand over her mouth as though to hold both inside.

"He's got scissors stuck in his belly," she managed to say.

Dieter for sure.

"Get out," Herr Mannheim was saying in a frantic tone. "Get out."

"A dead man?" Ignoring him, I bounded over and swept the curtain aside to see for myself before letting out a theatrical gasp. Truly, the sight was almost as startling as it had been last night. Better lighting revealed more details.

"Murder!" I said.

August let out a sob.

"What are you doing? Why haven't you called the police?" I demanded.

"They will arrest Herr Mannheim," August explained in a shaking voice. "Arrest us. We will be deported."

"Nonsense," Rose found her voice to say.

Except maybe not so much nonsense. She didn't know the

157

police as well as I did.

As though drawn by wires, we all stepped closer to Dieter's body, which lay on a ratty old blanket. He looked just as horrible as I remembered.

They'd moved him from where he'd been killed, leaving a bloody trail as they went, as if the original pool weren't enough. The scrubbing we'd heard must've destroyed any evidence the killers had left behind. And my own presence, as well. I must confess I couldn't help being a little relieved at that.

"What do you intend on doing with the body?" I asked.

Herr Mannheim began beating himself around his head with frantic hands.

I don't know what he was thinking. Bury Dieter and say nothing? Lord knows after five straight days of below zero temperatures the ground was too frozen to casually dispose of him just any old place. And since Mannheim said he didn't so much as own a horse, let alone a vehicle of any sort suitable for carrying the body away, I can't imagine what possessed the poor man.

What he did was begin weeping and crying. "Nein, nein, nein," he sobbed, as though we were going to torture him.

That much of his language I understood. He rattled on in what I later learned was Yiddish, while the rest of us observed his anguish in horrified sympathy.

I turned to August. "What is he saying?"

August wrung his hands, something I'd never before seen a man do. "He is saying he didn't do it. He didn't kill Dieter. He found Dieter this morning when he arrived. Found him dead. Blood, blood everywhere."

Well, I knew that, didn't I? Dieter hadn't died gently.

Herr Mannheim got down on his knees. "Bitte," he said. "Bitte."

Another word I recognized. "Please what? What does he want me to do?" Then, to the man on his knees. "Get up, sir, do."

"Bitte, do not tell." Mannheim remained on his knees, hands clasped.

"Tell who? The police? But you must report this death. Don't you want whoever killed him caught?"

Did I sound glib? Rose told me later that I did, but at least it got Herr Mannheim off the floor, sputtering more Yiddish.

"He is afraid they will blame him," August said. "He is afraid they will take his savings and confiscate this store. He says he is innocent." He puzzled a moment. "He is innocent. Me," his thumb pounded against his chest, "I am innocent, too."

Another thing I knew.

Rose stepped forward, shaking her head. "The police here don't hang innocent men. They will investigate and . . . and . . . well, not very often, anyway."

Mannheim's eyes, if anything, grew even wilder at the last part of Rose's attempt at reassurance.

Unfortunately for Herr Mannheim, the police might indeed accuse him, but they wouldn't take his store. Not right away, anyhow. And Rose knew that as well as I.

"You must notify the police immediately," Rose said. "Before you make things worse."

They already were going to be bad. We were all certain of it.

"If you don't call them, we will." I dreaded doing any such thing. Hadn't I tried to avoid this very development by running away and saying nothing last night? If Sergeant Lars Hansen found out I'd been here, he'd blame me and laugh at the opportunity. I'd be questioned. Doyle & Howe would be involved and Sepp Amsel dragged into it.

Nevertheless, if Herr Mannheim or August were accused, I'd have to admit to what I'd seen, when I'd seen it, and who those men were. Lars Hansen would have a heyday. He'd pretend not to believe me.

"Another body," he'd say. "They pile up pretty good when

you're around, don't they, China?"

Hell and damnation. Yes, they did.

Regardless of Herr Mannheim's state of mind, I had questions to ask, and it had to be done right now. I had to know how they were involved—innocent bystanders or partners in Anka's kidnapping.

"Who do you think killed your employee?" I stared into Mannheim's eyes. "Why would anyone do such a thing?"

Mannheim squirmed, his mouth twisting. He glanced at August as though in warning.

"A thief," he said, though not as if he believed it. "That is who. A thief."

I looked down at the body again and promptly wished I hadn't. "I don't know. Thieves usually break in at night. When did you discover the body?"

Mannheim thought. "This morning. Seven o'clock. Is when I got here."

Rose frowned. I don't know what she was thinking, but she said, "Did you expect this man to be at work?"

"Yes. But was killed in night," Mannheim said and shook his head in sorrow. "The blood. Can tell by the blood."

Indeed one could.

Meanwhile, Rose had raised a good point.

"Why was he here last night?" I asked.

"Why?" Mannheim looked around as though seeking inspiration. "I . . ."

"Working late," August said.

"Yes." Mannheim seized on the explanation, his head bobbing now. "Working late."

I studied him. "You seem surprised. Wasn't he scheduled to work late?"

"No. Last suit complete. Maybe," he brightened, "maybe he

waits for customer to pick up. Mr. Pierce's suit is finished. Maybe—"

"Perhaps you'd better check," Rose said.

Unfortunately, the suit was still behind the counter, wrapped in brown paper with a string twisted around it. There was a note attached to the string. *Hold for Mr. Pierce to pick up Friday.*

Well, that put paid to Mannheim's suggestion.

"I don't know," Mannheim said, nearly in tears again. "I don't know."

August's hands twisted. He, apparently, didn't know either.

"Your clerk's friends," I suggested to Mannheim. "Ask them if he stayed late to meet with them. See if they can shed some light on the situation."

But that was a dead-end street. The two went blank as white paper. Apparently, Dieter had no friends. Or none they wanted to speak of.

"Well, then," I said, "if you have nothing to hide, you'd better summon the police."

After a short argument, that, finally, is what he did. Or August did. He seemed to understand that Rose's and my advice was the only sensible course to follow. Between us, we persuaded Herr Mannheim to allow August to hail a blue-coated officer who conveniently strolled past. He turned away and vomited in a corner after viewing Dieter's remains. His first body, I suppose.

Rose and I acted our hearts out, a performance done as well as though we both belonged on the stage. Innocent shoppers, that's what we were, shocked and appalled and feeling faint. The officer allowed us to leave before Lars got there. Another body had been found in the snow, he told us, and the police were busy. I considered myself fortunate this police constable was new to the force and didn't recognize me.

"So, after all that, did you learn anything new?" Rose asked as we headed homeward, me limping with the pain in my hip. Her complexion was still a bit on the greenish side.

She had abandoned her plan to speak with Sepp as the morning headed toward lunch time. Snow began falling again in small, dry flakes—the kind that doesn't add up very fast. Nimble, the only one of us enjoying the excursion, scooted her nose through the powdery stuff, snorting and blowing like a whale at sea.

"Only that I'm reasonably sure Herr Mannheim and August aren't involved in the actual kidnapping. I do believe they knew—or suspected—Dieter was up to something, and with whom. Also," I added slowly, "they're afraid to speak of it."

"Yes, I thought so, as well. So, what are you going to do now?"

"I don't know. Nothing at the moment. My first priority is to find Anka, dead or alive, and return her to her sister. It's what I was hired to do. From there, if she is alive—and I truly think she is—I feel it's up to the police to deal with the people behind the killings."

Rose, from her greater height, patted me on the shoulder. "Good thinking. I'm relieved to hear you say so. Have you any idea where to start?"

"No." A sad admission. "But considering the people involved and the fact Dieter returned a very special Mamzelle purse to Jutte, I still think she was held in Mannheim's shop right after the kidnapping. But she's certainly not there now. Nor has she been for a while."

Rose batted snow out of her eyes. "What makes you think so?"

"More than just a feeling, you mean? First of all, the men

today weren't trying to hide anything but a body. And, secondly, once we explained things, they welcomed Officer Bell into the store without fearing too large of a repercussion. Not the action of someone holding a kidnap victim on the premises."

"I suppose you're right." She shivered and drew her collar higher around her neck. "But why kill Dieter if he was one of the instigators of the plot?"

I sighed. "Questions, questions. Rose, I just don't know."

Ice had built up on the step from the boardwalk to the road as we came to a cross street, and I lost balance, teetering as my boots skidded out from under me.

Rose grabbed my arm.

"Thank you." I caught my balance and went on talking. "At one time, I thought Dieter must be behind the kidnapping. While he was involved in the plot, I now doubt he was the brains behind it. I need to discover who his friends are . . . were. Where he might have met with them. Where they spent their time."

"Friends?" Rose cocked a brow. "Mannheim said he had none."

She had a point.

"Associates, then. But I suspect Mannheim didn't know his employee as well as he thought." Fretfully, I added, "I wish Gratton were here. And Monk. This is the sort of thing they do best. Men, especially foreign men, won't want to talk to me, and we don't have time to win them over. The ransom drop is scheduled for tonight. I have to free Anka before then."

Rose stared at me doubtfully. "Good luck," she said. "And be careful."

At the next corner, she turned onto Howard Street, hurrying now to prepare her café for any luncheon guests willing to brave the cold. I went on alone. Someone was waiting for me at the office's locked door as I approached. A welcome someone for a change.

"Philly! What are you doing here?" I gave her a little hug, and Nimble jumped up to place a snowy paw on her skirt. "I'm glad to see you."

"What happened to you? You look terrible! Are you hurt?"

I didn't feel up to explaining about the attack, maybe because I was still speaking with a bit of a lisp. "Slipped on the ice," I said.

Giving Nimble a pat on the head, she glanced about. "You always were a little clumsy. Anyway, I can't stay. I put an 'Out to Lunch' sign on the shop door, but I don't dare remain closed for long."

I am not clumsy! However, since this wasn't a social call, I glossed over the accusation. "What's wrong?" I asked.

Her dark eyes flashed. "Nothing with me—unless a certain somebody discovers I've been talking to you. But this business with Sepp Amsel's bride and her sister you were telling me about? I may have stumbled upon a tidbit you'll be interested in."

"A tidbit?" Digging the key from my coat pocket, I unlocked the door and urged her inside. She looked around, her gaze a little disparaging. Easy to see she wasn't impressed.

"Not so elegant as your shop," I admitted, at which pink tinged her high cheekbones.

Forced to look at the room through another's eyes, I decided Philly was right. The Doyle & Howe premises didn't amount to much. Gloomy, for starters, being lit with only the one electric bulb overhead. The woodwork was dark, the walls a drab tan, the windows overshadowed by the more imposing buildings surrounding us. Only the room's tin ceiling seemed acceptable. The oak furniture was not only heavy, but mundane. Nothing here to titillate one's imagination.

Of course, detectives depend on facts, not fairy tales.

Still, more cheerful surroundings might brighten up the thought processes. I determined to look into a bit of redecorating.

But that was for later. I waved Philly into the visitor's chair and, while she seated herself, thrust another chunk of wood into the stove. Nimble gave herself a giant shake, scattering a myriad of snow droplets before she flopped down in the circle of the stove's warmth and began chewing her feet.

"Coffee?" I asked Philly. "You must be freezing."

She shook her head. "No time."

Philly wore a classy, knee-length, black coat, a gorgeous concoction of a hat atop her shiny, dark hair, and carried a fur muff, probably of mink, over her bare hands. Ever so fashionable, if not particularly weatherproof.

But she was made of stern stuff and waved my concern aside. Shivering, she leaned forward in her chair as I sat down.

"You were asking about Sepp Amsel's bride and saying something fishy was going on?" She framed the sentence as a question.

I nodded.

"Well, one of the women—and I'm not sure which, as they look so much alike—came into the shop an hour ago. She looked around and bought a pretty ornament for her hair, one I'd made up only yesterday in a perfect color for a flaxen blonde like her . . . well, you don't want to hear about that. It's not the point." She took a breath.

"What is the point, Philly?"

"She met a man. An obvious assignation." Pausing breathlessly, her almond-shaped eyes rounded. "And he wasn't Sepp Amsel."

CHAPTER NINETEEN

Philly had always been given to drama, even when we were eleven.

I allowed myself to be surprised and impressed with her announcement. And I truly was. Impressed, I mean, that my old friend would venture out of her elegant environment, braving subzero cold to pass this newest twist along to me.

"Philly," I said, "you're a dear. How do you know it was an assignation?" My excitement roused Nimble, who pranced over to be petted.

Philly flipped an airy hand. "I know one when I see one. Lord knows I've participated in enough of them myself. The shifting eyes, the pinched fear mixed with glowing eagerness. The touch of hands so carefully disguised as a proper greeting. And always, an underlying expression of guilt."

I, too, could read between the lines. My heart faltered, thinking of the life she'd led. Even my own struggles with a stepmother who stole my inheritance had not been as demoralizing as what she'd endured.

"Oh, Philly . . ." I started, but she, knowing what I was about to say, shook her head so fiercely her hat loosened from its pin and slipped to the side.

"Never mind," she said. "That's over and in the past. I am Mamzelle now."

"Indeed you are."

We both were silent for a moment, then she adjusted her hat, thrusting the pin into the mass of her hair to anchor it. "Anyway, Amsel's bride and the man nodded a polite greeting, shook hands, then strolled about the shop ignoring one another so studiously anyone with eyes could tell it was an act. Then, over in the corner where the scarves hang—you remember, farthest from the cash register where I was standing . . . anyway, they came face to face again. She pointed at something, and he replied. Then he pointed at something else, and she replied. I, I may add, ignored them. Or so they thought."

She seemed rather proud of this duplicity.

"But then I had occasion to go into the back room, which— but how were they to know?—is right behind the area where they were standing. Only a drapery divides the two areas. A drapery with a convenient slit in it so I'm able to keep an eye on my customers without anyone knowing."

My breath caught. "Where you overheard everything they said."

She grinned. "Exactly."

She'd always wanted in on everyone's secrets, a trait, I daresay, that had probably served her well. Just like, I suspected, it was about to serve me.

Even so, I tried not to appear too eager. "And did your ears burn?" I asked with a smile.

Philly measured a pinch between her slim fingers. "This much, perhaps. But that's not what I found of interest."

"It wasn't?"

"No." She grinned, a wicked glint in her eye. "Although her husband-to-be might not agree."

"Tell me," I demanded as my impatience inched upward.

"Well . . ." She paused theatrically. "First, just clarify something for me. Mr. Amsel is marrying Jutte Kalb, right? And Anka is her sister?"

"Yes. It's been in all the papers." My impatience jumped

another notch.

"Isn't it interesting, then, that when this man greeted this woman and called her by name, she answered to Anka, not Jutte?" Philly was almost dancing.

I leapt to my feet. "What? Are you sure?"

A smirk curled her lips. "Of course I'm sure. I heard him very clearly."

My brain whirled as it absorbed this new information. "But this means Sepp isn't even marrying the right woman. Why would they do that? Trade places, I mean. What does it mean for Jutte? The real Jutte?"

Philly shrugged, as Gallic a gesture as from a true French woman. "Ask what it means for the real Anka while you're at it," she said, a wealth of meaning in her words. "Although—"

"Although what? What else did they say?"

"Just one little thing. And I don't know if it's important or not, but the man said, 'She needs . . .'; then I didn't hear the rest. But he handed her a slip of paper, narrow and a couple inches long. 'What is this?' she asked. Then, 'Oh, she always wants something.' It looked to me like it could be a shopping list. What does all this mean, China? Do you know?"

My fingers were clenching the edge of the desk. I was almost bouncing with elation. "I can guess." Even though I couldn't tell her yet. "What happened next?"

Another of those shrugs suggested Philly's agreement. "I know this sister took the list, glanced at it, and made a face. She said, 'Tell her I will take care of it.' They didn't say anything else. He left, and she came over to the cash register and yelled for me as if I were a dog to be summoned." She looked down and gave Nimble, who sat between us, a pat. "Not that I would ever do such a thing to this one. Anyway, when I came out of the back room—after a suitable interval—she had me charge her purchase to Mr. Amsel's account. Oh, and she signed her name J-u-t-t-e."

I rocked on the balls of my feet. "I knew there was something fishy about that woman. I knew it! And so did Rose." My ebullience excited Nimble, who raised her funny little head and, whippy tail wagging, took a quick turn around the office. I clasped Philly's hands and gave her another hug.

"Philly, you're a wonder."

She preened. "Aren't I, though? I assume you're pleased?"

"Delighted. You have no idea how much this clarifies the case."

"It does? I thought it made for muddier waters." She stared at me for a moment. "What case?"

"Oh, Philly, I can't tell you. Not right now, anyway. But I promise I will when I can."

"What are you going to do? How will you break the news to Mr. Amsel?" She frowned. "I liked him, China. He was polite and paid the bills those women ran up without even flinching. You ought to see the way some of the men—Well, you don't care about that. But really, I hate to see him hurt."

"Me, too. Although my guess is this won't be too much of a surprise to him. It might even be something of a relief. You see, he and my friend Rose—" I broke off. This wasn't my tale to tell.

Philly brightened. "This is twice you've mentioned her. Who is this Rose?"

"A friend of mine." I shrugged. "You'll have to meet her sometime."

She didn't answer, although a part of her shine seemed to dim, and she shook her head. I'd have to move slowly in introducing my friends. Philly may have cast off her orphaned waif history and rather checkered past to insist she'd become Mamzelle, but it seemed obvious a part of her early life still shrouded her.

I didn't press the issue. There was plenty of time.

Once alone in the office, except for Nimble, of course, I fetched myself a cup of warming coffee and sat at my desk with paper and pencil at hand. I still had plans to make. My investigation wasn't over, by a long shot. Because when you got down to it, Philly had only overheard the Kalb woman and a man, whose name she didn't know, greet one another and exchange a few cryptic words. For all I knew, Jutte, or Anka, or both, were bamboozling this man right along with Sepp. Philly hadn't actually heard much of their conversation. The note might have been about anything. Even something she'd dropped from her handbag and the gentleman had retrieved.

But, like Philly, I didn't think so. The man might have been anybody, but from Philly's sparse description of him I'd have bet money it was none other than Mr. Horst Werner. Not, I may add, the type of man to be taken in by a woman.

"Where do you suppose the missing sister is?" I asked Nimble, causing her to scramble to her feet and sit at attention, tail beating the floor, at my feet. "And is she a willing partner in a scheme, or is she indeed a victim in a nefarious plot? And which woman is she? This is the crux of the matter. I wish we were certain."

Nimble shook her head in a negative sort of way, the tappets on the ends of her ears fluttering.

"I wonder—" I got up and rummaged in a file drawer where Gratton kept a few items necessary to the detecting business. A telephone directory for one thing, although Central placed our calls. Also, a listing of city businesses for Spokane, Coeur d'Alene, Colfax, and Pullman. And, the item I needed, a map of the city.

Shifting the typewriting machine to the side, I spread the map on my desk and placed a thin sheet of tracing paper over it. Pencil in hand, I drew first a small circle around the kidnapping location, a second larger one, and then a larger one after that.

Yesterday, when Gratton and Monk scouted for information about an incident they dared not openly describe, they'd come up with nothing. I doubt the result would've been any different with more information.

The weather had been bleak Sunday morning. People with any sense stayed inside, leaving the downtown streets nearly empty. Even so, three men hustling or carrying a woman along in public still might've been noticed, especially if she were protesting, but Grat and Monk had found nothing.

So. This seemed to indicate Anka/Jutte Kalb hadn't been fussing. Also, that the kidnappers hadn't been abroad for long, which doubtlessly defined the distance they'd covered. Or . . .

I lifted the paper and traced the circle's parameters directly onto the map. Now I had a place to start looking.

"I can't imagine they went far"—I said to Nimble, squinting down at the hotel's location and studying the small circle around it—"for fear of calling attention to themselves. That's if the first premise is the correct one. Either way, I think they were lucky it was so cold, with the weather keeping most people inside. Nobody around to observe the so-called abduction. I'm told Jutte, or Anka, one or the other, insisted on her habitual early morning walk. I wonder if Rose stymied their plans when she showed up before seven o'clock? If they were afraid the alarm would be raised prematurely, prudence dictated they get off the street quickly."

My pencil touched on another address. "That would explain the haberdashery being used as a quick stop, and the purse being left behind."

The dog, no doubt bored with the talk, ambled over to the rug in front of the stove and flopped onto her belly.

Jutte had obfuscated the business regarding the purse, going so far as to buy another when I asked about it. Trying to fool me, I wondered, or Sepp?

I shivered. Two people were dead, murdered for the sum of five thousand dollars. Five thousand dollars their killers would never put their hands on if I had anything to say about it.

And what about Anka? Or Jutte? Or whichever woman was missing?

If she was actually missing.

CHAPTER TWENTY

Oh, how I dreaded going out into the cold again. I haven't the words to say. Unfortunately, I still had a job to do. Finding and rescuing, or maybe just recovering, Anka before 11 P.M. tonight meant pursuing whatever trail presented itself. Thanks to Philly, this new lead indicated I follow Jutte Kalb when next she left the hotel.

Praying I wasn't already too late, I bundled up, propped the Closed sign in the window, and ventured out again.

A breeze had kicked up, brisk enough to penetrate the seams of my coat the moment I left the office. It found every fissure in my knitted mittens and flirted amongst my petticoats as I strode along the boardwalk. At least the snow had stopped, if only for the moment. Maybe—I crossed my fingers inside the mittens—Gratton and Monk would make it home from the Silver Valley after all.

Meanwhile, the .32 was a comforting weight in my pocket.

I reached Jutte's hotel, stepping into the warmth of a lobby heated by two massive fireplaces, one at each end of the cavernous room. Stomping snow from my booted feet onto an already sodden rug, I had a clear view of the dining room, where several patrons were enjoying a fashionably late luncheon. The aroma of good food cooking wafted to my nose. My stomach growled. I'd been too busy for the thought of eating to cross my mind until this very minute.

Well, I was thinking about it now.

Jutte was one of the diners. She had her back to me, but I recognized her by her hairstyle, an intricate crown of flaxen braids. Alone at her table, her elbow raised and lowered as she shoveled food into her mouth with hearty appetite. I almost chuckled out loud when she took a couple fluffy rolls from the basket on her table and surreptitiously stuffed them into a commodious leather pocketbook lying conveniently by her plate.

Afraid of going hungry, or merely stoking up in an attempt to stave off the cold? Or did she take the rolls for some other reason? Heavy gloves and a cap fashioned of mink or some other dark fur lay on the table beside her place setting. A matching fur-lined coat hung over the back of her chair, a clear indication she planned on going outside. A tapestry valise sat by her feet.

Harrumph! No icy breeze searching out her neck or ears. Or up her spine or her throat. I only hoped she had cold feet. Too bad those fur-lined Eskimo mukluks weren't in fashion, although Sepp certainly would buy them for her. All she had to do was ask.

The only exit from the dining room was through the wide archway into the lobby. I found a chair in a warm inglenook by the fireplace and sat where I could watch her, becoming anonymous in the darkest corner.

And I waited.

Ten minutes later, having taken her time over lunch, she rose from her chair, donned her outside attire, and entered the lobby. The coat buttoned to her chin, the cap pulled over her hair, and the gloves on her hands, she carried the tapestry valise.

My heartbeat went into quick time.

Just as Philly's report had indicated would happen, Jutte was on the move.

As soon as she cleared the doorway, I got up, pulled my cap over my ears, and followed.

The part of Jutte's story about walking every day, rain or shine—or blowing snow—proved accurate. She strode along at a good clip, while I, puffing like a steam-producing boiler, trailed after her, rueing my somewhat overdrawn corset strings. A good thing for me she didn't turn around, or she would've caught me muttering to myself like a crazy woman. Although maybe I'd keep that in mind as a surveillance technique.

She took me on a meandering route that seemed to lead nowhere. We crossed streets, went through alleyways, and, once, slipped in through the back of one building, a hardware store of all things, and out the front.

It wasn't especially hard to figure out her plan. I often went parallel but kept slightly behind her. When the occasion called, I waited at corners while she crossed the street. Once I ducked behind a pile of goods being unloaded from a dray. I did wonder who taught her these techniques, as Gratton had taught me.

A few blocks later, I slowed. I didn't much care for the neighborhood we were entering. It grew seamier and seamier. Although I'd ventured into the tenderloin before, I'd never gotten in so deep or seen this section. I couldn't help thinking of the last time I'd been here, when I'd been knocked out and carted off by someone who planned to murder me. Not a comfortable memory, I daresay.

Cold or no cold, I removed my right mitten and stuck my hand in the pistol pocket. I'd shoot through my skirt if I had to. Even so, my confidence waned, while Jutte, a half block ahead of me, seemed undisturbed.

No boardwalks bordered the streets here. Drunken men, even at this time of day and despite the cold—or maybe because of it—spilled out of saloons. My nose wrinkled. A powerful odor of urine hung on the air, yellow patches of snow telling a tale of men too far gone on rotgut whiskey to think of keeping bodily functions out of sight. Rough-looking ne'er-do-wells whistled and called to Jutte as she passed.

She feigned not to hear.

As did I in my turn. Taking a page from Jutte's book, I ignored them, watching apprehensively from the corners of my eyes while fondling the butt of the .32.

Gratton would be so angry if he'd known I'd come here at all, let alone by myself. And Monk . . . well, my uncle would be shocked.

Best, then, if they never learned of it.

I started to wonder if Jutte, having somehow discovered she was being followed, was leading me on a fruitless chase when at last she left the road. After furtive glances to her right and then to her left, she stopped at a shop with a faded sign saying Krämer's Print Shop. Strangely, she neglected to turn around and look over her shoulder. If she had, she would've glimpsed me for sure.

Some conspirator! And yet, as a precaution, I darted into the doorway of a rundown grocery store where a lethal-looking icicle hung overhead.

The building she entered was dilapidated in the extreme, sorely in need of paint, its windows washed, and the step repaired. The door juddered across the threshold as Jutte pulled it closed behind her. Attempted to, at any rate, as the door stuck a few inches ajar.

Apparently, she didn't notice this, either. I busied myself in tying a boot lace, then, trusting she wasn't looking out the dirty windows, went up to the door and stuck my ear to the crack.

The place was silent. No voices. No clack of a printing press. No footsteps.

Ever so gently, standing to one side, I pushed on the door. It swung five or six inches inward with a slight squeak. Hardly noticeable at all.

I hoped.

Easing around until I could see inside, I peeped through the opening.

Empty. Not only of people, but bare of all furnishings except for the remains of a ramshackle service counter. And dirt. It smelled of mice. Evidently the printer's sign was old and the building long abandoned. But where had Jutte gone?

I had my answer in the wet footprints leading to a barely seen door opening off the main room.

What else could I do? I followed her footprints, testing the floorboards to avoid a squeak as I went.

The sound of voices rising and falling in an argumentative sort of way stopped me in my tracks. I recognized the speakers as Jutte, Werner—which I don't mind saying just about curdled my blood—and another woman. Once I thought I heard the mutter of another man.

You shouldn't be here. You should leave while you still can.

The voice in my head was loud. And wise. And yet I stayed.

"You took your time, sister," said the woman. Not Jutte, which meant she must be Anka. Or the woman we'd been referring to as Anka. Who else could it be?

"Do you care that it's almost freezing in here or that it stinks?" she whined. "There are rodents in the walls. And I am hungry. This man, he brings me a little greasy, cold stew and stale bread. And water. Plain water. I want my hot tea."

"Aw," the man not Werner spoke. "You been eatin' what I'm eatin', and I ain't bitchin' about it."

"You are a cretin," Anka said, her scorn of him clear.

The man grunted. "What the hell's a cretin?"

I knew him now. *Klein,* I answered, but only in my own mind.

Jutte or Anka—to keep them straight I decided to refer to them as introduced. So, the woman I knew as Jutte chuckled. "Do not complain so. I've brought food. Good bread from my own lunch table, and meat and even fruit. See? *Ein* orange. Do not forget, soon we will have money to burn. It won't hurt you to skimp a little now."

"Ja, but it is not your feet that are cold. Or your stomach that goes empty."

"You are too fat already."

Anka sounded near tears. "And you are happy it is so. Otherwise, would be you begging for food and me bringing it you."

"Oh, shut up." Jutte failed the sympathy test, which amused me no end. "At least you don't—"

Werner broke in with a snort somewhere between a chuckle and an indication of displeasure. "Quiet, both of you. You have food, Jutte. Eat. Your sister has brought the comb and brush and warmer clothes you asked for. It is only until tonight. At worst, one more day."

"One more day?" Anka's voice rose in a shriek. "Why one more day?"

Werner chuckled. "Tell your sister, Anka."

"My dear betrothed will soon receive, or perhaps already has, another ransom letter. I discovered he pays his workers on Friday, you see, after he withdraws money from the bank on Thursday. He keeps that money in his apartment safe. I want it."

Anka's reply came slowly. "How much money?"

"Usually only about five hundred dollars. But since our . . . the wedding is planned for Saturday, this time he plans on taking two or three thousand. Worth waiting for, yes?"

The other woman laughed. "Yes."

"Say thank you, sister." Jutte's mockery was plain. "Would you do as much for me?"

Werner laughed, and there was a smack—a kiss?—before he said, "Are you certain no one followed you here?"

I tensed, took a firmer grip on the revolver in my pocket, and prepared to run. My hands were almost numb with cold, fingers so stiff pulling the trigger might prove difficult.

"Of course no one followed," Jutte said as though such a thing were impossible. "I did as you said, dodging from one side of street to other and varying my route. Herr Amsel is a fool. He does not suspect. The female detective he hired is stupid, too. She pokes and asks questions but waits for Doyle to do her job."

Of course no one followed? Yet here I am, right on your tail, you fiendish woman. I barely suppressed an inclination to say so out loud.

Werner's attention shifted now to more important things than Anka's comfort or the sisters' arguing or even the newest extortion plan. "Has the body been found?"

The cretin man, Klein, took this as addressed to him. "No word, last I heard, boss. Funny, huh? Mannheim and the kid must've found him by now."

Anka's cup clattered, so I guessed she at least had a table in the other room. "Body? At Mannheim's? Whose body?"

Werner answered, off-hand and oh, so casual. "Braun. He was going to talk."

"T-talk?" Anka choked, her tone both shocked and pained. "How dare you? Dieter would never talk. Why would he?"

Jutte made a short attempt to ease the news. "Calm down, sister. He said he was going to tell. He said he is not a killer."

"Killer? But he—Who else is dead?"

Silence. Apparently, no one was willing to tell her. It occurred to me that she might be on the list. Perhaps it had occurred to her, too. The threat had certainly been in the ransom note.

"Who?" she demanded. I heard chair legs scooting on the floor.

"Sit down," Werner said. "No one important. A bellhop, is

179

all. He figured out about the kidnapping and wanted money for his silence." He paused. "Already too many know."

"But Dieter. This is not fair. You know he was in love with me." Anka sniffed. A giant sniff. Was she trying not to weep?

I could almost hear Jutte's characteristic shrug. "Be patient, sister. Soon there will be many men in love with you. Amsel's money will buy all the love you can use."

Werner laughed.

Klein muttered again, something about a shrew.

One of the men, most probably Werner, snorted. I heard the scritch of a match striking, and then the odor of tobacco smoke.

"Amsel will have no use for money where he goes." Werner sounded very sure of himself. "After the wedding, of course, when his wife becomes his heir."

Anger burned through me. And shock. The threat was there. Sepp was only safe until one of these despicable women married him, and then they planned on murdering him, too.

I thought their conversation must be winding down. Time for me to go. My body was cramped with the cold. It may have been above freezing in Anka's inner room, but not out here. Also, I hadn't taken a full, deep breath for at least five minutes.

Ever so carefully, I retreated, smothering a gasp as I spied the clumps of snow where I'd been standing. There was nothing I could do about them now.

Even so, I heard Anka's last petulant word.

"And it is not one more day. It is more than twenty-four hours until ransom is paid."

Hah, I thought. No ransom for you, my lovely. Not if I have anything to say about it.

Slipping through the outer door, I made my escape.

CHAPTER TWENTY-ONE

Once safely away from the derelict printer's building, my blood fizzed through my veins. Tinkling piano music followed my flight with the incongruous sound of "Church in the Wildwood." An unexpected giggle burbled in my throat. I'd solved the mystery. Sepp was indeed a victim of bamboozlement, and I knew the kidnapping for an elaborate scheme with the Kalb sisters willing participants, if not the original schemers. I knew the identities of the murderers.

I knew Sepp was their next intended victim. A crime we were in time to prevent.

The euphoria soon faded. Upon further consideration, my high spirits did not match the circumstances. I didn't, after all, know what to do about these discoveries.

Another detail preyed on my mind. I'd left traces of my presence via the snow fallen from my boots as I stood listening outside that door. Grat, if he found out, was sure to say I'd been careless.

Dangerous. Would anyone—read Werner for anyone—notice? If he did, would he assume it had dropped from Jutte's boots? And yet, even if he suspected an eavesdropper, he'd never know it was me. How could he?

Worry raised its ugly head as I hurried away from the seedy tenderloin district. I walked fast, casting more than one wary glance behind me as I pulled my cap more snugly over my ears and wrapped my green woolen muffler around my chin. A disguise, of sorts, as well as protection against the cold. I hoped.

I'd found Anka, or the woman we'd been told was Anka, heard what amounted to a confession of murder as well as the threat to Sepp, and lived to tell the tale, getting away unscathed.

So far. The first of my worries.

I pushed the thought aside, preferring to believe a successful conclusion to the case was at hand.

Truly? The second worry broke surface.

Who was I going to tell? Who should I ask for help?

The police? In particular, Lars Hansen? He'd delay moving on my information just to thwart me, and that's if I found him in a good mood. He might not even believe me.

Sepp Amsel? But he was the prime victim of the plot. An alive victim, at least for now, while the gang still expected to extort money from him. But with two bodies to account for, when all this became known, he might be in trouble for not going to the police in the first place. He'd hired me privately, on the quiet, a move that wouldn't please the higher authorities one little bit. Hansen was only one of those guaranteed to disapprove. The secrecy wouldn't go over well in a murder case if those responsible ever came to trial.

All of which left me out on my very own snow-covered limb. I needed Gratton. And my Uncle Monk. I needed them now.

Be careful what you wish for. The old axiom, which soon proved the absolute truth, came back to haunt me only a short while later. I daresay discovering two angry men pacing the floor and fretting over my absence isn't the stuff of dreams. Within minutes of arriving at the office, cold and out of breath from hurrying, I made up my mind to be more cautious with my wishes.

Gratton and Monk, back at last from Kellogg, were in no sweet temper. Their train had arrived at the depot about the same time I'd entered the tenderloin, giving them plenty of time to invent all sorts of dangerous situations to account for my absence. Accidents, kidnappings, jail time.

I pretended I didn't notice. It struck me as the wisest thing to do.

"Oh, good, you're home." I greeted my partners with a falsely bright smile as I shed my coat and hat. Hidden in its pocket, my pistol thumped against my thigh. "I'm glad. Did you learn anything new?" I had my doubts. It seemed to me all the activity had been right here under my nose.

A correct guess judging by Monk's scowl.

"Nah, might as well have stayed home and twiddled our thumbs," he said, choking back a cough. "Those men were just what they seemed; hard working boyos trying to make a living. We hopped aboard the first train back to Spokane just before it pulled out." He shook his head. "Turned out to be a freight hauler and, as it happens, the last train to leave Kellogg before another storm. We didn't know what we were in for."

Gratton correctly interpreted my puzzled expression. "The train crew had to fight a way through drifts blocking the rails through the Fourth of July canyon. Took all night. We pitched in to help with the shovel work where the snow was too deep for the plow."

Monk rubbed his back and creaked over to sit at his desk. "I thought we'd never get home. Earned our fare, I can tell you that."

"Sounds like hard work. And cold." I kicked off my boots and slipped on my rabbit fur–lined moccasins, so lovely and warm. My hip still hurt. And my shoulder.

"Where have you been?" Gratton demanded, not to be sidetracked for long. "Looked like you'd been gone a while when we got here, with the fire nearly out. Your dog was lonesome. And," he added in a severe tone, "you're limping, and you wince every time you move your arm. What's happened?"

Damn. With no way out of it, I had to tell them about the attack. Shall I leave it by saying neither he, nor Monk, were pleased?

"So, as you see," I ended my story, sort of offhand, "I've been busy. Oh, yes. And I've been following Jutte Kalb."

"Following her? What for? Sounds like as big a waste of time as our last twenty-four hours," Gratton said, and Monk nodded agreement.

"Really? What makes you think so?" A note of self-satisfaction crept into my voice. I allowed a pregnant pause to develop. "I found Anka."

"You what?" Monk barked out after a silent second or two.

"I found Anka." I'm afraid I smirked. "By following Jutte. Only, wait for it . . . Jutte is actually Anka, and Anka is actually Jutte."

I waited for accolades referring to my fine detective work. In vain.

"Jutte is Anka?" my uncle said at last, shaking his head side to side. "Are you sure? What makes you think so?"

Gratton scowled and gave me a suspicious look. He held his hands above the stove, now radiating heat like a forest fire. "Where'd you pick that up? Is it true? I'm not . . ." he hastened to add in view of my expression, "doubting your word, but China, that's kind of far-fetched."

"It's true," I said. I guess I sounded positive enough that it drove any doubts from their minds. Their follow-up questions seemed to take it as fact.

Is she all right? Yes.

Not a kidnapping? No.

It's a scam, then, right? Oh, absolutely.

How's Amsel taking it? I haven't told him yet.

How'd you think to follow Jutte? I had a reliable tip.

The most puzzling question remained unasked. *Why did they do such a thing? Why switch identities?*

The answer? I hadn't the least idea.

Their questions bounced off each other without leaving me time to give a clarifying explanation to any of them. Any explanation, really, let alone clarifying. Just as well. Until, unfortunately, they heard my reply to Monk's, "Where was she?"

Maybe I should've lied, but a fib wouldn't do much good when I needed their muscle. Even if said muscles were in bad shape. In fact, I suspected the unaccustomed, back-breaking labor of shoveling is what made their tempers so surly when they demanded I elaborate.

Wouldn't you just know? I asked myself.

"You were *where?*" Gratton's gray eyes seemed to snap. He started pacing again, boots clomping on the floorboards. "Do you mean to say that after what happened to you this fall you went back into the tenderloin? By yourself?"

I went over to stand by the stove as a distinct chill filled the air. "I didn't have any choice. And I had my pistol. Still have it." I patted my pocket. My goodness. If he was so upset over this little misstep, I shuddered to think what he'd say when I mentioned the murders and the threat to Sepp. They hadn't heard about those yet. News I couldn't keep to myself much longer.

Hell and damnation!

I drew the pistol and put it in the desk drawer where I stowed it during office hours. Truthfully, it's a little cumbersome, banging against my leg with every step.

Grat shook his head as though resigned. "Dammit, China, you need a keeper."

Monk's sharp nod suggested heartfelt agreement.

"I beg your pardon. Here I am, safe home, and I've brought

our client's problem to a satisfactory conclusion." I may have been exaggerating, since I hadn't spoken to Sepp as yet, and we didn't know what he'd want to do with the information. But at least we knew Anka was in no danger.

Or did we? Look at Dieter. He probably hadn't figured on being murdered, either.

"The thing is . . ." I took a deep breath. It must've been a noisy one since it earned a narrow-eyed look from Gratton.

"Yes? What aren't you telling us?" he asked.

"I'm afraid Sepp's problem is only part of the equation. There's also been . . . a couple murders." Did I mumble this last part? Apparently so.

"What did you say?" Grat, watching me intently, poked at his right ear like an actor making certain his audience understood the nuances of his actions. "You better not have said what I think you did."

Uncle Monk, whose ears really had been affected by his recent cold, whipped around. "What's going on?"

Grat's eyes never left mine. "Pretty sure I heard her say *murder.* Didn't I?"

My head bobbed. Yes.

"Hell," Gratton said. "And damnation."

My uncle heaved a great sigh, then coughed. "Lambie, what have you gotten yourself into now?"

I grimaced. "Sepp Amsel is an important man hereabouts. I suppose it was too much to hope his problem had a simple answer." Why did they always act as if a case turning sour was somehow my fault? Enough!

"But murder?" Monk sighed again.

Gratton, as usual, cut to the chase. "Who's been murdered? And what's it to do with Amsel?"

I seated myself in the desk chair to find Nimble already occupying the kneehole space. She sat up and pressed against my legs. "I doubt it's anything to do with Sepp. Or not personally, anyway. Just his money. It's these women he's gotten mixed up with."

"Poor feller," Monk said.

Grat, made of sterner stuff, kept his eye on the ball, to use one of his favorite sporting metaphors. "How do you figure?"

"Yesterday," I began my tale, "after you two left for Kellogg, I went to visit Jutte again. You know I distrusted her at first sight."

"Yeah, I could tell." The corner of his mouth tilted up. "She probably could, too. And she didn't strike me as a woman with a forgiving attitude."

I snorted. "Not exactly. Anyway, I wanted to verify a couple of her previous remarks to me so I went back. She could hardly wait to see me gone. But—you'll like this—in her hurry she let slip something that pointed me in a different direction. A more telling direction."

"Which would be?"

"I made up an excuse about wanting to show Anka's photograph around. She grubbed one out of a drawer, complaining the whole time. This is the funny thing. In her rush to get rid of me, she missed seeing another photo stuck beneath the first." I grinned in triumph and waited for one of the men to ask why.

After a pause, Gratton did the honors. "A major discovery?"

"Yes. I think so. One that's made me more cautious on how to proceed."

My uncle pulled his chair closer to the stove and sat at attention. "Most probably a good plan." He paused. "Cautious in what way?"

"What did the photograph show? Or should I say, who did the photograph show?" Grat demanded.

That's Gratton. Right on point, which is why he's such a good detective.

Hidden by the desk, my knees bounced with excitement. It felt good to have news of importance to relay. "The photograph was of Jutte and Anka—or a woman I assume is Anka—picnicking with a group of their friends. It was taken in Germany, not long before they emigrated."

Monk grimaced. "So they weren't quite the lonely waifs the newspaper write-ups reported?"

"Definitely not." I smiled at my uncle, who is also a good detective. "But I learned more than that."

"Don't hem-and-haw, China," Grat said. "Spit it out."

This was the part of the story I enjoyed telling. "Number one, the Kalbs certainly had friends in Germany. Number two, I recognized a few of them. Several of them are right here in town, and Jutte, or the woman posing as Jutte, has been meeting with them."

"I'll be damned." Monk frowned, clearly unaware of his language.

Gratton had a different take on the news. "I expect this puts a whole different complexion on things, doesn't it? Who are they, China?"

I checked names off on my fingers. "Dieter, the young tailor at Mannheim's, for one." Oh, how I dreaded imparting further news of him. "August, the clerk, who stood in the background of the photograph looking shy and as if he didn't belong. And another man, one who showed up here today. His name is Horst Werner, and he's a bad man. A very bad man."

Grat fixed a narrowed-eyed, steely gaze on me. "How do you know?"

It was almost as if he'd only heard those last four words.

I hesitated. "I'm getting around to that." Now came the hard part.

"I suppose it involves the murder you were talking about."

Monk's mustache seemed to droop, most certainly an optical illusion.

Gratton had a correction. "Murders, more than one, is what she said."

"So she did," Monk agreed, the mustache drooping even further.

"And I suppose," Gratton said to me, not like he supposed at all but knew for a fact, "you're the one who found the bodies."

CHAPTER TWENTY-TWO

Gratton knows me so well.

Or he thinks he does. In this case, his immediate conclusion that it was me who'd found the murdered men was only slightly off. I really don't know how he does it. Perhaps unwisely, I felt the need to defend myself.

"I beg your pardon? You think I found the bodies? Well, I didn't." Just as Uncle Monk's face started to relax, I gave up and added, "Nimble did. The first one, anyway."

Gratton said a very graphic word, one that sounded as if he'd been hobnobbing with my good friend Porter Anderson, who's been known to use logger parlance even in what should be polite conversation. Porter had saved me from drowning last summer and then gotten me inebriated. Quite an experience, I daresay.

Grat dropped into the guest chair in front of my desk and tilted the legs backward. "Where did your dog find this body?" he asked in a dangerously soft voice. There was a slight emphasis on the *your* part of the question.

"At the Majestic, stuffed into the dumbwaiter outside Jutte Kalb's room."

This piqued his interest. He sat forward, the chair coming down to rest on all four legs. "Ho. You don't say."

"I do say." Another thought occurred to me. "We weren't alone when we found him, so you needn't think there's anything dicey about it. Another bellhop was there. He was put out because he thought Eddie Barstow—that's the dead boy's name—had been neglecting his job and leaving this boy, Squirt, to do double duty. He complained to me of it."

"Eddie Barstow," Grat repeated. "That the kid we were talking to yesterday?"

"Yes. Not the most pleasant employee in the hotel."

Grat nodded, his mouth twitching upward as he said, "I remember."

"How did he die?" Monk asked.

"Bludgeoned. His skull crushed." A chill went through me at the memory, and I swallowed heavily. "It was . . . messy."

My uncle frowned. "Gawd, lambie. I hate for you to have seen that."

"What was Miss Kalb's reaction? Did she have an explanation?" Grat said.

"I don't know. She never opened her door to inquire about the commotion. Poor Squirt screamed, you see, and brought everybody else on that floor out of their rooms to see what had happened."

"Everyone but her?"

"Yes."

"I suppose no one heard a thing when the boy died." Monk's fit of coughing interrupted before he choked out, "Handy."

"Isn't it?" I know it made me glum. "And yet he had to have been murdered right there in the hall. I don't see how—or why—anyone would've moved him there from anywhere else."

"Except from out of a nearby room."

"Yes."

Gratton seemed to be thinking as his fingers beat a soft tattoo on the desk. Then he paused, looked up, and said, "And the second?"

"Second?"

"The second murder, China. What do you know about that one?"

How I wished to skate over those circumstances. As if Gratton, or for that matter Monk, would ever permit such carelessness.

"Nimble didn't discover Dieter—Dieter Braun. I did."

The corner of Grat's mouth curled up again. "Figured that, China. I asked what you know about how he died."

I had no reason to withhold the whole story. Except for how shocked my uncle would be. And how high and mighty Grat was sure to act. But they're my partners. I depend on them, and they depend on me. I had to share my information with them.

Hunching my shoulders, I started talking, beginning with my decision to scout Finkle's Rooming House. The more I revealed, the sterner Monk's expression grew. I expected I was in for a "talking to" about that.

As for Grat? For some reason, he was harder to read. I stopped my story where Rose and I had escaped from Mannheim's before the bluecoats showed up in force.

"So, nobody—the bluecoats, I mean—knows you were involved?" Grat summed it all up.

"I don't think so. It turns out Lars Hansen is in charge of the Mannheim investigation, too. He gave me the bum's rush with the bellhop, so I'm not privy to what they've learned and what they haven't at Mannheim's." Just telling about it made me angry all over again. And disgruntled.

Gratton got up and took his coat off the hook behind the stove where it had been hanging. Apparently, Mannheim's tailoring had held up well under the labor of shoveling copious amounts of snow, because the coat still looked good on him.

"We going somewhere?" Monk started to rise until Grat waved him down.

"Stay inside and keep warm, partner," he told my uncle. "Take care of your cough. I'll go see what I can find out from Shave Johnson. He's bound to have cracked the story by now, even if the authorities won't allow everything to be printed in the evening paper."

Johnson was a newspaper reporter who hung around the police station, deceptive in his eavesdropping as he managed to acquire the latest news. He always looked tired and bedraggled in his worn, shiny-in-the-seat suits that appear to have been handed down from a larger man.

I suppose it wasn't really surprising that he was one of Gratton's informers. A friend? I don't know. Most likely Grat had a hold of some kind over him.

Monk, uncharacteristically, nodded and settled back at his desk as he stifled another cough. Worry struck at me. Recovery from his cold had been slow. Was it turning into something worse? The train trip to Kellogg had done him no favors.

"I'm going to make you a toddy," I told him. "You should come upstairs where it's warmer and less drafty." I glanced at Grat. "I'll make you a toddy, too, when you get back."

Gratton, who'd paused to eye my uncle, took a breath. "I'll take you up on that. Make it with lots of butter and brown sugar, please." At the door, he turned. "And you can finish your story then. Oh," he added at my guilty look, "I know you left a few things out." He tied a muffler around his hat and over his ears. "A lot of things out."

The wind caught the door and slammed it against the wall as he left. The afternoon was fit for neither man nor beast.

Monk fell asleep over his toddy. Not surprising since I'd put enough Old Crow in it to quell his cough. He sat in his favorite chair with the leather seat and cushioned backrest, head canted to one side as he slept.

I put another stick of wood in the kitchen stove, lit a kerosene lamp instead of depending on the electric overhead bulb, and sat at the table. In front of me was a list detailing the things I knew versus the things I needed to find out. Nimble took up her spot at my feet, her funny wedge-shaped head resting on my toes. I reached down to pat her.

Paper rustled as I flipped over to a new sheet and picked up my pencil. I planned to write up my notes longhand and copy them on the Smith Corona typewriter when I went downstairs.

One, I wrote.

Sometime later, I started awake with my forehead pressed to the table, a blaze of blank white paper before my eyes. The room was dark outside the small circle of lamplight. Growling low in her throat, Nimble, ears arched forward, scratched my feet as she scrambled from under the table. She pointed her nose toward the stairs and took a step forward. I grabbed her collar.

I heard it, too. Someone was attempting to force the office door, the cold wood creaking.

At first I thought it must be Grat returning until my reawakened brain reminded me he'd be pounding on the door if he'd forgotten his key. The noise we heard was soft, secretive, as if whoever was there didn't want to be noticed.

Nimble pulled against her collar.

"Stay," I hissed.

Miracle of miracles, she did stay, leaning against me with her tail between her legs.

Blinking sleep from my eyes, I slowly rose to my feet. "Shh," I warned the dog, stilling her soft rumble so I could hear. I patted my empty skirt pocket.

I'd left my revolver down in the office.

"Hell and damnation." I merely breathed the curse.

My uncle was asleep in the living room snoring like a buzz saw, his nose clogged from the relapse of his cold. It almost drowned out the tinkle of glass breaking downstairs. I figured it for the window in the office door shattering.

A second later, the door banged against the wall.

Holding my breath, I froze and, with one hand, took a firmer hold on Nimble's collar. With the other, I put my fingers around her muzzle.

It seemed as if, down below, another entity echoed my rigid wait. Listening. Both of us just listening.

Monk slept on undisturbed, the rise and fall of his snores filling the bated silence. He kept a shotgun beside his bed, I suddenly remembered. Something he'd only had to do, or so he informed me, since I'd come to live with him.

In the office below, I sensed more than heard our clandestine visitor take a step, then another firmer one. He headed toward the stairway leading up to our apartment.

I had to get that gun and do it before the sneak thief reached me.

Nimble pressed against my skirt, matching my footsteps as I tiptoed past my uncle. A floor board squeaked, and I froze again but had no time to dither. I pushed into Monk's room.

The pokey little chamber was dark as a cave with only a faint glow from the kitchen lamp shining in the whole house, but I dared not strike a light and give away my position. Anyway, I knew where he kept the shotgun. The odd-looking six-shot pump with a 20-inch barrel hung from a bedpost. Like a blind person, I groped my way to where I'd last seen the holster.

Monk liked the gun because it folded up to half size, which for some reason didn't frighten Mavis as she cleaned and . . . er . . . did whatever else she did in that room. He also liked the gun because a quick wrist movement brought it into firing position.

I didn't expect the noise it made as I gave the Burgess a flick and it snapped into place. And I'd never have guessed the person just creeping from the landing into the apartment would have such speedy reactions. Or that he'd be carrying a cocked weapon in his hand.

In retrospect, I suppose I was as much of a dark blur to him as he was to me. I doubt he truly expected anyone to be awake. Not with Monk's uninterrupted snores filling the room. I probably startled him, what with appearing suddenly and the shotgun's metallic click.

Our shots sounded over each other.

I won that contest. The Burgess was loudest.

Monk leapt up with an unintelligible shout, his heavy chair going over backward and hitting the floor with a crash, somehow taking him down with it.

The person trying to sneak up on us also shouted. He turned and ran, footsteps faltering as he thudded down the stairs.

Nimble barked now, high pitched and frantic.

I said nothing at all. My jaw was clenched too tightly to allow speech.

"China!" My uncle tried to rise, tripped over the chair legs in the dark, and went to his knees for a second time. "China?"

"Uhhh." I forced a mumble. I was still on my feet, a good sign.

"What's happening?" Strange how his voice sounded muffled.

"Intruder," I replied. "He shot at me."

"Shot at you?" He paused, as if to catch his breath. "Are you all right?"

I wasn't any too certain, but I answered, "I think so. He missed. We both missed." My hold on the shotgun was slippery. Sweat? Or blood?

Not blood. And as it turned out, he missed. I didn't. Or not entirely, judging by the dribbles of blood we found on the stair and the door casing when we got the electric lights back on. Traces left behind as he plunged down the stairs and escaped.

A small round hole as precise as though bored by a drill marked the distance by which he'd missed me. Six inches is a lot when it means life or death. A head shot, no less. Unable to stop myself, I trembled so violently my skirts shook.

Uncle Monk put his arm around my shoulders. "You're a lucky lady, China. You know that? Tough, too."

My shot had caused a certain amount of damage to the wall. The pellets had hit at about shoulder height where the intruder had been standing. Some of my luck, I guess, that I'd hit him at all. But then it's hard to miss with a 12-gauge when you're only a few yards apart. The shot has a pretty good spread.

My uncle sighed and gave me a last squeeze. "Dang it, China, now I'm gonna have to get the wall repaired."

"I fix." Cosimo Pinelli appeared in doorway like a genie, making me jump. "Don't shoot, Miss China. Ima come in?"

With my ears still aching from the sound of the blast, I hadn't heard him coming up the stairs. And Cosimo is a big man. Funnily enough, I hadn't realized I was still carrying the shotgun.

"Yes. Come in." Monk, a little pale and visibly shaken, went over and poked his finger in the bullet hole in the woodwork. "Fix this one, too, before Mavis notices it."

"Did you see him?" I asked Cosimo. "Was it the same man from earlier today?" My legs still shook, a good reason to lean the Burgess against the wall before staggering over to the couch and sitting down. Nimble jumped up and claimed my lap. She was quivering, too. She hates any loud noise, voices most of all, but I suspected shots were rapidly gaining on the discomfort scale.

Cosimo shook his head "no." "Just a man who runs away. His arm, it hangs from shoulder like rag, so." A flap of his hand indicated the malady. "You one tough lady, Miss China," he said, almost echoing Monk's words.

Appearances can be deceptive. I daresay I didn't feel very tough just now.

One might've depended on this being the moment for Gratton to come pounding up the stairs. And I heard him, so, good news—this meant my hearing was returning.

He burst in, staring around with a wild look in his eyes. His arrival drew Nimble off my lap. She bounced over to him, jumped up, and placed one delicate foot on his knee. Funny how a twenty-pound dog can slow a man down. He stopped to reassure her. When he looked up, calmer now, he said, "I heard the shotgun from two blocks away. Figured the noise came from here. There's blood outside on the step. Anyone hurt? China? Monk? Pinelli?"

"Not us," Monk said. "We're good."

"How much blood?" I asked. I felt a little ill.

Grat studied me for a moment. "Some on the stair and a little in the snow outside. Not enough to kill anybody."

"But none of it's ours," Monk repeated.

Grat came over and knelt beside me. His gray eyes seemed very dark, but maybe it was because of the lighting in the room. "China?"

Shaking my head, I forced a smile.

"Good to see you're as handy with your Burgess as ever," Grat said to Monk. "Whoever this feller is, he got too damn close."

Monk coughed, his face reddening with the effort, and went to reclaim his chair, setting it upright and motioning Cosimo into the one next to him. "Not me," he told Grat. "Credit China. If she hadn't heard him when she did, we'd probably both be dead by now."

"Not me, either. Thank Nimble," I said. "She heard him first. She heard him in time."

Grat rose and, seeing the other chairs were taken, sat on the couch beside me. Close. Hidden by a fold of my skirt, his hand grasped mine and squeezed. "You figured out how to work Monk's trick shotgun?"

Why was he so surprised?

I tilted my chin. "Of course. I'm not stupid," I retorted. "Monkey sees, monkey does. I've watched him do it lots of times."

"Except I've never shot anybody with it," Monk said. "Never had anybody break in before . . ." He broke off, but I knew what he meant to say. He meant before I joined the agency.

CHAPTER TWENTY-THREE

"We need better locks," I announced. "And a stouter door." Really! Did my uncle expect me to take the blame for the criminal class's growing violence? I hardly thought their wrongdoing was my fault.

I forced myself to release Grat's hand, got up, and paced the room. I don't mind saying my feelings were hurt. To cover my distress, I threw a couple smallish chunks of wood on the fire and moved the teakettle closer to the front. Busy work. I refused to burst out crying, so I went on a rant instead.

"I'm sick and tired of every would-be killer or revenge-addicted miscreant in the area breaking in here whenever they take a notion." My voice grew louder with every word.

No one argued against these sentiments. Cosimo nodded, Monk coughed in a way that seemed to indicate agreement, and Gratton's mouth curled into a grin.

"How many times has this happened, lambie?" Monk asked. "Six? Seven? More?"

"Not that many. Don't get carried away." Even so, it had been more times than I liked to admit.

Cosimo, no doubt sensing some tension growing between us, cleared his throat. "Who is this man? You know, this mis . . . miscre . . ."

"Miscreant. I've got an idea who he is," I said. "And I suspect you've met him, too."

Cosimo's blue eyes widened. "Man who scared you?"

I brushed his scared comment aside, hoping Grat and Monk hadn't noticed. "I think so. Or if not he, himself, it might have been one of his thugs. Although, why would he decide to come after me . . . us . . . now?"

"Jutte," Monk said. "You must've left some sign, and they realized they had a witness."

I thought guiltily of those telltale tracks I'd left on the floor of the print shop as he added, "They all know Amsel hired you to find Anka, so you'd be the most likely suspect. And now Grat and I have taken a hand, we're three times as dangerous to their scheme."

"Or maybe you just rubbed her the wrong way," Grat added.

Uncle Monk went into another spasm of coughing, at which I got up to fix him another hot toddy. Extra water went in the teakettle to boil since I'd also promised Gratton a drink. It turned out Cosimo wasn't about to turn down Monk's favorite Old Crow whiskey, either, the least I could do to repay him for rushing to our aid. Again.

Gratton tasted his toddy and nodded approvingly. "Perfect. Got enough butter and cinnamon. Guess you could get a job as a bartender if this detective business ever goes wrong."

I couldn't help a little fizz of excitement. Not because I cared to be a bartender, but because he'd actually admitted I was a detective!

Or had he?

I opened my mouth to ask what, exactly, he'd meant, but he was already on to something else. A complaint, I think. Or maybe a simple observation. "We've got to put a stop to this damn breaking and entering business before somebody gets hurt," he said.

"Somebody has." I returned to the couch with my own smaller and weaker version of the men's drinks. "A bellhop and a tailor are dead."

201

"Aside from them. I meant either you or Monk. But I agree we'd better wrap this up before any more damage is done"—he shot a quick glance at me, then away, his gray eyes snapping—"by this bunch, anyhow. Have to wait and see what you come up with next."

"Harrumph." I had a question of my own. "So, did Shave Johnson discover anything helpful?"

"Don't know. Not much he was willing to tell me, at any rate."

We retreated into glum silence while Grat apparently mulled over whether anything he'd learned was worth repeating.

Cosimo Pinelli broke the silence. He'd been twirling his empty cup in his big hands. "These dead men, Miss China . . . They are bad men, or they are good men?"

Oddly enough, I hadn't thought to ask myself that question. I did now. And I had to think about it before answering, "Both, I think. Neither one good enough to count as completely innocent, but not bad enough to deserve killing." I huffed out a breath. "Which is probably what did them in."

Mr. Pinelli may have been a little puzzled by this evaluation, but Grat and Monk nodded.

"Don't pay for a thug to undercut or question his boss," Grat explained. "And trying a spot of blackmail can be dangerous.

"Anyway, one thing Shave had to say is that Hansen has been questioning the hotel's hired help. He's moving pretty slow with the guests, keeping things as quiet as he can. Turns out some bigwig from back east is staying there, and Hansen's orders are to not upset the fellow. Not over some peanut of a bellhop. Seems Eddie Barstow wasn't well liked by anyone. Not the rest of the hotel staff, and not the guests."

Monk grimaced. "That's a sad commentary for a young feller."

"What about Dieter Braun? Are they saying anything about

him?" I shouldn't have been surprised at Grat's report. Justice always seemed to go to whoever had the most money or was most popular.

Gratton set his cup on the floor in front of the couch. "They're calling that one a robbery gone bad. They're guessing Dieter got into work early and interrupted a thief."

"What?" My eyes, as the saying goes, popped. "But . . . the coroner. He'll know Dieter died before morning."

"Maybe so. Although they can argue that the cold temperatures made his time of death hard to pinpoint."

I looked around at the men, including Mr. Pinelli. "I expect, then, it's up to us to stop these people."

A short silence answered. Then, Monk exhaled noisily through his stuffy nose. "Think I need another toddy," he said.

Was that resignation I heard in his tone?

"Sí," agreed Cosimo, holding out his cup.

Reaching for his, Grat managed to kick it under the couch. "Yeah." He grubbed around, bringing forth a blob of dog hair along with the cup. "And add a touch more whiskey this time, sweetheart. Got a feeling we're all going to need it."

I do believe the next round of toddies aided in plotting our plan of action. I know it opened up my creative thinking.

Cosimo wondered why we should do anything since the woman hadn't actually been kidnapped but was a willing participant in her own abduction.

A good question.

"If nobody cares," he said, "then they will think, 'What is the use?' Yes? They give up scheme?"

"I see your point," Grat said. "And, ordinarily, I'd probably say the same thing."

Our neighbor's thick blond eyebrows arched. Isn't it funny how eyebrows can ask a question?

Monk agreed with Grat. "But if those women are the vindictive sort, Sepp Amsel could be in danger from them and their friends."

"I think he is even if he pays the ransom," I said. "Maybe especially if he pays the ransom."

Grat agreed. "Guess we'll know after tonight."

"We need to catch them red-handed and put them in jail," I said. "All of them."

"Yes." Monk coughed again. He held his cup under his nose and breathed in steam scented with cinnamon and whiskey. "Problem is, those women are going to deny everything."

Gratton nodded. "Could be hard to prove otherwise, too. Don't be surprised if they get away with their plotting."

I flounced to my feet, splattering a few drops of my toddy onto the floor. I ignored it. "That's just not right."

Grat's studied me a moment before breaking into a grin. "Nobody said it was."

"What he needs is a bodyguard until this is over," I went on. "Somebody the fair Jutte can't twine around her little finger even if she tries. Cosimo, do you need another job?" He adored his wife and new baby. I doubted he'd find either Jutte or Anka a temptation.

"You think we should let this play out?" Grat asked me, his head cocked.

"Yes. Catch them in the act. Even Lars will have to take action then."

"She has a point," Monk said. "I'm beginning to think this feud with Hansen ain't in our best interest. Or the interest of our clients."

Grat's mouth twisted. "Hasn't been for a while."

The problem between Gratton and Lars concerned a woman. A woman who wasn't me, and it had been going on before I arrived in Spokane. Not that either man ever admitted it.

"So," I said, sniffing, "I vote we make certain Sepp is protected, meanwhile going ahead with the ransom drop tonight."

"Amsel won't like it," Grat said. "He's the kind of feller who wants a say in his own affairs."

"Maybe we shouldn't tell him."

Monk scowled. "Not tell him? Lambie, don't you think that's a little dishonest?"

"It may be a little dishonest, but a whole lot safer," Grat said, surprising me with his agreement. "Who knows what he might let drop if the woman gets to questioning him."

"Exactly," I said. "Because I think she may be getting suspicious already. I do believe he's fairly safe until after the wedding, though." A bright thought occurred. "Perhaps Mamzelle's is Jutte and Werner's regular meeting place. If so, we can rely on Philly to contact me if they get together again."

Grat grinned at me. "I'm impressed, China. You're acquiring quite a posse of informers. And you haven't had to pay them a dime."

I tossed back the last of my toddy. "It's called friend helping out a friend."

We settled on a plan of action. Or perhaps I should call it a plan of inaction. Cosimo was going to keep an eye on Sepp this evening, striking up an acquaintance with him if possible, but without letting him know he was being watched.

Grat's job was to transport the valise with five thousand dollars to Finkle's Rooming House, placing the bag on the door knob at the proper time, then to watch who took it. A telephone call to Moseley's Saloon put him in touch with Bill Jackson, a former brand inspector often hired to do odd jobs for the agency. Mr. Jackson agreed to watch over Sepp through the night. They figured daylight hours should be safe. I begged to differ, my argument going unheard.

Monk announced he was getting too old to stay up all night and, leaving guard duty to the young fellers, was going to bed to nurse his cough. "If you need me, let me know," he said.

"What should I do?" I asked.

Grat winked. "Stay out of trouble. And don't shoot anybody unless you have to."

He kissed me good night when Monk's head was turned. A kiss that made me feel as if I were the only woman in the world.

Sleep would elude me this night, as I waited for the game to play out.

CHAPTER TWENTY-FOUR

Monk's incessant coughing kept me awake a good part of the night. Then, although I don't know if he quit coughing or I just closed my ears to the racket, I went to sleep and slept through until morning—a matter of two or three hours. Odd really, considering the unpleasant dreams that forced their way into my subconscious. I kept seeing a man—sometimes it was Werner, sometimes Dieter—standing in the doorway of my room, face contorted and with blood pouring from his midsection.

If dreams reflect reality, I hoped it was Werner I saw there and not Dieter Braun's ghost.

But then, it may have been two toddies spiked with Old Crow whiskey influencing those dreams.

Before we unlocked the door at eight o'clock, the Doyle & Howe Detective Agency, all of us, held a meeting, loosely gathered in chairs grouped around the stove. This time, along with Cosimo, Bill Jackson showed up for our conclave. Oddly, since I knew he'd worked with Monk for years, this was the first time I'd met him in person. He wore a bearskin coat that must have weighed twenty pounds, high-topped boots, and a Stetson hat.

He took my proffered hand as if I'd offered him something that might snatch him up and hold him captive, then released it as swiftly as though burned. Afterward, rheumy, blue eyes watched my every move, like he expected me to do something unexpected and explosive.

I hardly think you'd call my anxiety unexpected.

"What happened last night?" My first burning question went to Grat even before he sat down. "Did everything go all right? Have you heard if Anka has returned home?"

Gratton hadn't shaved, and a dark stubble pebbled his face. His eyes were bloodshot from lack of sleep. I wanted to throw myself into his arms. Of course I refrained.

He propped his feet up on his desk and tilted back his chair. "Nothing happened," he said, his disgust clear. "Nada. Zero."

"What?" Monk and I exclaimed together.

"I mean the pickup man didn't show. I waited all night."

"What does that mean?" I asked.

He spread his hands. "No idea."

We were silent as we all thought about this development, the general consensus being that it made no sense. I hardly thought Werner the type of man to let that kind of money go. Jutte struck me as too greedy, as well. They must have something else planned.

Gratton sent me a self-satisfied look when Jackson reported Sepp had poked his head outside his room and yelled for breakfast about seven. Surprised him, he said, since here he was thinking saloon men worked all night and slept all day.

I thought perhaps Sepp, like the rest of us, simply hadn't slept at all. We worried and acted like rats in a trap. Probably a little unease at the notion he might be in danger. Or that someone he would soon call family was in danger. And worried something would go wrong with the drop.

"Worst part for me was stayin' awake," Jackson said. "And stayin' warm. Durn near froze. Back part of Amsel's saloon is drafty as an old barn. No wonder he don't run a—"

"But no alarms?" Monk asked, overriding whatever Jackson was saying.

Run a what? A bordello? I wondered. I do hear what people say, after all, in their unguarded moments.

"Nope. Quiet as a graveyard." Jackson's face had turned the color of a red-roan horse, and just as blotchy.

Harrumph. Definitely a bordello.

"Just what I expected," Grat started, until Jackson gathered himself and cut across him.

"Except there was once," he said, "along about four A.M. Almost had me thinkin' I might see some action. Heard the floor squeakin', like somebody was tiptoeing over it and could've swore I heard breathin', too. I got up to see, but when I looked around the corner, twern't nobody there." His significant nose wrinkled. "Smelt somethin', though. Bay rum, so strong my smeller clogged solid."

I jerked erect. Werner had smelled of bay rum when he'd been here yesterday, powerfully so. There were probably a few hundred men in Spokane who, on any given day, visited a barber shop. I knew the potion was a standard finish to their services. But I believed it was Werner.

"You're remembering something, China," Grat said. "What is it?"

I hadn't gone into Werner's visit yesterday, but now, with Cosimo standing by, I had no choice. "Yesterday," I said, "Werner stopped by here." I glanced up and caught Cosimo's eye. "Did you smell bay rum on him?"

Cosimo, who'd been leaning against the wall again in a position that indicated it was the only thing keeping him upright, straightened. "Don't know bay rum."

"Men's perfume?"

I watched comprehension spread over his face.

"Sí," he said. "Stunk like whorehouse."

"Pinelli," Gratton barked, louder even than Monk's, "watch it. A lady is present."

I almost laughed. Why do men think women, even "nice" women, don't know about such things? I suppose I should've been horrified. Swooned or cried or something.

I did neither. Only managed to suppress the laugh. Two references in two minutes. My moment of hilarity passed because Grat was squinting at me with narrowed, gray eyes, while Jackson said thoughtfully, "Werner, eh? I've been hearing a lot about him. His name is going around."

"Around where? And what's being said?" Grat, as if he couldn't sit still, scooted his chair six inches farther from the stove.

Jackson shrugged. "This 'n' that. He ain't well liked, I can tell you. Locals are a little scared of him. Say he carries a wicked knife."

"Don't like knives," Pinelli said.

Meanwhile, my uncle, looking thoughtful, had already moved on to a more important aspect. "This Werner feller, he know who you are, Grat?"

Grat shrugged. "Not that I know of. The Kalb woman, though. She does."

Monk grimaced. "That's it, then. It'll have to be me."

Gratton and I both stared blankly at him. "It'll have to be you what?" I asked.

"Who meets him."

"Why—" I began, but Monk just shook his head.

"Got it," Gratton said. "Size him up on the sly. See what kind of man we're dealing with."

"A dangerous one." I must admit I got a little huffy. "I've already told you. He's a crook. A murderer. An evil man."

"Miss China is right," Cosimo said, earning my gratitude for his support. "Has got eyes like a wolf."

Even Jackson was nodding. "Reputation of one, too. Or worse."

210

"I have no doubt." Monk, knees creaking, rose from his chair. "But we all know Hansen won't stir himself on our word without compelling evidence. Maybe not then, especially since the five thousand in ransom money never got collected. You get it back to Amsel all right?" he asked Grat.

Grat nodded. "First thing this morning."

"Good. So, I guess we'd better get started finding evidence of murder."

"Yup." Gratton nodded. "And the best way to find anything out is by talking to the man himself. But Monk, I—"

Monk already had his coat on. "I know what you're going to say, but it's better . . . safer if I do it. He won't know me from Adam."

"How will you know where to find him?" I asked. "Or even recognize him?"

"That part is simple," Grat said. "Ask the barkeep. Might take a little . . ." He rubbed his fingers together, denoting a bribe.

Bill Jackson spoke up as Monk reached in his petty-cash drawer. "I'll go with Monk. No reason for Werner to know me, either. He might have a reputation as a man to steer clear of, but two of us'll be able to handle him. I know where he'll be, too. Hanging out with the bully boys at Manfred's Tavern down on Front Street. That crowd spends most of their time looking to pick up extra beer money, and they ain't particular what they do to earn it."

"What I do?" Cosimo asked.

Grat winked. "Finish that cupboard you been working on. Keep an eye on China."

Apparently, the men had courses of action planned out for everyone but me.

We'd see about that.

★ ★ ★ ★ ★

My investigation had progressed further by following Jutte Kalb than some people—all right, I mean Gratton and Monk—had with all their traveling hither and yon on the train. That also included their visiting most of the barrooms that catered to an eastern European clientele.. I reduced our demand for reimbursement of expenses, too, shank's mare being the most cost efficient form of travel there is. It always looks good on an expense report. I decided to put the form to use again. And again, I'd make Jutte my target.

Admonishing Nimble to behave herself and to hide if any dangerous individuals put in an appearance, I bundled up. Then, while Cosimo worked in the shed next door laboring over an intricate bit of sanding, I quietly let myself out the front.

Sunlight dazzled on fresh snow. My hurrying footsteps crunched and squeaked on the frozen crust. If I hadn't been going to the rather elegant Majestic Hotel, I would've worn my bicycling bloomer outfit and kept the breeze from blowing beneath my skirt. As it was, my legs froze, regardless that I wore two pairs of stockings.

Next time I trekked downtown, I vowed, I'd dress for the weather even if the snow was too deep for my bicycle. For now, the Waverley Belle remained hidden in the hall closet out of Nimble's view.

As it happened, I spied Jutte at a distance as I approached the hotel. She was leaving via the front, a uniformed man opening the door for her. Luckily, she faced away from me as she headed into the shopping district, but, after watching her from behind yesterday, I had no trouble identifying her by the way she moved as well as by her distinctive coat. I took up the chase, taking the opposite side of the street and staying a dozen yards behind her.

We hadn't far to go. Only the couple of blocks to Mamzelle's

Parisian Boutique. Having learned my lesson well from Gratton, I'd begun hanging back as soon as I reckoned her destination. A very good thing I did, too, as I caught sight of Horst Werner striding arrogantly toward us from the opposite direction. I whirled, gazing as though fascinated into a display window at Graham's Stationery Supply.

Of Monk and Bill there was no sign. Werner had slipped them, somehow. Or perhaps they'd guessed wrong about his hangout and were off in a different direction.

Werner, as reflected in the window's mirror-like surface, paused long enough for Jutte to enter the shop first. A short while later, by which time I was thoroughly sick of eyeing some particularly loathsome poison-pink colored stationery, he followed her inside. He probably would've noticed me if he hadn't been so intent on fishing out his pocket watch—twice in the two minutes. A man in a hurry, I assumed. Or a man impatient with the vagaries of a woman like Jutte.

I couldn't stay where I was. I ducked into the wide doorway of a general mercantile store and took up my post, hovering out of sight without blocking the entrance.

The wait seemed endless. My toes went numb inside my boots. My fingers felt like broken-off parts from the icicles hanging from the mercantile's eaves. The woolen cap covering my hair failed to keep my ears even remotely warm. My eyelids seemed frozen to the eyeballs.

After a while, Werner reappeared and turned to his right, moving rapidly back the way he'd come. A few minutes later, Jutte, carrying a package wrapped in Mamzelle's distinctive floral-patterned paper and tied with a burgundy-colored ribbon, exited the shop. She was smiling like a cat at the cream and not hurrying at all.

I imagined poor Sepp Amsel's account had just been raided again.

Jutte, on the street side opposite me, strolled toward the hotel as though she hadn't a worry in the world. Which she probably didn't, having, I felt certain, unloaded them onto Werner. They deserved each other.

I needed to talk to Philly and see if she'd learned anything.

As soon as Jutte was out of sight, I crossed the road. Much, I may add, to the consternation of a fellow driving a one-horse sleigh, as the horse slid on the snow-packed street.

"Stupid woman," he shouted at me. "You trying to commit suicide? Pick on somebody else, why don't you?"

"Oh, go buy your horse some ice shoes," I retorted, heartbeat a little rapid due to the rather large animal breathing down my neck.

Philly, standing where she could see out the shop window, was waiting for me, smiling a little and shaking her head. "Close call, China. You need to be more careful. Watch out for yourself. You're always in too big of a rush."

"Don't start. You sound like my uncle Monk." Basking in the warmth of the shop, I stomped snow from my boots and loosened my muffler.

She cocked her head. "Do they even have ice shoes for horses?"

"Indeed they do. And in this weather, all horses should be wearing them, particularly delivery animals. Poor things, stopping and starting those heavy wagons all the time."

She laughed. "We should make it a law. Put up a sign at the edge of town. 'No slick shod horses beyond this point.' But I don't think that's why you're here. Were you following Miss Kalb? Or her paramour?"

"Her. But I wasn't surprised to see him. I suspect they have a standing arrangement to meet here."

"Yes. This was the third time, I think. I don't mind since they each buy some little something. Him not so much. She, quite a lot, all charged to Mr. Amsel's account." Her shining crown of blue-black hair bobbed. "They think I'm too stupid to suspect. They seem to be under the impression that when I go into the back room, it's so they can be alone to canoodle."

She laughed, not in an amused sort of way. And only for a moment.

"Did you happen to hear anything interesting while you were being discreet?" I asked.

"Possibly. Certainly."

I leaned forward, eager for her report.

To my chagrin, two well-dressed ladies chose that moment to push into the shop, the chimes over the doorway announcing their arrival. For the next five minutes, while I chafed at the delay, Philly bustled about in the most genteel way showing off sets of unmentionables and touting their best features. Fortunately, she left the women on their own to decide which to purchase.

Though she kept an eye on the shoppers, she came back to me and lowered her voice, taking up where she'd left off. "I heard part of their conversation. An important part. The woman said, and I quote, 'I read in paper this morning as I practice my English. Two men are dead in red-light district. Bodies are found buried in snow.' China, I believe she was talking about murder. Two murders."

My blood ran cold, and I gave a tiny shiver. "Murders in the red-light district? Not unusual, I guess. I haven't seen the paper. What did Werner reply?"

"He said, 'The tenderloin is a dangerous place if you aren't careful.' She was accusing him, and he didn't deny it. And China, he laughed."

"Was Jutte reassured?"

Philly waved my question aside. "First, she says, 'Did Doyle show up with the money?' and he replied, 'Yes.' He laughed and said, 'I wager they wonder why I left them holding it,' and she says, 'You mean you didn't take it? Why not?' and he says, 'Bigger stakes, Anka. A bigger collection tonight. Much bigger. I'm composing another note for Amsel. He'll pay.' " Philly paused for a couple of heartbeats. "China, what in the world is going on?"

"Believe me, you don't want to know," I said.

Meanwhile, my question was the same as Anka's. Why leave the ransom? And what bigger stakes did he have in mind?

Philly, after checking on her customers, had more to report. "So, the woman said to him, 'My sister, she must be kept out of sight. But she must be safe. You won't let her be hurt, will you?' Jutte—or Anka, I can't keep track of who is who—appeared quite distraught. For a moment, anyway."

My mind raced. "Philly, I think you may just have heard a confession of murder along with all the rest. What did Werner say?"

"He didn't seem bothered. 'Don't worry about Jutte. It's tonight,' he said. 'Tonight the worst part will be over. We'll have the money, a lot of money, and nobody to take it from us.' "

Philly's dark eyes bored into mine. "It's an abduction, isn't it, China? Those people are holding Sepp Amsel up for money, and he's paying off. Am I right?"

I couldn't lie. I gave a short nod.

Philly emitted a short gasp. "Damn! I knew it," she said before going on with her report. "Anyway, Jutte gave him a funny look, but she still seemed worried. She repeated to him, 'Jutte will be safe. Yes?' And he said, 'Yes. Yes, I said she will.' "

Something about Philly's expression warned me. "But you don't think Anka thinks so. You think he plans on killing her. And perhaps the real Jutte, too. And she suspects?"

Philly's full lips compressed into a straight line. "I wouldn't be surprised if we read about a dead woman in the papers tomorrow. At least one."

But here we disagreed. "I think he has something else up his sleeve. Don't you suppose he'll wait until after the ransom is paid and the wedding takes place? If there is one. After that, nothing he does will surprise me."

CHAPTER TWENTY-FIVE

Philly's last words echoed in my head as I hurried away, leaving her to the sights and sounds of a couple happy customers pulling out saved-up pin money for new undies. A cheerier scene than the one toward which I rushed, to be sure.

Jutte's expressed concern for her sister's well-being eased my mind a little. The question remained: did she have any control over her paramour's actions? I sighed, puffing out a cloud of steamy breath, and headed toward the hotel. Somebody had to wise Jutte up to the danger she was in, and it appeared I was elected. But how? What could I possibly say that didn't give the game away?

At the corner in front of the Majestic, a newsboy, his nose crusted with mucus and in the process of turning white with frostbite, croaked hoarsely about some bodies found in the tenderloin.

"You should get inside and warm up," I told him. "I do believe your nose is frostbit."

He squished up his face and gave a mighty sniff. A tough guy, for sure. "Buy a paper, miss?"

I produced a nickel and received a paper, a section of which I handed back to him. "Stuff this in your shoes. It'll help insulate your feet from the cold." There was certain to be plenty of room for newspaper as the boots he wore looked at least three sizes too big.

Leaving him gaping after me, I continued on into the hotel.

Once again, the fireplaces blazed with heat and good cheer. Stomping my feet on the rug in hopes of invigorating their circulation, I proceeded to the second story and rapped on Jutte's door.

After what felt like a very long wait, the door opened a crack.

"You," Jutte said, her tone unwelcoming.

"Good morning." I smiled, making my own greeting sound friendly and cheerful—most assuredly no easy task. "I hope you don't mind me dropping in this way, but I had another question for you."

"I mind."

"Oh, you do? I'm sorry. But it's about the ransom. I imagine Mr. Amsel told you no one showed up to collect the bag."

"Ja."

"What do you suppose that means?"

"Do not know."

She certainly wasn't being expansive with her answers, which were no more than I expected.

"You do want to do anything you can to help find your sister, don't you?"

Her eyes shone like hard, blue marbles. The corner of her nose twitched. "Ja. Of course."

"Good. Well, then, do you and your sister—" I broke off. "May I come in?"

She had to think about it. I know she didn't want to, but she opened the door just far enough for me to slip through, waving vaguely toward the same slipper chair I'd occupied on my last visit. Coffee, its aroma rich and enticing, steamed in a cup on the table between us. A half-eaten cream-filled eclair sat on a pretty plate, showing the important doings I'd interrupted. She'd lost no time ordering up refreshments after her excursion. Once again, she didn't offer me a cup of coffee. Or an eclair.

"What do you want to know?" Seating herself, she sipped her coffee and bit off a chunk of pastry. Her accent, I noted, was stronger today.

I had to think of something. "First of all, do you and your sister look much alike?"

There she went, shoulders lifting in her characteristic shrug. "Not to me. You saw photograph. What do you think?"

I smiled. "I think you do, although you are slimmer." Hah. A dig. She wouldn't be for long if she kept eating Rose's eclairs. "Which of you is the elder?"

She didn't want to answer. If there'd been a window into her head, I'm sure I'd have seen cogs turning. I'd be willing to bet she was trying to remember if the newspaper reports had been so rude as to mention age. Setting aside the eclair, she said, "I am the eldest sister. What is this about? These questions are asked and answered before. What does it matter? The ransom is refused, and you don't find my sister." She paused. Her already hard eyes narrowed into a squint. "Do you?"

"You will be the first to know when she is found safe."

She relaxed enough to lick eclair crumbs from her fingers. At least until I said, "Have you had any word from her? A message from the kidnappers, by any chance, perhaps with fresh instructions after the drop last night fell through? New demands? Any reassurance as to her safety and well-being?"

"Why do you ask me? Kidnappers, they talk to Herr Amsel. He pays the money for Anka's ransom. Ask him."

"Oh, I intend to. I just thought the villains may have tried to extort money from you, as well. Do you expect Mr. Amsel anytime soon? May I wait for him?"

"No. Herr Amsel does not tell when he will see me. I go to dressmaker, stupid woman. Wedding gown does not fit." She looked at the clock. "I must go soon."

Harrumph. Caught in a bald-faced lie.

Anyway, I thought, there was no mystery as to why her gown might not fit. Eclairs are apt to do that to a woman who sat around eating all day. Furthermore, I wondered why she always referred to Sepp so formally, as if he were a stranger?

Even so, she was right about one thing. I needed to talk to him, apprise him of my latest discoveries, and find out what he intended to do.

I leaned forward and lowered my voice. "Perhaps I shouldn't tell you this, but I do have a possible lead on your sister's whereabouts."

She jerked. "News? What news?"

"You should know the Doyle & Howe Detective Agency has been busy. We've had people searching all over town for Anka. Yesterday, one of our informants came to us saying he'd heard a woman crying and raising a fuss in an old shop down on Front Street. He thought she spoke with a German accent. The noise came from a building that's stood empty for some time, so he investigated. He looked in a window, but it was so dirty all he saw was a woman with blonde hair. No real details. He thought maybe she was a prostitute who'd been left in the lurch. Or . . ." I paused dramatically, "she might've been your sister."

Face white, Jutte was on her feet. "Who does she talk to?"

"He didn't see, but he thought there were two men, and maybe another woman. He suspects the woman may be in danger."

Her fingers clenched, then, reaching out, she grabbed my shoulder. "We go look for her now."

"No, no. Not now. Later, perhaps, when Mr. Doyle can help. My uncle is ill. I can't leave him alone long." It wasn't all a lie.

"Now." Her fingers dug into my joint, painful even through the layers of clothing, her strength surprising.

I was thankful to be wiry, right then. Ducking out from under

221

her clutching fingers, I backed away. "I thought you had an appointment," and added, at her blank expression, "to fit your wedding gown."

Why, I asked myself, hadn't I transferred my pistol to my coat pocket? I might as well have left it in the desk drawer instead of buried in my skirt pocket under layers of sweater and coat for all the good it would do me now.

But in the end, I didn't need to draw it. She dropped her hand.

"You are right," she conceded. "What can we do? You go now. Bring Herr Doyle when he returns. We will look for my sister together. Later, maybe. Yes?"

"Yes. I will. We will." Time for me to go. I started walking backward toward the door. "Good-bye until then," I said.

She didn't reply.

Once outside, in the hall, I leaned against the wall. Squirt Williams, loaded down with a tray bearing a used coffee service for four and a mostly empty three-tiered china pastry server, was just backing out of another room.

Seeing me, he stopped short. "You ain't gonna find any more bodies, are you, miss?"

"I certainly hope not." I forced a smile. Shaken as I was by Jutte's intensity, it took effort to turn my lips upward.

He noticed. His nose pointed toward Jutte's room. "She's a scary one, ain't she?"

"That she is."

We walked down the hall together in an almost companionable way, he to take the server's staircase, me to take the public. Well met, I had a question for him. "Have the police discovered who killed Eddie?"

"Don't ask me," he said. "They don't talk to the hired help. But people been killed left and right the last couple days." He pointed to the few pages of newspaper sticking out of my coat

222

pocket. "Read all about it. Four murders, and the bluecoats don't know nothin' about nothin'."

"Four?" Oh, right. The ones Philly had told me about.

Too late. He'd dashed off, heading for the kitchen, if a lad with a heavy tray burdened with breakables can be said to dash. He must, I figured, mean Eddie and Dieter for two of the murders. But just who were the others, and how did they figure into the case? Or did they?

In the lobby, I found the darkest corner of the inglenook by the fireplace nearest the stairs and snapped open the paper. There was the headline. "Bodies Found in Red-light Area. Police Suspect Double Homicide. 'What is Spokane coming to?' " asked Mayor Horatio N. Belt in the article. " 'What are police doing to halt crime in our fair city?' "

What indeed? I wondered. It's about time somebody figured it out.

I squinted in the dim light, attempting to read the small print.

CHAPTER TWENTY-SIX

The article, under Shave Johnson's byline, didn't have a great deal to report regarding the murdered men. One was identified as Peter Boggs, a thug well known about town. He'd been found facedown in the snow with a needle dangling from his arm. According to the medical examiner, the evidence a little too obviously pointed to suicide. The reporter, investigating on his own, soon learned that Boggs apparently was not a regular at any of the nearby opium dens. The medical examiner's findings agreed with Johnson. He called it murder.

The article did not go into the hows and whys of those findings. *The Spokesman-Review,* after all, is a family newspaper.

Neither medical examiner nor reporter was as reticent about the second man. Shot in the back, there could be no doubt as to his manner of death. But nobody seemed to know who he was.

The police presented one slight bit of evidence they hoped would help identify this unknown man, believed to be of middle-European ancestry. A pretty, nine-inch hat pin had been found stuck through the lapel of his coat. The pin had an enameled cat's head as a stop.

My heart landed somewhere around my toes.

"Hell and damnation." My lips moved in a whisper. Merciful heavens! Was Werner getting rid of everyone connected with Anka's—or Jutte's—so-called kidnapping? Were both sisters expendable once he collected the ransom? I had no doubt Anka was sliding down a steep and slippery hill. Perhaps our—our meaning the Doyle & Howe Detective Agency—original task, to save the kidnapped woman, still held true. Perhaps she needed saving now more than ever.

And what about me? Klein's failed assassination attempt at Monk's apartment answered that question. Werner evidently felt whatever Sepp's hired detective knew or suspected was too much for his comfort. I was as expendable as a hotel bellhop or a hired thug.

Which brought up a singular thought. After Werner and Jutte used Mamzelle's Parisian Boutique as a meeting place, Philly might be in danger, as well. I needed to give her warning. Perhaps set a watch over her until we had these murderous people behind bars. Who should it be? Not Bill Jackson. He no doubt had his hands full with Monk.

Porter Anderson, my good friend the logger, came to mind. Again. It depended on whether he was still angry with me for coercing him into playing private nursemaid to a certain young lady a couple months ago. She'd managed to out-argue and outwit him at every turn.

If I, or Philly, rather, was lucky, he'd have forgotten his ire. He'd probably be bored by now, with logging operations closed for the winter. I'd give him a try.

Popping to my feet, I narrowly missed a waiter carrying a heavily-laden luncheon tray on his shoulder. The morning had passed without my realizing it. I'd best put my plans in order. Rally the troops, so to speak.

The temperature had dropped steadily as the day wore on. Shivering, I stopped off at the Western Union office, where a clerk sent Porter a telegram. Bundled in fingerless gloves and two sweaters—even though a small stove radiated heat waves in a losing battle against the frost-covered windows—the telegrapher tapped his key with digits stiffened with the cold.

Fortunately, my query was short.

A few minutes later, I slipped into the office to find Gratton standing with his rear to the Franklin stove and a crockery mug of coffee in his hand. He huffed out a breath through his nose at my appearance. A scowl denoted displeasure.

Nimble, on the other hand, cavorted joyously, happy to see me. I gave her a hug and received a face lick in return.

"Where have you been?" Grat reached over to set his cup on the edge of his desk and folded his arms.

I pulled the cap from my head, earning an unwilling grin from Grat as he studied the result. I sighed, wishing, not for the first time, that I was a beauty, like the daughter of Monk's lady friend, Mavis Atwood. Her daughter, Fern, was an actress on the vaudeville circuit. She was the woman Gratton Doyle and Police Officer Lars Hansen fought over for her favors.

"I've been doing my job," I retorted. "Investigating."

"Did you learn anything new?"

"I did, as a matter of fact." I shrugged out of my heavy coat and hung it on the corner rack. "How about you?"

"Yeah, I've got news, too. Come here." He crooked his finger.

I wrinkled my nose. Now what? Unable to resist, I moved closer.

Smiling, he tucked curls behind my ears and poked a couple wayward strands into the blob at the nape of my neck. "I don't know why you don't let it—" he started then, eyes with an odd little flash, finished, "well, maybe I do."

"Let what do what?"

He looked a little flushed, like maybe the stove was too hot. "Never mind. Now, how about your news?"

Stepping away, he went to sit on a corner of his desk, one leg swinging. "Well?"

I hardly knew where to begin. "Everyone had an objective

226

after our meeting this morning. Everyone except me. So I decided—"

"Didn't strike you that having you stay home and out of harm's way for a spell might be a good idea?"

I glared. "Do you want to hear this or not?"

He made a motion like sewing his lips shut. I nodded and started over.

"I found Anka yesterday by following Jutte. I thought what worked once might work again. And it did, Grat. Jutte was just leaving the hotel when I got there. Of course, I trailed after her. It didn't take me anywhere dangerous. We ended up at my friend Philly's shop. Mamzelle's Parisian Boutique."

"Girls' day out?" He sounded a bit sarcastic.

I smiled at him. "Oh, no. Don't you believe it. Jutte had yet another assignation with Horst Werner. Not two minutes after she entered the shop, he did, too."

His leg stilled its casual swing. "Either of them see you?"

"Of course not. I was careful. Somebody taught me how to change my stance and how to use windows and doorways for cover." Him, of course. "I've learned my lessons well."

"I hope so." He sounded grim.

"It was a short meeting. As soon as they left, I talked to Philly. She . . . ah . . . she managed to overhear part of their conversation, and, Grat, we need to make sure Philly is safe, too, because I'm afraid Jutte and Werner are going to figure out she's reporting their meetings to us."

He shook his head. "I doubt they'd be overly concerned about a shopgirl."

"You think not?" I straightened, my spine stiff and not touching the chair back. "You might change your mind when you hear two more men have been murdered, both thugs of Werner's. One of them is the man I stabbed with my hat pin. Even Jutte . . ." I hesitated. "She seems a little afraid for her

227

sister. She ought to be afraid for herself. And so I told her."

His leg had quit swinging. "Two more men? For God's sake, who?"

I gritted my teeth. Now I was in for it. "I told you. Werner's men. The man who attacked me, for one. He had my hat pin stuck through his lapel."

Gratton was gaping at me. "Your friend Philly heard all that?"

"Well, not exactly all that. But it's in The Spokesman-Review." I reached over and got the paper from my coat pocket. "Read for yourself."

He took the paper without looking at it. "And you told Jutte?" He sounded flabbergasted. "When? Why?"

"Well, I hinted, if not exactly . . . um . . . accurately. After I knocked on her door at the hotel and gave a little report."

"Hinted, eh?" He was beginning to look thunderous. "And you talked with her? Reported to her? What did you say, China? Sweetheart, don't you know you're asking for trouble?"

"Don't worry. I feel under no obligation to be truthful with criminals. I made up a story, and she bought it, top to bottom. I was careful." It struck me I'd already said this, about being careful, I mean. But was it true? Or true enough? "I implied a person in her position could be in danger. Oh, I didn't point my finger at her specifically but hinted that anyone connected with the kidnapping might be a target. I could tell she was thinking it over, too."

Grat reached a hand out to me. I took it and let him pull me close.

"You're a little bit crazy, you know it?" He tilted my chin up and stared into my eyes before slowly lowering his head until his lips met mine.

My innards seemed to melt, and I wished the kiss would never end.

But, of course, it did. People have to breathe, after all.

"Gutsy and crazy at the same time," he said, pushing me away as though the interlude had never happened.

Hell and damnation.

Not thirty seconds later Bill Jackson and Monk arrived, my uncle's cough wracking him again due to the frigid air scouring his lungs. He waved my concern aside.

"Wasted our time," he grumbled. "We hung around the bar for most of the morning, but Werner didn't show until just before eleven. He had one drink, studied on a table with several surly-looking fellers sitting around, and gestured a couple of them over. Hired 'em. Don't know for what. Took about two minutes and he left again."

"Said for them to meet him at the saloon tonight. He'd have a job for them then," Bill said, adding at the arch of Grat's brow, "I understand enough German to catch the gist."

"Probably gonna have them pick up the ransom," Monk said.

Grat nodded. "Possible, but count on him being close by. He won't trust any of those yahoos with five thousand dollars."

"True," Monk said. "What did you learn at the rooming house?"

"I learned China was right. Damn place has a rat problem. The landlady has already been warned and won't question when a messenger with the ransom shows up again tonight." He glanced at me. "And no, she doesn't know anything about a ransom. Apparently, she isn't real fond of her boarders, and she'd like to get rid of them. Lucky for us, it made her willing to cooperate for a small fee. I'll be in place early this time. One of the boarders works night shift at the sawmill, and I'll take over his room when he leaves. We'll catch whoever comes for the money."

"Isn't that kind of dangerous?" I broke in. "It didn't work last time. What about Anka? Will Werner turn her loose if he

229

doesn't get the money?"

Gratton shrugged, his expression grim. "Guess we'll have to wait and see."

"Have you talked to Sepp?" I said. "Did you tell him we know where she's hiding out? We can follow them there and, as soon as she's free, take the money back. And do a citizen's arrest. It should be easy."

Except right about then I remembered the lie I'd told Jutte. The one about the person who'd spied around at a supposedly empty building and found someone who might've been Anka. Or the woman we knew as Anka. Werner was bound to have moved her to another place by now. If she wasn't already dead. Unless—

Werner was on the move today. Maybe Jutte would fail to catch up with him in time. Maybe. But if he did, what would he do?

My fault if our plans for tonight went sideways.

"Easy, sweetheart?" Grat said after a thoughtful pause. He shook his head. "I'm afraid you're living in a dream world."

I suspected he was right.

CHAPTER TWENTY-SEVEN

Donning my outdoor things once more, I clipped on Nimble's leash and, after locking the office door behind us, slipped and slid over the icy boardwalks to Rose's lunchroom. The men had already gone on another mission—or so they said. I figured they intended to partake of the free lunch, with beer, at Moseley's Saloon, making plans away from my keen ears.

Moseley would serve the men thick beef on stale bread, fat dill pickles, and boiled eggs. Disgusting, to my mind, although they seemed to enjoy it. At Rose's café, I would have a bowl of wonderful homemade soup—chicken by preference, or maybe a chowder—and sandwiches made with fresh bread, thinly sliced ham and cheese, and mayonnaise. Plus a sumptuous dessert if I still had room.

My footsteps quickened at the thought, Nimble trotting to keep up.

The lunch crowd had thinned to almost nothing when we arrived at the café. I spied the very man I wanted to see first thing. Sepp Amsel perched, if a man his size can be said to perch, on one of Rose's thin wire chairs making quick inroads on a plate of chicken à la king.

Immediately, my mind changed from soup to what he was having.

"Come," he said, waving a hand expansively. "Come sit with me. I buy you lunch. Is goot. Frau Rose, she is a goot cook. Make a man a goot wife."

"She certainly is a goot . . . good cook." He'd get no argument from me on that score, although I didn't feel qualified to comment on the other.

I took the chair across from him, Nimble curling under the table at my feet and gnawing on the snowballs gathered between her toes. A report was due. Overdue, perhaps. I'd just wanted a little more time to form the direction I went with it. Break the news of Jutte's perfidy to him gently or dump it on him all at once? Those were my choices. I couldn't lie. My heart quailed. Fortunately, it didn't seem to affect my appetite.

Rose, looking . . . er . . . rosier than usual, I assumed from having Sepp in her lunchroom, appeared in the doorway of the kitchen. "China," she called, "what can I get for you?"

I pointed to Sepp's plate. "About half as much of what he's having."

"Hah," he said. "I am having pie for dessert."

Who could blame him when it came to Rose's raisin pie, a new recipe she declared she was trying out for Christmas. In fact, as the café emptied, she joined us to taste it for herself.

"Edible," she decided, "but it needs less cinnamon and more brandy."

Sepp shook his head. "No, no. Is perfect," he said.

Rose smiled, put down her fork, and, almost by accident, touched his hand for an instant. "Now, China, what have you discovered?"

There went any chance of putting off the bad news. I'd have liked to discuss my findings with her in private before reporting to Sepp, but he laid his silverware gently across his empty plate and looked me in the eye. The time had come. How to say what I had to say? The bigger question, how much to say? Hell and damnation.

I sighed. "About the drop falling through last night and why nobody showed up to collect the money. Do you know why?"

"Ja. Got another note. They tell me they want more money. Seven thousand, now." Sepp, accurately reading my expression, led the conversation, but I thought his announcement seemed a little prideful. Like young boys arguing over who has the most gruesome scab. There's something boastful about it.

Until his shoulders hunched. "You got bad news? Anka is dead?"

"Not that I know of. She was fit and fine yesterday, and I haven't heard any different."

This drew bug-eyed stares from both of them.

"You see her?" Sepp asked. "You are sure?"

"How do you know it was her?" Rose said.

"I heard her speaking."

"Heard her? You know it was Anka?" Sepp again.

"But did you see her?" asked Rose.

Apparently, they'd formed a tag team.

"I didn't see her up close, but I know it was her because she answered to her name." Technically she'd answered to Jutte, but that was far too confusing for now. The questions were growing closer to the bone. Under the table, my toe touched Nimble, and, in response, she sat up and placed a wet paw on my lap.

"Who says her name?" Sepp's blue eyes squinted, his cheeks going a mottled red.

Rose said nothing this time. I believe she'd guessed what was coming.

I took a breath, just a little shaky. "Horst Werner, for one."

Sepp's reaction showed me he recognized the name, his blue eyes squinting into narrow slits. "For two?"

"Her sister."

His eyes went from a squint to bulging. "Her sister? Jutte? Jutte knows yesterday? But she does not tell me. More bamboozlement, yes?"

Rose got up and placed her hand on his shoulder as though

to prevent him from jumping up and smashing her crockery.

"Let China tell us about it," she said.

"Where?" His voice rose to a near shout. "Where is she? I go get her. Put a stop to this."

"How did you manage to find her?" Rose asked in a soothing tone. "Sit down, Sepp, and listen. No need to go off without knowing all the facts."

The same advice she gave me every now and then.

I cleared my throat. "You may be interested to know the proprietress of Mamzelle's Parisian Boutique is an old friend of mine."

"Miss Philippa?" Sepp sounded surprised.

"Yes, her mother . . . well, you don't care about that. Anyway, she gave me a tip regarding Jutte and Werner. They've been meeting at her shop. I thought I should check on the tip. It chanced that I saw Jutte leaving the hotel with a valise, so I followed her."

"A valise?" Sepp seemed bewildered.

Rose snorted. "Evidently she didn't leave town. Do you know what was in the valise?"

They were zeroing in on the wrong thing. "I think I do, but the important thing is where she took the valise."

"Where?"

"Yes, where?"

"To an abandoned building in the tenderloin."

Rose's hand went to her throat. She gasped, "China! You didn't go back into the tenderloin! By yourself? What if . . ."

I waved this aside. "I had my pistol. And, as you see, I survived the experience."

"Who was in the abandoned building?" Sepp, at least, this time knew the right question.

"Anka."

My goodness, poor Sepp's face was so red he looked like his

insides were on fire. "Who else?"

"Horst Werner and another man, a thug. I believe his name is Klein. Jutte delivered the valise to her sister, saying it contained fresh clothing and some food." I did a little shoulder roll. "Anka complained mightily of being cold and hungry, but she wasn't tied up or anything. Just hiding out."

"Bamboozlers," Sepp said. "Just as I suspect."

"I'm afraid so."

"For shame." Rose plumped down on her chair, her shoulders slumped. "And two people have been murdered because of their greed."

I drew in a breath. "Four people."

Eyes wide, Rose repeated, "Four?"

"Two more dead men were found yesterday. One of them . . ." I choked. "One of them was the man who attacked me the other day. He had my hat pin in the lapel of his coat. The newspaper reported it."

"You were attacked?" This being the first Sepp had heard of it, he was visibly upset, his face set in harsh lines. "Why you not quit the job? I give them the money. And tonight they want more."

I leaned forward. "Is the drop on for the same place?"

"Ja. I talk to Doyle, tell him. More money, same place, tonight, it says. Seven o'clock." He thought a moment. "Train to Seattle leaves at seven thirty."

Suspicion struck me. "When did you get this note?"

He shrugged. "Hour ago, maybe two. What matter?"

And so I told him.

He seemed to take the situation calmly until his fist pounded the table, making the plates and silverware jump. "I fire you now. You not work for me anymore."

At this, Rose squeaked out a laugh. "China never gives up, Sepp. It's become personal. She's a regular ferret, and she's dangerous when cornered."

I sat up straight. "Believe it."

All this nonsense soothed him to the point he sat back and took a sip of his tea. I hoped it was calming chamomile because I had more to report. "The thing is," I started, then hesitated.

Two pairs of eyes swiveled toward me.

"The thing is, the women traded places. I have no doubt Jutte is the one who became your pen pal, Sepp."

He nodded. "Ja. We trade letters. Man at German Club has board on wall with women's names. Introduces peoples, some in America to some who want to come to America."

"But when the girls arrived here, for some reason they traded places."

Jumping to his feet again, Sepp let out a roar. "What?"

"I'm saying that Jutte is Anka and Anka is Jutte."

He scrubbed a large hand over his face, as though to rub away an undesirable vision, then, surprisingly, chuckled.

Rose's mouth moved like she was trying to put people and places in order. "So Jutte is supposedly kidnapped, and Anka is posing as Sepp's fiancée."

"Yes."

"Why? Why they do this? Why trade places?" Angry, pained, bewildered. All applied to Sepp, and yet he'd laughed, too.

"I have no idea," I said. "It all seems unnecessarily complicated. Maybe Anka is a better actress."

He pressed his palms to the table and rose from his seat like a man burdened with too much to bear. I swear the thin table legs bowed under the weight. "Engagement is over," he announced, and he didn't seem one bit sorry as he looked at Rose. "Throw out cake. Don't need it no more."

Her eyes widened. "But Sepp, I used eighteen eggs for that cake. It's a big cake that turned out perfect. It'd be a crying shame to waste it."

He shook his head like an angry bison. "I don't marry that woman. I marry a goot woman." He eyed her again. "One of dese days."

"Well, no, of course you won't marry her. You must tell her so as soon as possible. But . . ." She glanced at me, floundering.

It took only a small leap to clarify their situation when I asked myself a couple little questions. For instance, what was Sepp doing here, in Rose's restaurant, which mostly only ladies patronized? What was she doing, urging him to break with Jutte? What's more, she'd been hinting about a break ever since she met him. Why did her hand on his shoulder calm him, and why did he blush like a schoolboy when she smiled at him?

I guess I'm no fool. Glancing over at her, I winked and whispered, "Don't throw your cake out just yet, Rose. There may be a wedding after all."

My mission to discuss events with Rose (halfway a failure) and Sepp (saying more than I'd intended) eased my mind. And after a sound argument, I finally persuaded Sepp to go through with the ransom pay-off tonight, with Gratton putting a plan into action.

I also got him to agree to avoid Jutte—or Anka—until the business wrapped up. Sepp was no actor. One look at his face and any fool would know he was wise to the plot and see his anger. Werner was no fool. Anka, either, not when it came to reading Sepp.

Remembering the man who'd accosted me a couple days ago—now dead with my hat pin in his lapel—and acknowledging the danger may have ramped up with Werner and Jutte aware they had been overheard, I kept a close watch as Nimble and I made our way home. Nobody jumped out at me. Nobody even looked at me askance, as most had their heads down against the cold. I sensed nothing except the wind blowing under my skirt.

Nothing, that is, right up until I put my hand on the doorknob, and, without my turning it, the door creaked open. My slight pressure had broken the thin rime of ice holding it shut, but not latched.

The room was dark, and it smelled of blood.

Nimble drew in a breath and growled. Her little body trembled.

Hell and damnation.

CHAPTER TWENTY-EIGHT

My revolver appeared in my hand—and I not even aware of drawing it—as I pushed into the room. The lights were off, and the shades had been pulled down tight.

"Heel," I whispered to Nimble, without any real expectation she'd obey. She did though, sticking so close to my side I could barely take a step without treading on her.

It seemed to me I heard a drip, drip, drip, as though a nearby faucet had a slow leak.

I wished. We had no faucets on this floor.

Voice shaking, I said, "Uncle Monk?" and thought I heard the slightest whir of sound in return. Except for that one small, maybe imagined, reply, if one could call it that, the room was silent. Dead.

No, oh please, no.

The dark was not my friend. I reached behind me for the light switch, bumping the pistol barrel on the wall. Facing front, my pistol pointed left, right, ahead as the fixture warmed. Light appeared gradually, until it blazed down on the puddle of blood seeping onto the floor behind my desk.

"Cosimo," I gasped, for the large mound slumped facing me from my desk chair could be no other. "Mr. Pinelli!"

Nimble broke free of her palsy and ran ahead, jumping up to stick what must've been a very cold nose in his face. A muffled groan rewarded her. Rewarded me, too. The stink of blood yes, but not the reek of death.

Hardly knowing how I got from the door to his body, I dropped to my knees beside him.

He'd been gagged with his own handkerchief, which I'd last seen hanging from the back pocket of his britches. I yanked it out of his mouth. He sucked in a draft of air, and then another. *Alive. Breathing. So far.*

His arms were bound behind him with his own belt, which had then been buckled onto the chair back. Bad to be sure, but it was the knife lying a few inches away that had me gritting my teeth. Its blade shone red and gooey under the light. The hole in Pinelli's belly showed why, and also why I heard the drip. Blood oozed from the slit in his side to the floor.

The similarity to Dieter's death struck home.

Pinelli's eyelids flickered as I said, even though I doubt he truly heard me, "Hold on, Cosimo. I'm getting help."

The telephone was on the desk. I picked it up, waited for Central to answer, then yelled for help. I didn't notice I was crying until the operator mentioned it.

Cosimo had already been carried off to Sacred Heart Hospital down by the river when Gratton showed up. "Get out of my way," he demanded when the bluecoat guarding the door attempted to keep him out. Needless to say, the policeman failed in his mission.

"What the hell's going on?" From the doorway, Grat's stare blazed around the room, taking in everything. The blood, me, Hansen. He didn't seem pleased about anything except Nimble, who went immediately to his side.

I felt just like the dog. A sense of relief swept over me, I was so glad to see him. Lars never cows Grat.

I stood by the stove waiting for the room to warm while Sergeant Lars Hansen went through the motions of questioning me. He sat at Monk's desk twirling a pencil in his fingers as he pretended to take notes. I'd have said he was badgering me, except that's too mild of a word.

"I'd gone to Rose's for lunch," I started, but Lars interrupted.

"No talking," he said.

I ignored him. "When I got back I found Cosimo unconscious and tied into my desk chair. He'd been stabbed."

"Is he hurt bad?"

I gulped. "Yes. He's been taken to the hospital."

Lars blathered something about scene of the crime and suspects, but we weren't listening.

Grat wasted no time. He barged on in and, disregarding my hands still covered in Cosimo's blood, swept me into his arms. "Don't tell Hansen anything about Amsel's business," he said into my ear.

I nodded, my forehead brushing his chest. Did he think me stupid or completely undone?

Aloud, Grat said, "How is Pinelli?"

"I don't know. Dr. DePaul wouldn't say. You know him. He just grunted." My breath caught. "At least Cosimo is alive. Grat, we'll have to get hold of Agnes. She'll be so upset."

Lars Hansen, overhearing us, chuckled. "Half-breed like her? My guess is if he dies, there'll be another man in her bed within a week. Probably another ignorant Eye-talian. They seem to go for . . ."

Grat whirled to face him. I couldn't see his face, but whatever Hansen saw made him stop in midstream.

I swear, the man grew more despicable every day! How I ever tolerated him long enough to dabble with a flirtation puzzled me no end nowadays. All just to compete with Fern Atwood, as if such a thing were even possible for an ordinary person like me.

Grat and I, as smoothly as though we had a prior agreement, turned to each other and took no more notice of Hansen. He didn't know what he was talking about, anyway.

"Do you know what happened?" Gratton asked. Without waiting for an answer, he found a cup, poured a sluggish stream of stale coffee into it from the pot sitting on the stove, and handed it to me. "Here. Have some of Monk's cowboy coffee. Put some sugar in it. It'll buck you up. Warm you from the inside out."

Steaming coffee slopped over the side of the cup, but I hardly felt it. Sipping, I made a face. Monk truly makes the most awful coffee.

His back to Lars, Grat winked at me. "All right now?"

No, but I nodded as he guided me over to sit at his desk. I found Nimble already hiding in the kneehole. Poor little pooch, she's afraid of Lars. Even so, she brushed by me to sit by Grat again. Glancing down, I couldn't blame her. Cosimo's blood had soaked through the hem of my skirt, along with splotches at knee height where I'd knelt trying to stop the bleeding. Even my dog was repulsed.

Gratton took a position leaning against the desk corner with his arms folded across his chest. He may have appeared relaxed, but I felt tension vibrating through him.

"Now, I'm asking again. What exactly happened to Pinelli?" He gazed down at me, a worried gleam in his gray eyes.

I opened my mouth to tell him, until Lars butted in.

"Shut up and sit down, Doyle," he said. "I'm asking the questions here."

Grat's lip curled into a snarl. "Then get off your butt and look alive. Have you even bothered to look for evidence?"

Hansen flushed an unbecoming crimson. "Evidence? What for? I figure China can tell us. The hell, China. You stab your neighbor in the gut? He try to get too close?"

Who knows the havoc anger can stir in one's soul until tried by somebody like Hansen? Not me. I went icy hot, sweat breaking out on my forehead, but feeling as though ice ran through my veins. Ever so slowly, I drew the .32 from my pocket and set it atop the desk.

"You'd better put this away for me," I said to Gratton.

Huffing out a snort, he tucked it away in his desk drawer. "Go on upstairs, China. Have a jolt of Monk's Old Crow and try to settle down. Soon as Monk gets here I'll send him up. We'll all talk then."

Nodding, I rose, as stiff and jangled as a marionette. I didn't look at Hansen. I figured I'd start clawing at his eyes if I had to see him.

"Wait a minute," he blustered. "She's staying here until I know everything she knows. Try sneaking her outta here and I'll throw both of you in jail."

"I don't think so," Grat said, cool as mint. He smiled at me. "Go ahead, sweetheart. And take Nimble with you. She's scared."

She wasn't the only one.

I guess respect for authority is ingrained in me for some reason, regardless of police officers like Lars Hansen. At the doorway into the hall where the upstairs access begins, I paused, though Nimble raced up the stairs by herself. "I went to Rose Flynn's café for lunch," I said to Lars, repeating myself. "When I got back I found the office door ajar. The shades were drawn and the lights off. When I turned them on I found Mr. Pinelli tied to a chair. He was unconscious and bleeding. I called for the police and a doctor, then got him loose and laid out on the floor, where I used pressure to try to stop the bleeding. There was no one else here. Other than that, you know as much as I do. Mr. Pinelli is unable to speak."

Hansen stopped me as I took a step forward. "What was Pinelli doing in this office when none of you were around?"

Grat answered for me. "Being a good neighbor," he said.

"Keeping an eye on the place."

A snort fit to rival a dray horse replied, though Lars let the remark pass. "Did Pinelli say anything to you, China? Tell you who stabbed him? Say what they wanted?"

I shook my head. "I told you. He was unconscious."

"So you did. I forgot. I didn't say I believed you. Has anything been taken?" His chilly blue gaze drifted around the room, which inspired my own to do a quick search. Gratton's, also, checking for anything he might have missed before.

I didn't see a thing out of place. The file cabinets were closed and locked, as secure as they ever are. A quick scan of the hall closet showed everything intact. Even our desks were in the same condition as when we'd left. Mine clear and tidy, Monk's with pen and paper and contract form sitting ready for use, Gratton's with a clutter of paper snippets, an empty pen, an ink well with the cap askew, a flutter of cigar ash in a tray. The one spot I avoided looking was where Cosimo's blood chilled to a sticky red goo on the floor.

"Nothing I can see," Grat said, and I nodded.

"Nothing? Strange," Lars said when my attention returned to him. "But there is one thing you might be missing."

"Really? What?"

His lips twisted into a smile. "The fact that whoever did for Pinelli was in your office. The Eye-talian was tied up at your desk." His grin widened. "Yours, China. What have you been doing to make a man like that come after you? A man who would stab another man in the gut and leave him to bleed out? Because I doubt Pinelli was his intended victim. I'd guess you were." He sounded as if he were genuinely concerned.

I didn't believe it.

Unable to bear any more, I dashed up the stairs to my bedroom. I'd never tell him so, but I had no doubt he was correct. The only active case the agency had right now was Sepp

Amsel's, and I was the principal hired to help. My acrimonious dealings with Jutte pointed straight at me. Furthermore, I knew Horst Werner to be a cold-blooded killer who liked using a knife. Or if not him, the man I'd seen him with. A cretin, according to Anka, which applied to both of them. Too mild a description, would be my guess.

The sooner this ransom transaction, and the irrefutable evidence proving Werner's guilt, took place, the better. But not with Lars Hansen horning in.

Gratton must've tracked Monk and Bill Jackson down while I was upstairs, because they returned to the office within the hour reporting their errand unsuccessful.

"This Werner must have a good hideaway," Monk said as he bellied up to the stove. "Folks say they haven't seen him in any of the German hangouts."

Lars and his bluecoat had gone by then, Grat telling us, once we all gathered around the stove in the parlor—nobody, meaning me in particular, wanting to deal with the blood—that the police hadn't appeared terribly interested in solving the case.

"Just like Dieter's murder." My jaw clenched.

Grat managed a "not quite" grin. "At least he sent that young officer to sit by Pinelli so he can be questioned as soon as he wakes up. Maybe Hansen'll take some action then."

"If Cosimo wakes up." Tears filled my eyes again. He'd looked terrible, which I'd seen but the men had not.

Monk patted my back. "He will, lambie. He's a strong feller." He coughed and abandoned the stove to sit in his chair. The rest of us trailed after him, finding our usual seats.

"Immigrants. They don't got money; the bluecoats don't care much what happens to 'em." Bill Jackson's blue eyes seemed sadder and wetter than ever. "Reason I changed my name soon as I got to this country."

"You're an immigrant?" Even Monk looked surprised. "I didn't know that. Can't tell by your accent."

Bill's chin lifted. "That's on account of I ain't got one. Name used to be Jung. Means young." He laughed. "Long time gone."

After a brief silence, I ventured to ask, "Are we still on to nab whoever collects the ransom and chase these people down? Or, after what happened to Cosimo, should we abandon the whole enterprise? Go to Sepp and tell him that since the kidnapping is a set-up to begin with, he should drop it."

"Hell, no," Grat burst. "Let these mutts get away with murder? Not on my watch. Not while one of my friends is a victim."

Monk nodded. "Yep."

"Count me in," Bill said.

Three sets of eyes settled on me.

I sat up poker straight. "I guess you all know how I feel."

Even Bill Jackson nodded.

CHAPTER TWENTY-NINE

I daresay we weren't terribly concerned about the murder of Werner's henchmen, nor even the bellhop and tailor, beyond what it meant to Sepp Amsel's case. I don't know what that says about me, or any of us. And, for now, our concern all centered on Cosimo, and he wasn't dead. Or not yet. I put my faith in Dr. DePaul's expertise to see him through. So did Grat and Monk, although their assurances to me on that score seemed a bit overdone. Besides, they hadn't seen him before the ambulance carried him away. I had.

A terse message from Dr. DePaul a few hours later did little to allay our anxiety. *Out of surgery, still alive,* it said. *Bad shape. Pray.*

The only thing of consequence to occur during those hours filled with guilt and restlessness was Porter Anderson's arrival. He burst in through the front door shedding fresh snowflakes like a molting snowman. Standing with hands on hips, he glared at me and announced, "What do you want now? Something that'll get me killed, I 'spect."

I froze. No I didn't. Not another of my friends. I opened my mouth to send him home, but Grat took over before I had a chance to speak.

"Not if you're careful. We figured as long as you're not doing anything else you might keep an eye on somebody for us. We don't know she's in any danger. Just don't want to take any chances. It's only for today. Maybe carry over into tomorrow."

"She?" Porter scowled and unwrapped a ten-foot-long muffler from around his neck. "The female isn't Neva Sue O'Dell again, is it?" He shuddered. "Gawd, I hope not. You can count me out." He seemed horrified at the mere thought.

I had to laugh. "No, it's not Neva. It's a lady, a businesswoman, named Philippa Kim. I doubt she's in danger, but we just want to make certain. All you have to do is loiter in her nice warm store and keep watch. It'll be easy."

"Yeah? That's what you said about Neva."

"Not up for a challenge?" Grat mocked him.

"Challenge, hell," Porter replied.

Stronger measures seemed called for. "I'll pay," I said.

"How much?"

I thought a moment. "Ten dollars?"

Porter's scowl cleared. "Well, hell, I'm here now. Might as well. Long as the job's inside." Another item to go on Sepp Amsel's bill.

"Good man," Monk assured him.

Before long, Monk and Bill departed once again to try to find Werner. If successful, they'd keep watch on him. Gratton went off to cadge another official-looking satchel from Sepp before the ransom drop, filling our employer in on the latest developments. Oh, yes, and mention the charges to his bill. I doubted Sepp would quibble.

Catching Grat before he left, I took him aside, upstairs where Porter had no chance of listening in.

"You'll warn Sepp to stay in his saloon, won't you?" I plucked at Grat's sleeve. "Somewhere there's a lot of people. No matter what, right? Even if somebody comes in and says his house is on fire."

He was building a house, a fine, fancy house for his new bride. *Who'd never step foot in it, if I had my way.* If the bride was Jutte Kalb, at any rate.

"I'll tell him. Or if some yahoo starts a gunfight, I'll tell him to get down on the floor behind the bar and stay there."

"Yes." Heavens, I hadn't thought of this, which made another thing to worry about.

Gratton took me by the shoulders and stared into my eyes. "And you, sweetheart. You're going with Porter to stay with Mamzelle, correct?"

"Correct."

He shook me. "You won't wander around, poking your nose in where it don't belong? You'll stick with Philly where people— where Porter—can see you. Correct?"

"Correct."

"And you'll take the dog with you."

"Of course."

He sighed. "Then I reckon we're all set. All we got to do is wait for zero hour."

We went back downstairs, where Porter and Nimble were waiting for us. A moment before we stepped into the office, Grat stopped and drew me toward him. He planted a kiss, a big kiss, dead center on my mouth.

"All right," he said when we came up for air. Since I came up a little lightheaded, he pushed me into the office ahead of him.

"Take care of her," he told Porter with what I'm sure he meant to be a meaningful stare. Twenty seconds later he went on his way.

Porter smirked.

Before we left, I sent Porter over to Pinelli's cabinet shop to make certain the fire was banked and his door locked. With Porter out of sight, I reloaded my pistol and jammed it into my skirt's specially reinforced pocket, dumped a few extra shells into my pocketbook, and bundled up. Last of all, I fought Nimble into her red sweater and clipped on a leash.

The wind was blowing again as we wended our way toward

Mamzelle's, snow rising in slow swirls. Drifts that looked like white, ocean-washed sand had begun piling up in front of shop doors; the streets were nearly empty of both vehicle and foot traffic. Gratefully, I accepted Porter's bulk between me and the elements.

"So," Porter said, steam puffing out his mouth as he spoke, "this is a helluva situation. Good thing Grat was to home. You weren't going to tell me about the murders, were you?"

"What a poor opinion of me you must have." I blinked snow from my lashes as I looked up at him. "You have to know how to protect us. And yourself! Of course, I'd tell you something so important."

"Huh. A relief. Just not right off the bat, I guess."

He had me there. I forced a smile. "Didn't want to scare you off."

"Scare me off," he muttered. I think he was offended.

After a block and a half, he reached down and picked Nimble up. We made faster progress when she no longer had to struggle through the deepening snow, and in no time at all we reached Philly's store and went in.

The place was empty. Wide open, so anyone could walk in, but empty.

I mean yawningly, lights-out, and silent. Not a single customer, not a single clerk. Most of all, no beautiful, ebony-haired Philippa Kim.

Porter put Nimble on the floor. "What the hell?"

My stomach lurched in my belly. Nimble shook snow from her ears and tail and sat on my boot, refusing to stir.

"I don't know," I said in a whisper. But I was afraid I did. Footsteps lagging, I stepped ahead.

No Philly, even though I looked all through the storeroom, the fitting room, the tiny kitchen area where she often made tea for her favored customers.

What I found were signs of a struggle.

A rack of scarves turned over onto the floor and trampled underfoot. A stack of embroidered corset covers strewn across a display. And, in the kitchen, close by the back door, a cup shattered into a thousand pieces on the floor while a container of honey dripped into the crockery. Twin drag marks, as if made by the heels of narrow shoes, created a path through the sticky shards.

What there wasn't, was blood.

Porter breathed in and out through his nose like a stalled steam engine. He seemed unaware of holding onto Nimble until she struggled in his arms. I hadn't been aware he'd picked her up again.

"Looks like we're too late," he said. "They've taken her."

"Yes."

He eyed me. "What do you want to do?"

"Go after her."

"Go after her?"

"Yes." I flapped a hand. "Feel. It's not cold in here. The honey is still dripping. She hasn't been gone long. There's still time." *Please. There had to still be time.*

"Do you know where she might be?"

"Maybe. Or maybe I know somebody who does." I was unconscious of patting at the pocket holding my .32 until I noticed him watching. "If you're squeamish, you can go back to the office and wait. But I'm taking Nimble. She knows Philly. She can track her."

Porter's already ruddy face turned a shade brighter. "You ain't going anywhere without me. The hell? I ain't having Gratton Doyle on my wrong side."

His speech would've impressed me more if I hadn't known he didn't give a hoot what Grat thought.

251

CHAPTER THIRTY

Porter and I went directly to the hotel. The Majestic, I mean. Werner was just walking away, his strides long, as if he were in a hurry.

"That's him," I gasped to Porter. "That's the man who has Philly."

He gaped down at me. "We don't know for sure who has her. Anyways, we can't see his face. How do you know this feller is Werner?"

I'd been explaining the murders, the extortion, the players in this crime, to Porter as we walked.

"I know." It didn't make sense he'd brought Philly to the hotel. Too chancy by far. And he was moving very fast, as if he were on a mission. I felt certain, due to the timing, his mission had to do with Philly. And, obviously, also implicated Jutte, or he wouldn't have stopped by the hotel.

"You should follow him," I said.

"Me? While you do what?"

"Keep my eye on the woman. If we lose Werner, she's our best chance of leading us to Philly."

Porter shook his head—vigorously. "Grat said to stay with you no matter what, and, missy, that's exactly what I'm going to do."

"But Philly—"

"Don't know Philly. I'm sorry for her, but my job is to see nothing happens to you. Monk and Jackson are looking after

252

Werner. They're probably watching him right now and got us in sight, too."

Porter's excuse didn't stand up, to my mind. I knew Monk would never have allowed Philly to be taken if he'd been on hand.

I glanced around with a meaningful look. "Do you see Monk and Jackson anywhere around?"

"No," he said, "but it doesn't mean they're not close by."

He may have been right. As I've often said, my uncle is a good detective. He knows how to tail a suspect and not be seen himself.

The whole question quickly became moot. We'd lost the window of opportunity as Porter and I argued. Werner had turned the corner a block away and disappeared from sight.

I'd become such a regular at the hotel no one seemed to notice as I peered into the dining room. It was empty of customers at this hour except for one bored-looking man drinking coffee and playing a game of solitaire. Waiters were sweeping up fallen lunch debris and setting tables for the next meal. The lobby also suffered a dearth of clientele, due no doubt to the ongoing storm and dreary weather. Just like Rose's café, only on a larger scale. Bad weather, I observed, is not generally good for business.

A couple boys wearing the hotel uniform came into the lobby with a wheeled cart full of short logs. Drawing it over to the fireplace closest to us, they proceeded to stoke the fire. One of the boys was Squirt. I called him aside.

"Do you know if Miss Kalb is in her room?" I asked.

He made a face. "Well, I ain't seen her leave. Yet."

Yet? What did that mean? "Has she had any visitors?"

His palm came out. Knowing what that meant, I grubbed in my pocketbook and extracted a quarter, which I placed in his hand before repeating my question. "Has she had any visitors?"

Ready now to cooperate, Squirt nodded. "A mean-looking feller. He's been here before, usually at night." He leered. "Dresses like a gentleman, but ma'am, he's no gent. He just left. That's why me and Dave are late with the fires."

"How'd he make you late?" Porter asked.

I expect he wondered, as I did, if Werner had paid them to disappear while they wafted Philly up to Jutte's room.

But no.

"He was around the day Eddie got killed," Squirt said, almost whispering. "We think, Dave and me, he did it. He killed Eddie."

My breath caught. "What makes you think so?"

He shook his head. "Well, we got no proof, but me'n Dave talked about it. The time. See, it was him called Eddie up to the woman's room. Nobody saw Eddie after that. Not alive. So we stay out of his way."

Easy to see he remembered the sight of Eddie dead the same as I did. So I gave him another two-bits as a bonus and my thanks. But he wasn't finished.

"She's all packed up, you know."

"Packed up?"

"Yeah. I took coffee to her room a while ago." He stopped and thought, his face screwed into a living question mark. "Know what? I ain't seen the sister in days. But she was stuffing all those things she bought into containers ready to transport but not taking much care about it. Her and her sister's things. Got a lot of boxes and trunks and valises."

"Well, she's probably preparing for her wedding on Saturday."

"Huh. Don't look like it to me. Not getting married to anybody in Spokane, anyway." He smirked. "She don't know it, but I got a good look at some of the boxes. They have an address on them. Want to know what it is?"

My heartbeat accelerated as Porter nodded. "You bet we do,

sonny," he said.

Squirt leaned forward. "San Francisco. Some hotel there. The Palace."

"Well, maybe her sister . . ."

"No, ma'am. Everything is going there."

Dave, unabashedly listening in, wiggled and nodded. "He's telling the truth. She had me go out and hire a feller to transport everything to the train station tomorrow morning."

"I'll be damned," Porter breathed, fishing in his pocket for a couple more four-bit pieces to give the bellhops. "What do you suppose this means?"

"Nothing good I'll be bound. For Philly or for Sepp." It puzzled me, too. And worried me. If these crooks were abandoning their scheme, why had they taken Philly? More importantly, what had they done with her?

I turned, catching sight of Jutte Kalb as she started down the stairs. Bundled up to the eyeballs in luxurious dark fur and rich cashmere wool, she glanced neither right nor left as she descended. She looked angry. And maybe a little scared.

I whirled away, hiding Nimble in my skirts and grabbing on to Porter's sleeve. "Look. That's Jutte on the stairs."

He stared openly since she'd never seen him before. He probably wasn't the kind of man she'd give a second glance, anyway.

"Looker, ain't she?"

"Harrumph. Perhaps, if you're attracted to a woman like that."

He laughed. "You want to go search her room, or should we trail her? See where she goes?"

"Trail her and see where she goes. I don't think they'd leave Philly in a hotel room, even if she's . . ." I couldn't go on with the rest of my thought.

Porter settled his hat and gave his muffler, overly long and in danger of tripping him, another wrap. "Come on, then. We don't want to lose her."

And, indeed, she departed at a brisk walk, almost as if the boardwalks weren't slippery with ice and snow. We followed.

If I'd thought Werner in a hurry, Jutte came in a close second as Porter and I hastened to keep her in sight. She didn't head into the tenderloin, as I'd expected, but turned east on Main to Howard, then went south as if she were going to Rose's café.

And then she really did go to Rose's café.

I grabbed Porter's arm, stopping him about half a block away. "What in the world?"

"Huh? What?" he said, shaking me off. "Ow."

"Jutte. What is she doing here?"

Porter gazed down at me with a baffled expression. His nose was red with cold—better than white, which would've signaled frostbite. "She's going to a restaurant. Nothing strange . . ." He stopped. "Well, yeah, I guess it is odd, coming from a hotel and all. And in this weather." He thought a moment. "And considering what's going on."

He finally grasped the extent of my agitation. "You gonna tell me why you're in a twist and why you about paralyzed my arm?" Putting on an act, he flapped the offended appendage as though to wake it up.

"Don't be a baby," I said. "And I'm in a twist because Sepp Amsel is about to give up on Jutte and Anka Kalb and fall in love with Rose Flynn." I pondered a moment. "If he hasn't already. And because Rose just so happens to own the Cozy Corner Café."

He stared at the café with its tidy little sign. "Oh," he said. "Well, it's a good thing the place is closed and Jutte can't get in."

The blinds were drawn and locked up tight, something I'd never seen before. But as we watched, Jutte tapped on the door.

A man's thick finger moved the blind obscuring the window aside. A second later the door opened, Jutte slipped inside, and it closed behind her.

"Hell and damnation," I said. "They've got Rose, too."

CHAPTER THIRTY-ONE

"Got Rose?" Porter echoed. "How do you know?"

I glared at him. "Trust me. I know." My mind was racing at a furious pace. Dear Lord, what were we going to do now?

He huffed, breath steaming. "You mean to say these people have kidnapped two women in the last hour? Right under our noses?"

I was so angry I thought I might burst. "That's what I mean to say."

"Well, hell," he said, "we can't let 'em get away with terrorizing our friends whenever they feel like it, now can we?"

"No, we can't. I'm glad you agree."

"A'course I agree. And if it was you they'd taken, China, I'd agree even more."

"Thank you," I said. "But, Porter, there's something else. These people, apparently, they have a habit of murdering anyone who no longer serves a purpose in their schemes. So that indicates . . ."

He was quiet a moment, then said, "Shows this Werner prolly doesn't intend for the ladies to live."

"He won't want to leave any witnesses. Look what happened to the bellhop. And a dissenting cohort, and even two of his paid thugs. So, it's up to us. We've got to get Rose and Philly out of there. In one piece." I touched the pistol in my pocket. "Sooner rather than later."

"Goes without saying," he said.

But how? That was the question.

Nimble, seeing what had become one of our regular haunts ahead, tugged on her leash, wanting, no doubt, to get in out of the cold. I held her back.

"We need to see what's going on inside the café," I said. "I can't do it. It'll have to be you."

"Yeah? What if they kidnap me, too?"

"I'll rescue you. I promise. Anyway, they won't. Why would they? They don't know you. All you have to do is walk up to the door and knock. Just like you saw Jutte do. Yell a little bit. Say . . ." I had a hard time thinking what he could say persuasive enough for Jutte and whoever was in there with her to open the door far enough for him to look inside. After a moment, the right phrase came to me. "Say you've got a reservation."

Porter's eyes bugged. "A reservation?" He studied the café. "There? In case it escaped your notice, the joint ain't what I'd call a gentleman's hangout."

I daresay I sort of flounced. "Say whatever you have to in order to spy them out. We need some sort of hint as to what's going on. See where they're holding Rose and Philly." *If they aren't already dead.*

He blew a great heaving breath through puckered lips. "What I don't go through for you, China Bohannon. From fishing you out of the drink to having my head bashed in. And now I suppose I'll get a knife in the gut."

"Don't be so dramatic," I said, even though he'd voiced exactly what I was afraid of.

I drew Nimble behind one of Mr. Thomas Elsom's cedar telephone poles, hoping between that and the now thickly falling snow we'd become invisible, while Porter went on to the Cozy Corner. Peeking around the pole, I watched as he hammered on the door. I could no longer see if anyone looked out at him, but, after a fraught minute, the door opened. He strong-armed it a foot or so farther, listened to whoever spoke to him, talked a bit himself, then listened again. His head hung as though dejected. As though giving up, he nodded, turned away, and trudged up the street, away from me.

Smart, I decided. They'd be watching him as he drew any potential notice away from me.

Three or four minutes later, when I figured nobody would be paying attention, Nimble and I went back the way we'd come. After a while, Porter met us at the corner. He gave Nimble, who acted as though she hadn't seen him in a month, a pat.

"Well?" I said.

"The women are in there, in the kitchen, not the dining room. All I saw is a foot, sitting in front of a chair. It was moving, like somebody trying to shake off a bug."

I had a little experience with a certain situation, where a person tied to a chair tried to loosen his bonds. This sounded similar.

"So they're alive," I said.

"Yeah. One of them, anyhow. I only saw the single foot. Pretty good-sized one wearing a black, low-heeled shoe with laces."

"Rose," I said, a little cheered. "Who else did you see? I saw you talking."

"I argued with a big burly feller, scarred up like he's been in plenty of fistfights. Is that Werner?"

"No. That must be the man who was keeping an eye on Anka. The cretin." *Yes. And the one who'd killed Dieter, broken into Monk's apartment, and who probably had stabbed Mr. Pinelli. Although it probably took both Werner and Klein to overpower Cosimo.* I thought I'd keep that bit of information to myself. "Did you see Jutte?"

"No. I expect she was in the kitchen keeping the women quiet."

"Yes." I went silent, trying to think what to do next. Nothing much came to me.

"We going in after them?" Porter asked after a few seconds.

"I don't think we have any choice. Do you have a gun?"

"Hell, yes." He patted his hip. "You don't think I come into Spokane without my pistol, do you? I ain't so stupid." He eyed me. "You got your little pea-shooter?"

I'm not so stupid, either. I nodded.

"So, how we gonna get in? Storm the door? You go in one way, me the other? I saw the place has a back door when I went through the alley behind the restaurant."

"There's a more hidden door than that. Rose showed it to me. We'll go in that way. Hopefully take them by surprise. Maybe Rose can help us. And Philly, too. She's small, but she's tough and resourceful."

Porter nodded. "You're the boss."

I wasn't any too sure I wanted to be the boss. A good thing my anger buoyed me along.

Admonishing Nimble to be quiet and not give us away, I anchored her to a pillar holding up the stoop overhang on the business next door. Porter and I then crept through the alley to the back of the café, where a high wooden panel hid not only Rose's waste barrels, but the secret entrance. Most people saw only the visible door and didn't know there was another one there, exiting from a storage room. Our stealth only wasted some time.

As we approached, we saw the main door stood open, a frightening sight in itself, and, though we rushed in with our pistols drawn like gunfighters in a penny dreadful, the place was empty and already growing cold. No trace of Rose or Philly, but no bodies, either. And no blood. Only Jerry the cat, poor thing, huddling behind the door as if terrified.

There were some tracks.

I swung the café door closed in utter disregard of the way it slammed. Then, untethering Nimble, Porter and I followed the tracks until they hit the street, where they disappeared.

Porter swore, loud and imaginatively, like the mighty logger he was. And he didn't apologize.

"We've lost them," I said, dejected beyond describing.

We stood in the street as snow swirled around us. It didn't matter. The streets were quite empty. I shivered.

"I hope Rose and Philly are wearing coats." I had a hard timing imagining Jutte or Werner being considerate enough to appropriately garb their captives for the weather. Worry nagged at me as I berated myself for getting my friends involved. Then I remembered it had been Rose who called on me. But Philly, she was certainly blameless.

"It's colder than—" Porter started, then stopped. "Look at your dog. What's she doing?"

I glanced down to where Nimble, nose to the ground, was pulling on her leash. Pulling me, I was certain, in the direction Rose and Philly had been taken.

"She's tracking them!" I cried in delight. "Rose, anyway. She loves the way Rose smells."

"Smells?" Porter frowned at me, probably thinking it was an insult.

No insult intended. "Rose is the cook in her restaurant," I explained. "She smells of baking and soup and all sorts of good things."

"Ah." He grinned. "Then let's follow the dog's nose."

So that is what we did, down two blocks, up three, then down another two and a half, until we came to a small house that needed some upkeep. The party's footprints, which had dwindled away as the snow fell, showed more clearly here. Porter and I had depended solely upon Nimble's tracking prowess, but we were certain we'd come to the right place.

We stopped half a block shy of the house.

"Looks like somebody is here. Now what?" Porter peered toward the house, where a wisp of dark smoke curled from the chimney and was whipped away.

I fished my pistol from its pocket. "Do like we planned at the restaurant, I guess. But this time you go in the front. I'll work my way around to the back. Give me a couple minutes, and we'll hit them at the same time."

"What if there's more people than the two we been following? What if Werner is holed up in there? That's too many for just you and me to handle."

I steeled myself. "We can do it, Porter Anderson. You know we can."

He could tell my mind was made up.

"Start counting, then. One hundred and twenty from now." He huffed steam into the air and tracked through the snow toward the windowless side of the little house. Nobody could see him, but that worked both ways. "Go," he said softly.

I cut down the side yard, went past the house next door, and came in through a totally untrammeled backyard. Actually, I was relieved. It meant both places had been empty until now.

One minute was gone as I kicked through the last drift and mounted the porch. Only when Nimble whined did I remember she was still attached to my wrist by her leash. Nothing for it now. She'd have to come with me to prevent her setting up a howl. I lifted her over the snow onto the porch.

Grasping the knob in my hand, I'd begun to turn it, ever so slowly, when I heard people talking inside. The door was thin, easy to hear through.

"What took you so long?" a woman said, high-pitched and angry. "Is freezing in here. Horst has put me to stay all by myself *und* I can't get the fire to burn. House is as big a pig sty as other place. Old, cold, and stinks."

I recognized her from hearing her complaint before. Anka.

"Calm down, sister," a different female voice replied. Jutte. She sounded nonchalant, and not particularly soothing or sympathetic. "He found this house abandoned. A temporary stop, only. All will soon be done."

"Done!" Anka said. "What is done? All for nothing, Horst says to me. Amsel knows is trick, he says. No five thousand dollars."

Wait a minute, I thought. Only the day was changed. That and the price had gone up. The ransom drop was still on, and she didn't know?

So the others lied to her, which meant her days were surely numbered. A sudden decision? I wondered. Or the plan all along?

"Circumstances have changed," Jutte said. "The plan has changed. Horst has made new plans. Now we have these two, and Herr Amsel will pay more for them. But—" She laughed a little, as though anticipating.

"But what? Why do you not tell all this before?"

"I'm telling you now. First, we pick up the ransom money, then we have Sepp Amsel open his safe at his home. Hah. We didn't know about that one until two days ago. Is reason for the delay. He keeps much more money there."

Anka struck me as being disgusted. "Why delay? Why not make Amsel open his safe now? Be done. We take the train and go."

Jutte laughed. "Detective Doyle is watching the boarding house. Klein will go there, kill him, while Horst takes care of Amsel. Fool them all."

"Ja. Fool them. But Dieter is dead."

"Dieter." I could almost see Jutte's accompanying shrug. "Forget him, sister."

"I don't want to forget him. And now these women. What are we to do with them?"

The question hung there unanswered, unless one called the clatter of a stove lid an answer. Then I heard another voice, a stifled one, that only made a *mmmmmmm* sound. Even from outside the door I recognized it. Rose.

"Quiet," one of the women said, harsh and cold.

Time was up. The two minutes had passed, and Porter must be set for action. More than set.

I spun the door knob and burst in, brandishing my pistol and screaming like a madwoman. Nimble, taking her cue from my noise, barked vigorously enough to make my ears hurt.

A glance showed me everyone's position. Rose and Philly were tied to rickety chairs along one wall. Good. Out of the line of fire.

Anka sat at an oilcloth-covered table facing me, pinched with cold but plump as a Thanksgiving turkey and gnawing a pastry of some sort. Ironically, probably one of Rose's baking.

Jutte, just beyond Anka, was bent over the stove stuffing a few sticks of kindling into the fire box. She turned. "You!" she said.

Speeding up, I kept right on going. Grat has told me people often mistakenly slow their momentum and turn themselves into a target instead of a force. I plunged forward, toward Jutte, reaching out as I went past Anka and, with a thrust that wrenched my arm, tipped her and her chair over onto the filthy floor.

Nimble, delighted, pounced on top of her, at which the woman screeched like an angry hoot owl.

Vaguely aware of noises followed by at least two quick shots from the front of the house, I dodged the cast-iron stove lid Jutte threw at me. I'm afraid I flinched, losing my forward timing as she rushed me.

She didn't count on Philly, closest to her, scooting her chair into Jutte's way.

Jutte fell. Hard. Philly fell, too, but she rocked the chair, banging it into the side of Jutte's head. Lord only knows how badly Philly damaged herself in the fall.

"Mmmmmmmmm," said Rose.

Philly banged Jutte's head again.

Anka had her pudgy hands over her ears as Nimble nibbled at them with her sharp little teeth, tasting, no doubt, the remains of the pastry.

Jutte managed to push Philly aside then and, cursing loudly in German, which I had no trouble understanding, sprang to her feet. The thing is, she rose up right into the barrel of my Smith and Wesson.

"Yes, me," I said, jamming my .32 into her belly. I wasn't gentle about it, either. "You, you fiend, are going to jail."

Silence reigned in the other room.

"Porter?" I called softly.

A moan answered.

CHAPTER THIRTY-TWO

My heart seemed to stop at the sound of the moan. "Porter?" I yelled.

A couple seconds went by. More than a couple, maybe. It felt like a lifetime.

Then he yelled back. "Hold on, China. I'll be there quick as I take care of this yahoo."

I sagged, like all the starch in my spine melted. But nobody hollers as loudly as he did if they'd been hurt. I understood him to mean he'd put the cretin out of commission but needed another minute to utterly vanquish him. Relief washed over me; a pent-up breath released.

Meanwhile, I was stuck in the kitchen guarding the Kalb sisters. I kept my pistol pointed at Jutte as I searched through a drawer until I found a rust-pitted knife with only half of a handle. Enough of an edge remained on the blade to scratch through the rope binding Philly to the chair. The rope must've been something they found in the house. Something like half-rotted old clothesline. It cut through in seconds.

Philly's mouth, once freed of the gag that had been stuffed in it, shook with cold, her teeth clacking together. Her lips were a blue-colored hue, whether from the pressure of the gag or the cold, I don't know. I do know she was shaking so hard she could barely hang on to the knife when I passed it to her to free Rose. She had no coat or gloves or hat. As I'd feared, she and Rose both wore only indoor clothing, although Rose, at least, had a heavy woolen sweater on over her dress.

I'd have freed Rose myself, but at this point didn't think I'd better trust Philly with my pistol. Oh, not just because pure fury might cause her to shoot Jutte—I didn't care so much about that—but because, with the way she shook, Rose or I might've become an accidental target.

"Will you be all right?" I asked her.

"I'm freezing," she said, her teeth clacking together.

"I know. I'm sorry." A quick glance showed me what to do. I pointed my pistol at Jutte. "You. Take off your coat."

She wore the one made of cashmere and fur. Toasty warm, I figured, and carrying her body heat.

Jutte's eyes widened, and she stiffened. "I will not."

I smiled, although it may've looked more threatening than pleasant. "You will."

"Mmmmmm," Rose said with enough emphasis I figured she meant she wanted to help peel the woman down.

"Yes," I told her, reaching across with my left hand and pulling away her gag. Blood tinged the corner of her mouth, making me mad all over again. "Luckily, we have two sources of warmth. A coat for you and a coat for Philly. That one," I nodded toward Anka, still fending Nimble off, "should fit you well enough. A little short, maybe."

"Short is fine with me." Rose, stalwart that she is, laughed as Philly finally cut through the clothesline and her hands came free. She stood up and shook Philly's hand.

"How do you do?" she said. "I'm happy to meet China's friends."

Philly's shivered all over, like a horse shaking off flies. "Charmed."

Introductions over, I handed the pistol to Philly, even though her hands were so stiff she barely held on to it. "Aim at that one." I indicated Anka. "If this one gets too feisty, shoot the sister."

Philly nodded grimly.

Anka, no surprise, shrieked.

Rose and I soon wrestled Jutte out of her elegant coat, not without Rose receiving an elbow in her stomach, and me a smash across the mouth. We prevailed, naturally, and handed the coat off to Philly. As a testament to her strength, she resisted donning it until we'd divested Anka, who went so limp it was like undressing a rag doll, of her plainer garment. Rose didn't care; she got it on in five seconds flat and took the gun from Philly.

"Your turn, my dear. And well deserved."

The sound of clapping drew everyone's eyes to Porter Anderson, who stood just inside the kitchen, observing the goings-on. He threw up his hands as the pistol pointed his way.

"Don't shoot him," I said. "That's Porter."

"Hell, China," he said, "is everyone you know tough as nails?"

I grinned at him. "You bet," I said, but the grin soon faded. I'd already started worrying again. In view of Anka and Jutte's discussion, Gratton, Monk and Bill, and Sepp Amsel were not out of the woods. They were out there with Werner planning on murdering them. Grat and Sepp, anyway. We needed to warn them. No. What we needed was to stop Werner.

The streets outside showed empty in the snow's reflected light. I wasn't terribly surprised when no one came to investigate the gunshots from a house supposed to be empty. Not in this neighborhood. Which meant one of us had to go for help. By general consensus, my three friends selected me. It made sense, I suppose, since Philly and Rose both were still too cold to venture out, and Porter needed to keep track of the cretin—or, more precisely, the murderer Herr Klein—and the Kalb sisters.

Perhaps I should be ashamed, but I couldn't help thinking it was too bad Porter's shot hadn't done more damage than merely shattering the man's shoulder. At least Rose had good advice for me.

"Try the corner of Howard and Riverside," she said. "That's Bill Shannon's beat, and he usually patrols along there about this time of day. Besides, he knows you by sight. He'll help."

Twisting my muffler higher on my neck, I nodded. "Keep Nimble here, will you?" I pulled open the door that someone, I don't remember who, had eventually had the presence of mind to close. "Someone will be here soon to help."

Philly nodded. "We're counting on it. And China . . ." She waited until I faced her. "Thank you. And your friend Porter is right, you know. You are tough as nails. Just don't depend on it too much. Be careful. Please, be careful."

"I will, I promise."

Leaving Nimble with my friends, much against her will, I might add, I stepped out into the night.

A few lights shone in the scattered houses, beacons in the darkness with their silvery glow. Snow still fell, lighter now, floating down like the softest of dandelion fluff. The wind had eased as the temperature dropped, which should've been warming but wasn't.

The few blocks to the corner where Rose had directed me seemed endless. Shannon was nearby, though, just as she'd predicted. I found him walking on Howard about halfway between Riverside and Main.

"Officer Shannon, wait for me," I called, forcing my stiffened legs into a trot as I attempted to catch up. He turned, and, if I felt frozen after fifteen minutes outdoors, he looked like a hand-rolled snowman. His eyebrows and mustache were white with frost, the shoulders of his coat with an icy crust, his blue hat weighted with snow.

I'd be willing to wager he was the only officer actually doing his assigned beat on an evening as cold and snowy as this.

Warily, he watched me approach until I was close enough for recognition to dawn. "Miss Bohannon. What are you doing out? You should be home by your fire."

"I only wish I were." I gave a shiver. "Mr. Shannon, I need your help."

He cocked his head.

"Rose Flynn needs your help, I should say, and Philippa Kim—Mamzelle—and, I think, Sepp Amsel."

These names turned the trick where mine did not.

"What's happened?" he asked, sharper now. "What's their trouble?"

"A murderous gang kidnapped Mrs. Flynn and Miss Kim this afternoon. My friend, Mr. Anderson, and I have since freed them, but they—my friends—in turn are holding the kidnappers until they can be formally arrested. Can you come quickly and take them, the kidnappers, into custody?"

"Kidnapped?" he repeated, as if he hadn't heard the rest of my concise relating of events.

"Yes. Apparently, Mr. Amsel's fiancée is not the lovely woman he deserves. She and her sister, along with some others, have been victimizing him." I took a breath, coughing as the icy air heavy with smoke from the city's chimneys bit into my lungs. "The gang is guilty of the recent murders of the bellhop at the Majestic Hotel, the clerk at Mannheim's Haberdashery, and the two transients in the tenderloin. That's over and above the kidnapping and extortion."

His whitened eyebrows contracted, but he didn't move. "Murders? Extortion? That's a pretty lengthy list of crimes." He thought a moment. "How do you fit in, Miss Bohannon?"

"I agree, it is a lengthy list. I was hired to look into a suspected case of extortion. The murders are a surprise." I didn't know what else to say without actually saying Sepp Amsel's name. And that is just not done in the private inquiry business. "Please, sir. I can give you the address where Mrs. Flynn and Miss Kim were held. They're still there, along with the criminals. But I'm worried for them, afraid those people will turn the tables on them."

"This ain't a trick, is it?" He still seemed doubtful. "Something to do with Hansen? Payback of some kind with Doyle getting even?"

My temper flared. "Officer Shannon, I never joke about death or kidnappers, no matter what I, or Mr. Doyle, or my uncle think of Lars Hansen. I believe you know that. Please, time is wasting. And there's at least one more of these crooks, the ringleader, on the loose. If we hurry we may catch him, too."

Breath gusted in a steamy cloud from Shannon's mouth. "I suppose you know who that is, too."

"Why, yes, sir. I do."

He folded his arms across his chest. "Then you'd best be telling me."

So I did, words tumbling over each other in their hurry.

Quite soon Shannon's whistle split the night as he called in the closest officers to aid in bringing in the Kalbs and the cretin. He had the address. As for me, although Shannon protested vigorously, I was already scurrying toward Finkle's Rooming House, my footsteps a rhythm beating out, "too late, too late."

People, mostly men, were out and about in this section of town, even at this time of day. Many of the poorer working-class folk lived here, some whose jobs took them far into the night. As for me, I just hoped there was safety in the number of people still abroad.

The rooming house, as I approached, hadn't improved since my first visit here a couple days ago. It was just as run down now as it had been then, although, once again, the stoop had been recently swept. According to what I surmised from scrutinizing the steps, no one had passed in or out since the sweeping. I told myself it was a good sign, that I must be in time to warn Grat of Werner's intentions toward him. I doubted he'd be surprised.

The door, when I tried the knob, opened with a soft snick. Cooking odors, cabbage and onions predominant, penetrated the hall. The swish of water and a woman's steady cursing at stuck-on grime came to me. Mrs. Finkle must've been washing the supper dishes. Her cursing, although not so very imaginative when compared to Porter Anderson's, covered up any small sounds I might have made. Or so I believed until a dog barked twice beyond a closed door.

I froze in place. The woman cursed at him to shut up, and he, good dog, obeyed. Presently, when nothing else stirred, I scooted up the stairs on silent feet.

I don't know what I expected. For Grat to pop out of a room and embrace me, I guess. Naturally I was wrong. The upper hall, so chilly and dank I thought the residents must sleep wrapped in a half dozen quilts instead of only one or two, was silent as a tomb. If I hadn't been sure Gratton was on the job somewhere, I would've thought the place empty. At least until I heard a man's snorting gasp for air and the squeak of bedsprings.

Harrumph. One of those good beds the landlady touted, no doubt.

"Grat," I said in a stage whisper, which is louder than one might think. "Grat?"

Floorboards creaked from across the way. A latch clicked on the door to my left, opening a scant inch.

"China?" The crack between the door and the jamb widened. "What are you doing here? Go away. I'm expecting the drop soon."

Little did he know. On the premise it wasn't a good idea to

be bandying words across the hall, I went over to where he stood inside the dark room. "I came to warn you. The plan may have changed. It has changed."

"Changed?"

Although his face was barely visible, I saw him look right and left before he yanked me into the room.

My nose wrinkled. The room smelled of unbathed man, unwashed bedding, and general funk. Unpleasant, to be frank.

"Whose room is this?" I asked, only to receive a shrug.

"Some feller who wanted to make a dollar. He thinks I'm spending the night. It doesn't matter. I asked what you're doing here?"

He took my hand and held it. How did he manage to still have warm hands? The room's temperature must've been near zero.

I skipped over his question to ask one of my own. "Do you know where Monk and Bill are?"

"Sure. Tagging after Werner. Following the plan. You shouldn't be out, China. It's too cold. It's too damn dangerous."

If he only knew. As far as the cold goes, in thinking back, it seemed I'd been outside a good part of the day. "Listen to me, Grat. Werner knows we're on to him. He doesn't mean to give up on the money, though. He plans on killing you when he comes to pick up the ransom. Then he's going to find Sepp and force him to open his safe. He intends on murdering Sepp, too."

He went silent. "What makes you say so?"

"I don't have to say so. Jutte and Anka say so. And the cretin."

"The who?" He shook his head when I started to speak. "Never mind. Tell me about it. How'd you hear all this?"

Although he urged me to sit on the edge of the cot, I refused. I daresay bugs lived in the quilts and mattress. Perhaps even rats. With the room so dark, the varmints may have been invisible, but I knew they were there. Remaining standing, I explained.

"You and Porter, eh? Gonna have to hire him on to the agency." Suitably impressed, Grat went over to the window to check his pocket watch.

"Seven right on the nose," he said, "too late for you to leave now. Werner might see you." He took up his station by the door again. I nestled in behind him.

Silent now, we waited.

They say women have better hearing than men, and it may be true because I was aware of the soft opening and closing of the front door several seconds before Grat. I poked him in the back with my finger and pointed downward. He cocked his head, listening.

Wood squeaked as a foot trod on the stairs. Then again. Someone heavy. Or, unless I was mistaken, two someones. I heard a muffled gasp. An equally muffled grunt. These secretive visitors made a lot of noise, considering.

Maybe it wasn't Werner. Maybe this was all in vain.

Below us, the dog barked out a short volley, violently this time, and, once again, Mrs. Finkle hushed him, good watchdog that he was.

No, I'd been right the first time. Horst Werner had arrived right on time. But who did he have with him? Another henchman? One I didn't know about?

I grabbed onto Grat, stood on tip toe, and said, my lips touching his ear, "He's here. Two people."

For once Grat didn't argue but nodded agreement. He detached my clinging arms from his waist, pushed me to one side, and drew his pistol. Didn't cock it, though. Too loud by far in what struck me as a waiting silence.

We listened for Werner to go into the other room, the one I'd looked at in my guise of a boy, but he didn't. Feet shuffled. I heard another grunt, which raised my curiosity even higher, then Werner spoke.

Not what we expected.

"Come out, Doyle, and bring the money. I've got a surprise for you. A package I'll give you when you hand over the ransom."

Gratton felt like a statue, he went so still where I touched him.

"Oh," Werner said, "throw your gun out the door first. Otherwise . . ."

We didn't move. I know I held my breath.

"Quickly, now, Doyle. I haven't got all night." He chuckled. "My friend here hasn't all night either."

We heard a thud and a muffled groan.

"Dammit." Hand on the door knob, Grat turned it. The door opened. I had no view, but Grat did. He stiffened even more, if that were possible.

"Sure, Werner," he drawled in the Irish brogue that came to the fore when he was under pressure, "and you're a tricky bastard, aren't you?"

Werner seemed to find this funny. "I told you it was a surprise. Throw down your gun, and bring out the money. We'll make a trade."

By stretching my neck and peeking under Grat's arm, I caught a glimpse of the hall. Dim as it was, and as narrow as the gap, I saw two men standing there, close together. Not, I expect, by the second man's choice. Sepp Amsel's hands were bound behind him, while Werner held either a knife or a gun, I couldn't tell which, on him. Werner pressed the weapon into Sepp's back, causing Sepp to utter a sharp sound through the cloth tied around his mouth.

"See what I mean?" Werner said. "A fair trade, ja?"

I almost snorted out loud, causing Grat to reach back in

warning. He didn't want Werner to know about me.

Did Werner really expect Grat to believe him? Not that he cared. He knew he held the ace card.

Hell and damnation.

CHAPTER THIRTY-THREE

"Throw out your gun," Werner said again. "It's not hard to slit a man's throat. Takes only an instant. Or shove the blade through his back. The knife goes in sideways, between the ribs, you see. Punctures the lungs and the heart. Easy as killing a pig. Easier."

Apparently, he'd had lots of practice, to be so precise in his method.

Gratton knew it, too, and made up his mind in an instant. "Hold on. I'm coming out."

I grabbed onto his coat, but he was already bent over his boot, transferring the mate of my own .32 to his coat pocket under the pretext of picking up the bag with the ransom. He turned to me, put his fingers to his lips, and breathed one word. "Hide."

He set his Colt on the floor and shoved it with his foot, sliding it out into the hallway.

"Wise," Werner said, a chuckle in his voice. He picked up the pistol as it stopped near him, transferring what I saw was a knife to his other hand. He had Sepp in a headlock, with the knife actually touching his neck. "Bring the money."

Poor Sepp. Not so pleased, he was making indecipherable sounds of protest behind the gag. I can't say as I blamed him. I'd seen the way Werner and his henchmen operated; ruthless, fast, but here's the thing: maybe a little careless.

He didn't bother searching Gratton for another weapon. Too

difficult, I expect, what with holding Sepp prisoner and keeping Grat under the gun. Anyway, I believe guns are not so common in Europe. It would be rare for a man to own more than one. At any rate, his attention moved from Gratton to the bank bag he carried.

"Open it," Werner demanded, shoving Sepp forward, the better to see. "Strike a match," he told Gratton when the light proved too dim. "Here, there's some on this table."

Obligingly, Grat moved from the room's doorway to a rickety hall table with a coal oil lamp sitting on it. He struck the match and set it to the lamp's wick. A weak flame trembled in the drafty hall, but it was enough for Werner to peer into the bank bag. He nodded.

"Good," he said. "Excellent. Count it out. Do not try to cheat me."

Cheat him? What nerve.

Grat didn't like it, but he followed orders. There were a good many small bills, having come directly from the cash register in Sepp's saloon. They counted out to exactly seven thousand dollars.

"As agreed," Grat said, stuffing the bills in the bag again. "Take the money and go. I'll care for Amsel." He still stood by the table, the lamp throwing his shadow on the wall in front of him. His every move was magnified.

In the strange way one has of noticing odd things in quiet moments, I became aware of the sleeping man's snores, unbroken through the exchange. He must've been exhausted. And I was also aware that below us, the landlady made certain neither she nor her dog interfered.

"About Amsel," Werner said, "I'm afraid I have another use for him. He's going to open his safe for me. The one in his apartment, not the one in his saloon. So your job is done, Doyle. I have no further use for you." He stepped more clearly into my view, shoving Sepp in front of him. His back was to me now, which meant Sepp's back was as well. Streaks of blood marked Sepp's coat, dark stripes on lighter fabric. Werner's method of control showed clearly.

I bit back a gasp, but, even so, Werner must have sensed my presence. "Who . . ." he started, but Grat was already moving, slipping out of the lamp's glare, drawing the .32 from his coat pocket. Still, he was a half second too late.

Werner slammed Sepp in through the half-open door of the room where I sheltered. Sepp knocked into me, sending me staggering backward. The thing is, I'd had my pistol out of its pocket since Grat left the room. Even Werner, charging hard under the shield of Sepp's body, couldn't beat the fraction of a second it took to yank back the hammer and pull the trigger.

The bullet took him in the chest. A look of pained surprise mixed with anger crossed his face.

"What?" he said. "You?" Then, "No."

He lunged toward me.

I was about to shoot again when something in his face stopped me. The suddenly blank expression, I think. The slackening of all his muscles.

I stepped aside as he staggered past. One step, two. On the third step, he fell, collapsing as if all the bones had been drawn from his body. Body fluids flushed. A stink filled the room.

Grat followed him in, holding the lamp high.

The snores stopped. A man shouted, "Wha . . . ?"

Downstairs, the dog howled once.

I closed my eyes on the sight and trembled.

After a moment, Grat moved to free Sepp's hands, and Sepp dragged the gag from his mouth. A trickle of blood seeped from a gash under his chin as he stared at me.

"Rose," he said, after a silence that seemed awfully long. "Rose, she is a wise woman. She tells me you are a good detective. Firety. Smart." He looked at Grat. "This one, she got guts." And a moment later, "Thought I was gonna be dead."

I'd thought so, too. I'd known so.

The pistol in my hand shook, as though too heavy for me to hold. Grat set down the lamp and took the gun away, removing it from my grip before gathering me into his arms and pressing my face into his shoulder.

"Come on, sweetheart. Don't look," he said. He rested his cheek on my head. "Don't think."

I burrowed deeper, eyes shut tight and hoping the after image of Horst Werner's body would become blacked out.

I killed a man. Horror colored my first thought, followed by another. *He deserved it, the evil, wicked man.*

The knowledge didn't help. What did was Grat's arms and the bellowing of Bill Shannon from downstairs as he burst into the rooming house. "Police here. I heard a shot. Everybody stay where you are."

I heard the clatter of doggie toenails on the stairs, and Nimble raced into the room. She jumped up, snowball encrusted chest and legs and all. And somehow, between Grat and me, we caught her between us.

Five days, five men dead. All for a few thousand dollars.

A big day arrived come Saturday morning. I fired the boiler in the cellar and ran hot water upstairs into the bathroom. I bathed and washed my hair, rinsing it first with lemon juice followed by a second rinse of rose water. When the time came, I donned my best afternoon dress, a teal-colored affair. Gratton had told me once it matched my eyes. I hoped so. The dress was a pretty color and looked good on me with its bell-shaped skirt with a ruffle-trimmed overskirt, full sleeves, and a short capelet. My gloves were dark-blue kid, and I wore a dark-blue velvet sash at my waist that had a concealed pocket sewn into it. The pocket wasn't quite big enough for my .32, only a tiny, single-shot derringer. But that was all right this one time. I'd have Grat to protect me today if, by some chance, I needed protecting. As a final touch, I clipped a concoction of Philly's she called a "fascinator," made of satin, netting, and peacock feathers, into my high-piled hair.

Bill Shannon had reported to Monk this morning on the status of the case. I thought about what he'd said as I dabbed the slightest blush of rouge along my cheekbones.

Officer Shannon certainly had a fine tale to tell regarding Jutte and Anka Kalb. They were chatting up Lars Hansen and his officers with determined purpose, he said, the whole story coming out as they tried to put themselves in the best light.

Turns out they'd traded places because, on the way to America, Anka got horribly seasick, lost twenty pounds, and decided she would fare better with their mark than her much plumper sister, who contrarily had gained a good many pounds during the voyage. The real Anka was in love with Horst Werner, himself fleeing prosecution in Germany. She gladly took over the role of bride hoping to please him, the pair having larceny in mind from the start.

Poor Sepp Amsel had always been only a means to the end. The end being their enrichment. Monetarily, that is.

Sepp's planned end had been death, although originally that was supposed to happen after the marriage. His bride and her paramour had planned to inherit it all.

Murder? Werner certainly didn't shrink from it. I guess Anka didn't, either. Only Jutte did, at least as far as Dieter was concerned. The rest? Just the hired help. They didn't matter.

I shook my head at the thought, poking an errant curl behind my ear.

Oh . . . the reason I was primping and dressing up in my best? Because of the wedding taking place at one o'clock this afternoon. Not my wedding, of course, although I'd stand with the bride.

Sepp Amsel, just as planned, was the bridegroom. The bride was Rose Flynn.

ABOUT THE AUTHOR

Carol Wright Crigger lives with her husband and two feisty little dogs in Spokane Valley, Washington. A big fan of local history, all of her books are set in the inland Northwest and make use of a historical background. She is a two-time Spur Award finalist, in 2007 for Short Fiction, and in 2009 for Audio. She also writes under the name C.K. Crigger. She reviews books and pens occasional articles for *Roundup* magazine. Contact her through her website at www.ckcrigger.com.

The employees of Five Star Publishing hope you have enjoyed this book.

Our Five Star novels explore little-known chapters from America's history, stories told from unique perspectives that will entertain a broad range of readers.

Other Five Star books are available at your local library, bookstore, all major book distributors, and directly from Five Star/Gale.

Connect with Five Star Publishing

Visit us on Facebook:
https://www.facebook.com/FiveStarCengage

Email:
FiveStar@cengage.com

For information about titles and placing orders:
(800) 223-1244
gale.orders@cengage.com

To share your comments, write to us:
Five Star Publishing
Attn: Publisher
10 Water St., Suite 310
Waterville, ME 04901